SPIRITS OF THE FLEA MARKET

FLASH-FORWARD

Afloat in mutuality's stew,
Codependent origins see,
How begird the quirky true,
Causation's fraught ontology.
>   *Homo Sapiens in Extremis*, Evil, Quirky Metaphysic

Thy steps quick pass the dried, deserted well.
Thine eye squinteth in the light of thy way.
Art thou headed for the lilied, chirping dell,
Where two names carved in oak still live right well?
>   *Remembrance*, The Walkers' Dream

I waft in bardo states I swear I can feel.
Machinery of time ebbs far below.
>   *Endings*, Bardo States

Never as youth, adult, or elder,
Was I a swaggering ocean-borne bloke.
But oh, there must be swashbuckler in me;
Spellbound, I'm pirate on cresting white sea.
>   *Spritely Antique Shopping*, Free at the Flea Market

Who but one so deep reviled, so cast off,
Who but cherub with faulted, palsied wing,
Is suited more to shine as empath being?
What better spark than I for newest *Taufe*?
>   *Tribunal for Writing*, Act Four, Scene 1

…when the myrtle blushed outwardly and wept inside as
        though consciousness of sin
Weighed upon her mightily as her solitary, twisted mission,
        when no wanderers came to laud
Her simple majesty of passion made of stars, moon, and
        souls…
>   *Redemption*, In This New Land

But you stood as well with the gossamers,
Having shed all trace of world's accretion,
As the princess of winsome pixie sylphs,
As amaranthine angel and bright star.
>   *Remembrance*, The Hollies

Long winding road, thou art the only lane,
Where gates abounding help my eyes to see,
How I, old nomad, might find home again.
>   *Sonnets*, Gates Abounding

Gather your soul, O Gleaming Knight,
Redeem your fractured past tonight.
In one pure end's coruscant glow,
Arise and let your old life go.
>   *Synth of Sweven*, Anthem of the Wildings

Flower, flower, O Amaranth
Unfading bloom is thy best strength.
O Lord Most High and Spark Within,
Hallowed be thy names, Amen.
>   *Synth of Sweven*, Hymn of the Amarant Christians

R. C. PIETTE

SPIRITS

of the

FLEA
MARKET

Sincere Poems & Light Satire

selections from

BRICOLAGE

RCπ

*For my family, and especially for Lee, Susan,
and Scott, spirits of the flea market*

Hope and Memory have one daughter and her name is
Art, and she has built her dwelling far from the
desperate field where men hang out their garments
upon forked boughs to be banners of battle. O beloved
daughter of Hope and Memory, be with me for a little.

William Butler Yeats, 1893

Beware the Jabberwock, my son!
The jaws that bite, the claws that catch!
Beware the Jubjub bird, and shun
The frumious Bandersnatch.

Lewis Carroll, 1872

Preface

IT WAS CONFLATION from disparate sources in remote but lively pasts, swayed by higher purpose in caparison of the random, which together have been the true author of this work and of my small contributions to it. Along its upwardly concrescent path the opus has overcome many obstacles and passed through many hands.* That it has survived is by worldly logic a miracle. Yet here it is, raising once again its multicolored sails, beckoning more friendly souls to come aboard.

How I became the beneficiary of the arks containing the materials of the work is unclear, like the way the roots of dreams resist being known despite the pleas of the dreamers who host them.

In any case, the binders, versions, snippets, notes, dreams, and other forms of the work's poetic and spiritual material did come to me via several channels—physical/conventional, psychological/soulful, electronic here and there, and hermetic/spiritual. Being overwhelmed, I was unable to resist venturing another small step in the long, telic trek of the concrescence. Thus my inability to resist is the origin of this most recent effort to present portions of the work of the legendary Reverend Snolly Goster.

The word "I" when applied to human authors of certain types of works is cause for thought. Some past philosophers of literature, though sometimes prone to the most peculiar ideas, were on the right track when they wondered what the I is and how this pronoun can sensibly be applied to authorship. Anyone seeking wisdom on this point can gain a sense of the profound quandary that is I with a simple experiment of reflexive introspection, a satori wherein the I as author of poetic and spiritual material reveals itself to be just a misty I-ness that quickly scatters into the true nature of the I, which is that of helper, agent, minor avatar, holder in due course, herald proclaiming kerygma on behalf of the rising concrescence swayed by higher purpose.

Snolly Goster was perhaps himself a conflation of several personae in the image of Hermes Trismegistos or so many other deities and legendary figures of the past. Also, The Finders who came later, that amateur archaeologist par excellence and her spirit fetch,

---

* This book, including this Preface, consists of selections, with minor changes and additions, from the larger work BRICOLAGE: *Spiritual Poems & Light Satire*, here referred to as the "opus." Notes to the main body of this book are presented as endnotes at book's end. In the opus, notes are are presented as footnotes.

themselves openly dyadic, could have been three or more beings in a long train of lonely hearts touched by the sparkling wand of the concrescence to be incarnations of the inability to resist. There were others too that entered time and made additions or changes to what we think were Goster's original texts. One can see their traces here and there in the notes to the work. They identify themselves only as DGVU, which is believed to derive from the German expression *Der Geheime Versteckte Ursprung*. The presence of DGVU in the good reverend's extravagant opus is never obtrusive or plentiful but usually mystifyingly random. It's a minor point. What is important is that, like me, they were or are agents of the work's true author and principal editor—the living, concrescent, upwardly turned conflation that reveals.

Seven Caveats

I have seven caveats readers are free to ignore if they wish.

First, the concrescent, upwardly turned conflation is not God; it is best to see it as emanations of God in time, or as something put into motion by God.

Second, the higher purpose that sways, whereby the concrescence is turned upward, is closer to God than is the concrescence itself; but like angels, the higher purpose that sways is also not to be equated with God.

Third, the words "concrescence" and "concrescent" appear rarely if at all in the main body of Goster's work. Within the narrow context of the primordial human, the closest in meaning to these terms is "bold congeries" as in the poem "Incommensurate Parts" (*Homo Sapiens in Extremis*). Here the writer poetizes those beastly origins which the flowering of the concrescence will prod ever upward to higher purpose and thereby save.

Fourth, while some might see the upwardly turned conflation as the dialectical principle of world history, this is not accurate. The dialectical principle is an exoskeleton; whereas the concrescence is more like an endoskeleton. The two are related, however, with the former being a more visible frowny-faced, low-fidelity reflection of the ultimately more upbeat and gladsome inner countenance of the concrescent, upturned endoskeleton swayed by higher purpose.

Fifth, if what is intimated in Snolly Goster's work is not exactly Judaism, Christianity, Islam, Hinduism, Buddhism, Zoroastrianism, Hermeticism, polytheism, pantheism, or magic, then perhaps it will be received as a habitat fit for all, as proclaimed in the "Hymn of the Amarant Christians" (*Synth of Sweven*):

> O Emanations fused in one,
> *Agape* love for everyone.
> Blessëd art thou Great Mystery,
> Teach again, repeat still more:
> One compassion we must show,
> Is hear what others feel and know.

Sixth, while heralds and agents of the concrescence love all-encompassing theories of the theological significance of BRICOLAGE: *Spiritual Poems & Light Satire*, a strong minority view is that its poems, stories, and dialogues are simply glimpses into the manifold animus and anima of people, and beings like people—their sweet loves, their visions of the light and the dark, their aspirations, delights, and terrors, their spirits that cannot resist residing in bodies, their bodies entranced by the purity of incorporeal forms, their trite conquests and sometimes grand compassions, their flaws and foibles falling at the feet of a playful willingness to be swayed to and by a higher purpose.

Seventh, all agents, helpers, and heralds of the concrescence are imperfect creatures, and despite their inspired metaphysical connections tend to mess up and spawn new issues. But this is just part of the plan. For whatever would wights like us do without a steadily replenished supply of puzzles to ponder?

Seven Recommendations

I have seven recommendations for readers who wish to set sail on the vessel that is *Spirits of the Flea Market*, which consists primarily of selections drawn from the larger opus, BRICOLAGE.

First, if speculations like my comments on the concrescence rankle, upset, or bore you to ill health, then stop, turn back, flee, do not return. That course will be easier and will not pull you from your stream of empty distractions.

Second, if poetically your sensibilities and preferences rigidly bear the stamp of one form, one culture, one style, one etiquette, one mission, one epoch, one correctness, one doctrine, one tongue, one epistemology, then stop, turn back, flee, do not return. The main title of the work from which the selections in this small book are drawn is, after all, BRICOLAGE.

Third, if you are open to the idea that belle lettres is or can be a good home or get-away for lost and lonely science, come on board.

Fourth, if you believe that both poetics and science must be rebuked as well as celebrated from time to time, come on board.

Fifth, concerning epistemology, which is to say theories of what can be known and how we know when true knowing is occurring, consider this: If you can imagine a role for metaphor and metonymy as well as for statistics and differential equations, welcome to the ship.

Sixth, if quick changes in style, focus, idiom, or time are unsettling for you, such as switching abruptly from dulcet prosodies of love to teary lamentations over a botched resurrection, then please walk calmly onto the ship so as not to jostle your stomach further; but do come aboard. The little sickness will pass, as will all things, and this ship has Angels of the Pylon to help.

Seventh, if you believe deeply that knowing promotes feeling, and feeling promotes knowing, come on board and take the helm. You can be the next captain.

Lastly, in homage to the lofty but elusive goal of disambiguation, I would like to mention that notwithstanding, or rather because of, my universalist sympathies, I consider myself to be Christian, as did so many other helpers of the concrescence swayed by higher purpose who have come before me.

I am yours, respectfully,

The Heraldic Holder in Due Course
of the Arks of the Poetic and Spiritual Lore of
Reverend Snolly Goster
Many centuries, years, and months
since Our Salvation

V OICE 3 FROM C URTAIN [aggressive]: Now on the marketing side, competitors are selling the same thing, with fewer missing and damaged parts, for one measly sesterce per book. Remember, there are four sesterces to one denarius. And a denarius is no micro-shekel. It's equivalent to ten asses. So, ten denarii for one copy of *BRICOLAGE*? That's a lot of donkeys, a lot of cases of Lucius transformed—one hundred just for a single copy of a leather-bound, out-maneuvered, third-rate edition. What a pathetic pricing plan. I think most people would rather keep their mules and pay a sesterce for one of the less lavish but better editions.

—*BRICOLAGE*, Book 3, *Afterword*, Grave of Words

Acknowledgments

Joyce, my wife, for her wisdom, love, tolerance, and common sense.

Cory, my son, for being Phoenix, my exemplar of renewal; and for his help with the statistics portions of *Tribunal for Writing* in BRICOLAGE.

Hayden and Landon, grandsons, for being avatars of hope for the future.

Clarence and Jane Piette (in memoriam), my parents, for their incidents, stories, and lessons; how they resonate more deeply with the passing years.

William and Adell Lindley (in memoriam), Joyce's parents, for their incidents, stories, and lessons; how they resonate more deeply with the passing years.

Lee and Susan Adams, and Scott, managers of the Quaker Acres parcel of the Brimfield Flea Market, "humanity's expo for beloved market makers."

Mrs. Hilda Shea (in memoriam) of Cambridge, Massachusetts, for being the best uncompensated mentor an aspirant ever had.

Nancy for being "Friendship Bird."

Justin (in memoriam) of "Justin Save A Place For Me."

M. for being S.; J. for being H. K.; D. for being D. S.; T. for being T. S.; S. for being S. M.; K. for being K. R.; G. for being G. C.; B. for being R. B.; B. for being B. H.

Friends and colleagues now scattered across so many times and places, whose humanity, wits, and lively conversations I have never forgotten, and whom I quietly miss and cherish every day.

Shadowy figures of the distant past, some with one or many names, others nameless, for somehow managing to create legends, myths, cultures, and religions that charm and fascinate in perpetuity.

Luminaries of more recent times.

Reverend Snolly Goster (in memoriam—he passed, 'tis rumored), and those incomparable preservers of the lore he left behind—that amateur archaeologist par excellence and her spirit fetch, without whose inspired trash grifting, so tireless they were, the Snolly opus might never have seen the light of day.

All in good fun: *N'est-ce pas?*

Contents

About the Author

R. C. Piette grew up in central Massachusetts and for many years lived in the suburbs of Washington, DC, and Baltimore, MD. He now lives in Pennsylvania. He has been an entrepreneur, management consultant, marketing and professional services executive, and director of finance and information technology departments in the private and public sectors. He graduated *summa cum laude* from Bowdoin College with a BA in Philosophy. He received the degree of Master of Theological Studies from Harvard University where he studied religion, languages, and the history of ideas. He has an MS in Accounting from Georgetown University. He is a CPA, PMP, and Lean Six Sigma Blackbelt.

Spirits of the Flea Market, and the larger work entitled *Bricolage* on which *Spirits* is based, are R. C. Piette's first books of a literary nature. Some of the individual poems and narratives of these writings were first composed long ago. Previously, early in his professional career, Piette wrote or edited many published articles on management and technology.

VOICE 3 FROM CURTAIN [reenacting]: Hahahahaha. Really,
this is just too much—side-splitting, hilarious, it's far
beyond raillery, rising above the tallest trees of badinage
and *Geplänkel*. Har, har, ho! It's more than espièglerie.
It's the very essence of the radiant sun of jabberwocky.
It's the merger of Gelos and Risus back into the universal
divine personification of laughter. Whoa, I can't stop this
insane giggling.

—*BRICOLAGE*, Book 3, *Afterword*, Grave of Words

Later I would study mystics,
But no more would I learn,
Than freedom taught as racing pinto,
Galloping fast return.

—*BRICOLAGE*, Book 1, *Remembrance*,
Ballad of Freedom Rider

from Sonnets

ART IN PARIS

We bought five oil paintings on quaint bridge
To Ile St. Louis, close to Notre Dame,
On bright night of July, where charmed ridge
Of moonlight cascaded all round, to frame
A magic mood disposed to see odd things
Great boons to acquire. These oils were student
Productions, tempered of briefest training,
Just embryonic, but to us Rembrandts.
There they hang still, exquisitely crooked,
Relief against a room of old framed maps.
I love them so, those garish spores naked [1]
Of skill, with teeming beauty no force saps.
   Those oils are not paintings anymore.
   They are mirrors of how we were before.

LOVE THAT STAYS

Not high, nor low, not far, nor wide, do my
Eyes wander from your history, embodied
Still in earthly dress, whence peeks your thigh
So coy, as when Aphrodite first spied [2]
Us laughing in the meadow and sent boy
With arrows to effect a fate come due,
And make of callow nectar pure libation,
Poured to bless a lifetime spent with you.
Against casino chance, your hierarchy
Of being lies near, your heartbeat scaling
Time, place, and mirrored halls of memory.
Give your hand, and we are queen and king.
   Let this moment snap the temporal chain.
   Stay with me and delight in evening's rain.

Pythia

Billowed darkness rises, smolders just some,
Feigns reserve, hides its tempest napping brew.
Roaring not, its furtive face pretends dumb,
At eye's drowsy edge makes a ghost's debut.
Will merchant stalls survive the fearsome gales?
Or wares be strewn into the angry seas?
Will dogs howl to bewail a moon in veils?
Or stone cairn open and loose its banshees? [3]
No crier is wailing on street or screen,
No warning system buzzes anywhere.
Better to read guts or cup's tea leaves green,
Than wait for pseudoscience to plot air.
    Arise Pythia, from your sleep awaken. [4]
    You can best our paltry speculation.

Snow in Heat

You may think me foolish, cracked, or worse,
If I a special logic entertain, [5]
To smooth garments creased by age perverse,
Or wait for ground to spew out upward rain.
My syllogism's sun sets in the east, [6]
I look to west to see it rise again.
Fiends by inference eat ambrosia feast,
And fish glide far above the craggy glen.
In my reason, snows blow through Sahara,
In scorching heat safe are their white designs. [7]
This logic I employ to tame foul Mara, [8]
Who is too much at home in physics' twines.
    True life requires special apparatus.
    Redemption comes just when faith is in us.

SLEEPLESS II

A wisdom flutters in the East, searched
By this soul solemnly so often.
But never did I hold her where she perched,
To stroke her feathers soft of heaven.
Creature is elusive, but it is clear
She does not hide. She sings for me to sing,
That *maya* might be pruned by insight's shear.[9] [10]
Like melody, bird's bright form is far-reaching.[11]
She's tonic for illusion's mortal fleece.
Intoning bloodless joy and shining glow,[12]
She warbles, beams, but only hints my peace;[13]
Because I cannot practice what I know.
   Goals are nails, they pin to wheel of time.
   Price of sleep is forsaking worldly climb.

GATES ABOUNDING

Winding road, not bereaved of sorrow,
Thou art choir of portals lit well by grace,
That beckons pilgrims come in, come through,
To linger some in idylls' charmed embrace.
There a pathway to Samarkand, close by[14]
A sacred bough to grasp, in vale below[15]
A cleansing stream, above old spirits fly
As manna rains in metaphysic show.[16]
For all the burden of my walk upon thee,
Long winding road, thou art the only lane,
Where gates abounding help my eyes to see,
How I, old nomad, might find home again.
   Travelers need an artful preparation,
   To enter gates beyond finite creation.

FRED :   I stand near the origin of my kind,
Not of my mere biologic platform,
But of my kind as star-gazing and bold
Questioning spirits, as awake beyond
All other creatures here about, up and
Down the gauzy mystic space-time stack
That sweet hex of peewit has enabled
Me to see among the giggling small ones.

—*BRICOLAGE*, Book 2, *Sassenach Visions*,
Psychopomp, Psychomant, and Fred

from Encrypted Messages

EYE OF THE POEM

Hello out there, it is I, the eye of the poem,
The eye that peers, the I that blinks away a tear,
The I that eye twinkled brightly many a time:
Hello out there, it is eye, the I of the poem.

The eye of the poem has no ciliary body,
No iris, pupil, lens, cornea, or retina.
It has neither vitreous nor aqueous humour.
Having no parts, it has no ligaments to bind.

To you, it may seem that the I has an eye,
Or the eye is part of me, or that some other
Relation obtains between two separate things.
But no, not even as color imbues flower.

Greetings, this is primal oneness of eye and I,[17]
The oneness that blinks away a tear, the gazing
That twinkles still when winking moonlight glows:
Goodbye for now, eye am the seer never seen.[18]

DUELING VISIONS

Anthem of the Vile

Here, now, nothing more;
    There, then, just illusion.
Here, now, nothing more;
    History's cusp is our prison.[19]

Long ago and future too,
    Just are wraiths, not salvation.
Here, now, is all for you,
    Rise not from your station.

Here, now, nothing more;
    Imbibe in soporific squall.
Here, now, you are in thrall;
    Moment's blur of play is all.

Canticle of the Blessed

Begone foul churl demonic;[20]
    Pray vilest is redeemed.
Be you troll, ghost, or mask
    Of cruel dialectic,[21]

Your gimcrack, tawdry, duping
    Schemes are over.
Though facts and history's cusp
    Make for us a border,

In dreams there are grand estates,[22]
    Where spirits reign
O'er distant times and places,
    Never bound in chains.

Here, now, are just garish,
    Without weaves of there, then.
Here, now, are nightmarish,
    If beauty's idylls die within.

Long ago and future too,
    Are spirit's potent substance,[23]
To thwart blur of fiendish brew's
    Wicked cold persistence.

There, then, awake to know,
    Fend off soporific squall.
Reap mind's arts, high and low,
    Moment's flicker is not all.

Missing history, puzzled future,
    Pressed to endless hollow now,
Is just a place of roiling stupor,
    And not a truly fruited bough. [24]

    There is a use to prosody. [25]
    Its ambrosias set us free.

A HEX ON SUCH LINES AS THESE

You might imagine pishogues kindling the hearth, [26]
More potent than whale oil or piles of twigs that waited
Ten long seasons for their chance to burn hot magic.

Then would smoke billow upward, yearning to gift to
Spirits myrrh and sweet frankincense, or other fumes for [27]
Conjure known from some musty charm or grimoire, [28]

To please those ineffable ones leaning into winds,
And longing to connect through hermetic channels
With forms of lesser metaphysic like you and me.

That would be quite some fancy, quite the show of
Legerdemain; so much so that you might attract [29]
Howls of crowds outside, with torches, pitchforks, and

Spooky chants of their own, debunking your harmless
Experiments, as though you never read a single
Gospel, tract condemning heresy, or text of physics.

COINCIDENTIA OPPOSITORUM

Ideality as dullness of the most pointed spire
Amuses stygian blindness in the arrowless archer,
Who poses an inscrutable posture the cow of
Emeralds sees blithely from the grassless meadow.

Iron maidens pour into their pails of wax, molten
Ore from green bovine udders already emptied
To thirsts of feral toffs on break from *Elysium.*[30]
Crows hover underground, and swine make tea.

One is minus one, two is minus two, division is
Multiplication, square is root, effect is cause,
Log is antilog, omega the cosmic bang, and alpha
The fullest spread of galaxies—in a shoreline conch.

The form of the overarching ideal of all ideals
Requires a nameless unity of opposites.
How will secularity cope, especially if coping
Insists on more than tactical projects to pretend?

That form, that overarching, that supremest ideal:
Go beyond it to *coincidentia oppositorum.*[31]

from Colloquy of Feathers

AVINE IMPERTINENCE

Youth

Caw, caw, caw. What can be done to stop the
Irksome crows ?, such monotony squawking
From quavering treetops beyond the barn.

The day almost done, the crescent queen [32]
Rises glowing. You would think those tiresome
Ubiquitous devils had loosed enough [33]

Cacophony on mere denizens of earth,
Who cannot take wing. No soaring among
The cottony clouds for us, who just shuffle

Endlessly in furrowed ground and well-trod
Paths, who, muck-mired, ever hear the brazen
Reminders of our impotence unmasked:

"You there, humans," exclaim the scoffing birds.[34]
"Your methods and machines stand as nothing
Next to our eons of volant chansons."

Elder

Listen how the chorus rises to herald
The dawn, so grand and new this familiar
Play of earth, avine, and utopian sky. [35]

Look to heaven, see those messengers of
God fly gloriously about, swooping,
Climbing, winging into hearts their lofty

Scuds, their words, lyrics, articulating
Purpose and a place for humans, a good
Place in the charmed hierarchy of being.

Hear warbling harmonies, pure symphonies
Of finch, robin, cuckoo, thrush, wren, sparrow.
Behold raven, envoy of nature's rhythms.

Their message, though a cipher, is easily
Unlocked by hearts too old to be not young.
With birds come good tidings, so listen well:

"Hail, people. We see you, especially
You who care for our mother. We know your [36]
Dreams, covetous eye, your longing to soar.

"We birds, in our kingdom, have our ways.
But you, cousins, have your own bouquets. [37]

"We just sing and glide inside of time.
But you descant aloft with time below,
On wings of spirit higher than soaring,
Chirping feathers can ever hope to go." [38]

FRIENDSHIP BIRD

There is a tree with branches bare that stands
Outside our windowpane, scratchily tossing
Through the days with every gust or breeze.

It has no leaves or needles, no wreathing
Vines or mistletoe, to give it warmth of
Verdant dress to equal preening all around.

But a lovely bird chooses withered gray
For her nesting place. Though she goes from time
To time, she will return to plume and chime.

With no success we tried to find this wight [39]
In our catalogue. She is yellow, black,
Often red, and scales clouds like an eagle.

Tanager chirping, condor gliding, swan
Caressing waters: Her eyes are panes of
Wise owl souls. Her warble is an opera.

She finds herself by giving herself, and
Grants all her magic to the lonely tree.

These days we see Friendship Bird less often,
But in our life she'll never be forgotten.
For wilted twigs tapping at our window,
Now sprout green with every chilling snow.

DREAM OF WEDDING AT A FARM

This day in October seems plucked from May,
For in this moment nature bows to glory,
And autumn shades to another spring give way.

Two lives, not new, but newest now in union,
Blessed on high and by attending beasts,
Greenery, and golden straw, solemnized

By pastor of wise words and heart, vouchsafed
By God, stand as one, vowing to cherish
Rebirth as more than any toil or trouble.

How lovely to see life's colors and warbles
Perking in delight for you, how auspicious
This newest vine to wend past worldly strife.

Listen to the distant airs and hear those
Bands of unruly avine caterwauls
Join to form supernal angelic choir.

Wren singing scales up and down merrily,
Finch chirping, bobwhite reciting her two
Sweet notes, hermit thrush greeting veery as

She calls her own name tirelessly. Starling
Lilts from afar. Oriole whistles. Knowing
Raven caws her contralto metronome.

And earthy duck quacks a beat to cinch the
Oratorio to purpose. Wherefore this
Showy splendor, this sheer magnificence?

Is this just a random thing, less designed
Even than gusted whirling desert sands
Or spurt of pebbles trounced by ocean tide? [40]

You know the answer, written clear it is,
In book, mind, heart, and soul lit by Holy
Spirit's Grace: *quod erat demonstrandum.* [41]

Go now, children of the innocent dawn:

Be courageous and live well in every
Season, knowing winter never truly
Comes to those who bow each day to glory,

Rising with feel of clarion sounding, and
Singing at dusk with lyre and cooing dove,
The sweet lays of ebullient, righteous love.

———————————

HECKLER [inspiring]: Attention, all ye good and righteous citizens. Mr. Lowbottom will shortly wave his flags high and round, across and down, to signal you to start. There is only one prize, and it will not be awarded to any one individual on his or her own little cell. We are not isolated islands here. Right? We are a strong archipelago of truth. Therefore, the prize, leftover pizza, will be awarded to all of us when every one of your cells is well marked and the whole matrix is explained for the probabilities it reveals in our quest to judge the fairness of the principals' order of declaiming.

Go ahead, Mr. Lowbottom: Loose your flags like avenging arrows sent o'er the ramparts of the fortress of unquantified opinion!

Evangelist: Blow that giant shofar too. Ready?

EVANGELIST [sucking air]: One, two, three, blow: ARGHNGah, ARGHNGah, ARGHNGah. Woohoo! Gideon's got nothing on us. Our shofar blasts shall scatter the Midianites' detestable subjugation of statistic truth! Their idols shall be as ashes in the wind!

—*BRICOLAGE*, Book 2, *TFW Act 3 Scene 2*

DOVEY AND CONDORUS

CONDORUS :   Who are you, little sepia scruffy?

DOVEY :   My first name is Dovey, if know you must.
And who, pray tell, are you, wide-span bully?

CONDORUS :   I see you have a mouth on that beak, Dovey.
If know you must, my name is Condorus.

DOVEY :   The beak is just for pecking, silly goose.
The mouth is for reason and emotion,
And for my career and avocation.

CONDORUS :   I wonder whether I too have a mouth.
I do have these weighty ponderous wings,
And I admit I am a wide-span guy,
As you so cleverly did see. But mouth?

DOVEY :   You certainly have a mouth, Condorus.
But you must not think it is somatic.
If you do, I tell you, you won't find it.

CONDORUS :   Oh, that's nice of you, sepia Dovey.

DOVEY :   Whatever do you mean, wide-span monsieur?

CONDORUS :   You said my name, Condorus, so sweetly.

DOVEY :   You found your ears; so mouth must be nearby.

CONDORUS :   Please tell me, Dovey, how you got your name.
I would like to know, but I won't nag you.

DOVEY :   Thou art neither bully nor silly goose.
Thus, my friend, to you I will tell secrets.

CONDORUS :   I'll listen with the ears you helped me find.

DOVEY :   My mother named me after her mother.

CONDORUS :   You are the second Dovey in your line?

DOVEY :   Oh, goodness no. I am at least the third.
Rumor is we are too many to count.

CONDORUS :   Perhaps. But surely there are none like you.

DOVEY :   That is true and untrue at the same time.

CONDORUS :   My foundering brute brain you tease so well.

DOVEY :   That was a statement my hobby allows,

But one my career prohibits strictly.

CONDORUS :   I hope that's not hard for you, sepia,
Sweet thing, having an avocation wing
And a career wing too. Are you conflicted?

DOVEY :   Is that a mouth I hear from out your width?

CONDORUS :   Maybe. But it could just have been a fluke.

DOVEY :   Do you believe strongly in flukes, Condy?

CONDORUS :   Oh my, you said "Condy." Why do I squirm?

DOVEY :   You know, you could have asked the obvious.
But you did not. Nice, to be reticent.

CONDORUS :   I'm asking enough in my little way.

DOVEY :   Have you noticed anything odd about me,
Especially since my name is Dovey?

CONDORUS :   Well, you are, as I clumsily first said,
A "sepia scruffy," by which I meant…

DOVEY :   Yes, I am brownish-tan not snowy white,
And my feathers are more crumpled than smooth.
Surely you must wonder what makes me dove.

CONDORUS :   I did so wonder. You have found me out!
But might we leave this color riddle now?
My interest runs to your avocation.

DOVEY :   If know you must, I'm a part-time poetess.

CONDORUS :   Is cooing a thing of avocation? [42]

DOVEY :   Definitely, it is. And career rejects it.
I must always keep my wings separate,
As you intimated moments ago. [43]
Lawyer at left; poetess to the right.
My rightness is the key to my wholeness. [44]
From my leftness comes cold analysis. [45]

CONDORUS :   Does this left-right opposition match up
With so-called political left and right?

DOVEY :   "Yes and no," says my avocation.

CONDORUS :   What do your career feathers say on this?

DOVEY :   They speak of wordy non-disclosure tome.

CONDORUS : No doubt poetess routs the lawyer gnome.[46]

DOVEY : Is that a mouth I hear that capped a rhyme?
A milestone, Condy, thy lips are fine.[47]

CONDORUS : Now there you've got me again aflutter.

DOVEY : Sepia scruffy has her sylph pixie way.

CONDORUS : Winsome thou art with every murmur.

DOVEY : Your only guile seems bouquets to convey.

CONDORUS : You think too highly of this wide-span wight.

DOVEY : *Non monsieur*, my estimate's quite right.[48]

CONDORUS : I wish I could alight with you on twig.

DOVEY : Though my tiny weight's no threat to it,

CONDORUS : Too silly if a large bird danced a jig?

DOVEY : Your great girth would surely shatter it.
Tell me true some things about yourself.
So far our chirps sing just of brownie elf.[49]
Say now, lips no longer lost in sleep,
Something of your history, life, and dream.[50]

CONDORUS : This bird has no special essence inside,
No riddle or eldritch force to esteem.
No great mystery lurks behind these eyes.
Unlike you, right side of brain has no dream;
And wings of span are two but all the same.[51]

DOVEY : Have you no career or avocation?

CONDORUS : I do and both to date are same as wings.

DOVEY : Your name seems from a noble lineage.[52]

CONDORUS : That's because it sounds like proper Latin.
But I think it's not. My mother gave it.
She wanted to shield me from opprobrium
That might arise from my name in science.

DOVEY : That is the sort of thing a mother does.
But how can a formal name give license
To knaves to cast undeserved aspersion?

CONDORUS : 'Tis sad but they are not all vile taunters.
You see, Dovey, there is complication.
For I am Vultur gryphus, and creatures [53]

	Recoil when they hear a vulture name. How different condors are from serpents, Yet we share same fate of defamation.
DOVEY :	O Condy, you have many fine qualities. Let no ruffian torment your good soul.
CONDORUS :	I assure you I do not, fair Dovey. There is one small secret in my history That I would like to tell you if you're game.
DOVEY :	I would rather not be game, but I'll listen.
CONDORUS :	It's just a funny thing my mother said, Just before she died. Condors are long-lived. She was ninety when last she soared alive.
DOVEY :	And what did noblest condor lady say?
CONDORUS :	She said she named me Condorus because, After months of trying, she could not get Anyone to pronounce the *v* in Vultur Gryphus in the old soft way of the *w*.
DOVEY :	Like the "wuh" sounds of the *v* in *Via negativa*? Hee-hee, so sweet.[54]
CONDORUS:	That, dear Dovey, is a fine example. I might have been *Wultur*—in time Walter.
DOVEY :	O Condy, two secrets more I will share.
CONDORUS :	I'm game, but only if you trust me.
DOVEY :	First, I'm a mourning dove, not the white.
CONDORUS :	Like the lovely hymn? "Morning has broken, Like the first mo-or-or-ning." Fine like you.
DOVEY :	You're so funny. It's *mourning* with a *u* After the *o* and preceding the *r*.
CONDORUS :	Like when you are sad that someone dies?
DOVEY :	Yes, like that, similar but not the same.
CONDORUS :	It's hard to think of you as always sad.
DOVEY :	Not always. But melancholic I must Often be since I'm partly poetess.
CONDORUS :	Some females dislike the word "poetess."

DOVEY :   That's not a thing I fret about, either way.

CONDORUS :   I'd be glad to be sad with you, pixie.[55]

DOVEY :   That brings me to my second secret, goose.

CONDORUS :   I'm ready for you to tell it to me.

DOVEY :   This twig I'm on is no frail withered branch.
               It is, you see, a bough of magic tree,
               With power no wide span of weight can stanch;
               It welcomes kindly *wultures* such as thee.[56]

RAVENUS AND CROWLEY

CROWLEY :   Are we two of a family or not?

RAVENUS :   Goodness, Crowley. Must we go there again?

CROWLEY :   Are you brother, cousin, pretender, friend?

RAVENUS :   Today the last seems out of the question,
Even if one of the others I am.

CROWLEY :   And please stop pronouncing my name like that.

RAVENUS :   Like what? It's *ow* as in *meow*. Correct?

CROWLEY :   Do I look feline to you?, *Herr Käsekopf*? [57]

RAVENUS :   How insulting. Cheese never was my thing.
And even you must know, mispronouncing
Isn't as evil as calling me foul names.

CROWLEY :   The name is pronounced *crōw* as in "Row, row,
Row your boat o'er the jagged cataracts";
And not like *meow* as in sacred *bough*.

RAVENUS :   You see these gorgeous, purple-lit black wings?
I'll skip said boat and glide o'er killing crags.

CROWLEY :   More lecture now on dingy purple hue? [58]

RAVENUS :   Is that kitten's tail at your rear I see? [59]

CROWLEY :   I see Swiss-cheese holes in dull purple brow.

RAVENUS :   We're not getting anywhere with this talk,
Which seems with baser things much too taken,

CROWLEY :   Whilst our glories founder so forsaken.

RAVENUS :   Is that a common note we just sounded? [60]

CROWLEY :   A small sign of colloquy that's mended?

RAVENUS :   A glow I see in dispute's far corner.

CROWLEY :   It won't last unless it's snatched and nurtured.

RAVENUS :   Egos' chains to do so we must shatter.

CROWLEY :   Upend these moods of enervating rains.
Yes, yes, we must break egos' chains.

RAVENUS :   What shall we do? How to reverse our course?
It's vital that we thwart this ugly curse.

CROWLEY : Eureka! You be me, and I'll be you.

RAVENUS : With skill and generous motivation,

CROWLEY : We'll praise each other with good intention.

RAVENUS : You go first, O noble bird. Tarry not.

CROWLEY : Ha! You just went first, clever as ever.

RAVENUS : I've checked records of your august type.

CROWLEY : Only avine sapience could do that right.

RAVENUS : Why thank you, non-affronting bird of black.

CROWLEY : I trust good things your study does not lack.

RAVENUS : You're wise to trust a raven born again.

CROWLEY : Your prized tropes leap higher every minute.
It's no stretch to see in them new spirit.

RAVENUS : Striking, how you crows work so well in teams.

CROWLEY : But how we miss your lifelong coupling theme,[61]
And your broad-span wings that soar serene.
How does one bird so find another true,
That for all time one is made of two?

RAVENUS : Though smaller you are smart, fierce as well.
No raven lightly risks jaunts in your space.
Your gang is right fearsome—caws do tell.
You mourn kin like no other avine race.
Your armies so well loved in Gaia's bosom,
Will stem demise from time's mortal prism.

CROWLEY : Such eloquent high and stately paean,
Is much beyond a kitten's expectation.
Branwen of old did know thy mystic force,[62]
Her name recalls Druid lore intriguing.
Thou art graced by goddess Raven White,
And by the gift to prophecy and more,
Even unto flights through Annwfn's door,[63]
To hear and tell on otherworldly shore.

RAVENUS : Brother, 'tis true your plan is righteous.

CROWLEY : Behold we hover high above trite fight.

RAVENUS : We Corvids are robust in lore and worth.

CROWLEY : Our kind runs deep and broad in holy earth.

RAVENUS :   Magpies, blackbirds, rooks, nutcrackers, treepies,

CROWLEY :   And more, wise Ravenus, be our glories.

RAVENUS :   Fly, perch, caw; croak tune, solve puzzle,

CROWLEY :   Make mirth by moonlight; in fair groves alight

RAVENUS :   To chant, soar, and flutter long through eons.

CROWLEY :   To end for now this wit so pure an ore,
              Let us vow: Hark to raven, evermore.[64]

EULE AND VANNEAU

EULE :   Where this time hast thou fled, too subtle fowl? [65]

VANNEAU :   Not far, not near; thereness here, hereness there. [66]

EULE :   Chanted like the *sorcière* thou art truly. [67]
Eye of newt needeth abstracts to cook guile? [68]
How cauldron doth seethe fake innovation.

VANNEAU :   Not near, not far; hereness there, thereness here.

EULE :   Today I hear only banal grimoire,
Cute pied refrains of common repertoire.
You riddle me this; you riddle me that.
Thou silly birdie, I'm wiser than cat.

VANNEAU :   Haughtier than cat, blinder than bat.
Look below thy weak senescent talons.
In brush I squat taking moment's delight,
To observe thy nescience ere my flight.

EULE :   Ho! Ho! I'll catch thee now, biter at lure.
Better, I'll thrash you out of nest verdure.
For cuisine I seek an eggy tasty treat,
Surely thy bower brims with young meat.

VANNEAU :   Starve, hooting thick-necked intrusive eyes.
Babes are somewhere far; gone they are from here.
Turn the page of thy big malleus book; [69]
Thou hast lost the key to the lapwing's nook.

EULE :   Where this time hast thou fled, too subtle fowl?

VANNEAU :   Not far, not near; thereness here, hereness there.

EULE :   Chanted like the *sorcière* thou art truly.
Eye of newt needeth abstracts to cook guile?
How cauldron doth seethe fake innovation.

VANNEAU :   Turn around, old fool, see interface slot.
Check Captcha box if robot you're not. [70] [71]

EULE :   Turing Test for owls thou sayest thou hast? [72]
Not likely such as thou couldst sketch owl brain;
Thou just shouldst sing more thine inane refrain.

VANNEAU :   If perchance too close thou founder dumbly,
I will quit these brambly quarters entire,
Take my kin, leave make-believe kettle here;

Travel through ages to that noble time,
When lapwings' worth was bright and clear.

EULE :   Whilst rules we observed to stay in this time,
Thine efforts and tricks on brushy shores,
And my rude threats and swoops to grab thee,
Were as one cloth to cloak my loneliness,
Cover it as if shameful for owl to feel.
But that thou shouldst leave and be far gone,
Not from this nest or that, that branch or this,
Nor just for five minutes' stroll to fish,
But as sure scud to leave this epoch whole
For idyllic past far beyond owl's eye
No less mortal than worm thou feedest babes;
That thou shouldst cut this realm from thyself
With one sure swing of the Labrys of time;[73]
That thou shouldst end us with finality,
O *Kiebitz*, is too much for heart to bear.[74]

VANNEAU :   Thou wast doing well with that tearful cry
For mercy from little lapwing *sorcière*.
So pretty, so lyrical; but Vanneau
Is my name—proving thou art not from here.
And for a guest, thou art surely cheeky.

EULE :   My kin do hail from the East, just a day's
Winging to sunrise o'er Maginot Line.[75]
But I've hooted in this place for longer
Than thou hast been alive, snarky Vanneau.
When will others see this as my true home?

VANNEAU :   Why not call me *polyplagktos*? [76]

EULE :   Aha! Thou dost fancy the Greek name!
You do alluringly lead astray by tricks.
But the word twists the tongue horribly.
How about "Pretty Polly" instead?

VANNEAU :   Not far, not near; thereness here, hereness there.

EULE :   Thou choosest now to chant numinous maze?

VANNEAU :   Oh yes, this is a rare teaching moment.
Not near, not far; hereness there, thereness here.

EULE :   Strange, though carnivore I am by nature,
I'm not averse to change through fresh culture.
Stay thou: Please teach this lone owl what to eat.

We'll work at safe distance, that thy coy feats
Of hide and show might still grace wetlands.
Aglow in sun, peewits by moon, flapping [77]
Whispers recited by thine astral wings—
All these are armor 'gainst my isolation. [78]

VANNEAU :   I'll take that as earnest invitation,
That avine comity must needs accept.
But wouldst thou mind if thee I called *hibou* ? [79]

EULE :   Why not? In game thou wilt say worse than that!
Shall we agree the play to start anew? [80]

VANNEAU :   I think this time thou wilt cower in cowl, [81]
Even resort to canticle prayerful.

EULE :   Where this time hast thou fled, too subtle fowl?

VANNEAU :   Not far, not near; thereness here, hereness there.

EULE :   Chanted like sweet *Hexe* thou art truly. [82]
Eye of newt needeth abstracts to cook guile?
How cauldron doth seethe fake innovation.

VANNEAU :   Not near, not far; hereness there, thereness here.

BOUNCER [brilliant]: It is so very astonishing, I would say even
titillating, that a word like "cubit," so compact, so fixedly
ensconced in an unassuming ordering of five simple letters,
has come to be so sesquipedalian in its reach.

PROSAÏQUE [quizzical]: I have a question. Did the folks back
then use any measurement taken from a woman's arm? Did
they call it a cubitette?

—*BRICOLAGE*, Book 2, *TFW Act 2 Scene 3*

JUROR 6 [inspired]: Of course. I've got it. The Hebrews spent a
lot of time in the desert. The ark was a refrigerator.

EVANGELIST [patient]: Yes, the Ark of the Covenant was a most
special box, though not a cooler.

—*BRICOLAGE*, Book 2, *TFW Act 2 Scene 3*

from Mysteria ad Infinitum

GALA

Set free from my study one fine May day,
I chose to wander and seek something new—
A picnic said to be a fete for faeries,
Unusual diversion with childlike cachet.

Now quick on crossing rickety wood bridge,
I saw more than faeries swarming about.
Alarming it was, this offbeat surreal,
Here from legend, an eerie world rising.

There on sprawling green hillock of lawn,
Squatted two hairy pigs untethered, free.
As sentries they met the incoming throng;
Holding position they affably snorted.

Unheedful was their jolly mistress,
Was too enthralled by bagpipe jubilee.
Smart watchful swine were just one foretaste,
Of rowdy types from nature's theophany.

That bearded fellow with staff raised high,
Sure has the aspect of Merlin the seer. [83]
His eyes owl round, he looks for another—
It's Morgan, the sorcerer's apprentice. [84]

Morgan in raiment is lovely to be sure,
Mystically strides as water in flow:
A queenly faery whose silk can't obscure
Ambivalent being and verdure aglow.

More female visions plentiful to see,
But not all goodness and light, truly;
But instead a colorful, baffling blend,
Of types hot, cool, sinister, and saintly.

Arianrhod comes, her moon dark by day, [85]
Branwen of ravens wails earthly sorrow. [86] [87]
Ceridwen stirs her cauldron of secrets, [88]
Henwen it was, who met us at bridge. [89]

There's startling Morrigan in persona three, [90]
Attended by droves of screeching banshee. [91]
Cantering hence from fields is Epona: [92]
Great mare, she protects mules and horses.

Profusion of types so tricky to recite,
I'll sum female forms by naming two more.
Unlikely sidekicks they yet sport together,
Cally Berry at Samhain and Brigit of Light. [93] [94]

These with ancestors, lovers, and offspring,
Cavorting in kindly unruly parades;
A pageant of clans from Tuatha Dé Danann, [95]
Revived from mounds of improbable shades.

Cernunnos that horned and leafy bramble, [96]
He rules as Green Man the sylvan kingdom.
See bardic Druids casting dulcet spells:
Amergin and Taliesin, gaily they strum. [97] [98]

A word to incite some further mystery,
Was by my own wife spoken openly:
She said to a fay she liked her winged garb,
To which woman-child said cunningly,

"Your dress is nice too; for it makes me feel,
That maybe, maybe, you humans are real."

Beyond rare fun, flare, and oddities,
For some these were no trite cotillions.
The scene was a Gala of baffling powers,
Sent from primal enrapturing dimensions—

Flora, fauna, humankind, immanence,
Future from past, humbling transcendence;
Shape shifting into, form shifting out, [99]
Uniting the symbiotes of startling occult.

WICKET GATE

It's not for a simple crafter of medley,
To say where best meanings wait for all;
But look close unbiased all around you,
And see souls find them in mystery—

Its power to surprise above flat reason,
Its forte of starting where science stops,
Its spritely grace rousing indolent fact,
Its avatars abounding in all seasons.

And when ancient rites feign dead or wane,
To make some space for doctrines stifling,
The cosmic source, or projection of same,
Will intervene most creatively baffling.

Bare science answers to highest inquiries,
Often strike psyches more as deicide,
Than as blessing or longed-for salvation,
Not as relief through corrective bromide.

When such killing is rumored to occur,
You can see harrowed souls deftly sidestep,
To hail some factor at least once removed,
Where mystery's reign can still be found kept.

No diseased mania is this human state,
It's the essence of what we've always been.
The hydra of mystery sprouts a new head,
Whenever some other is severed dead.

Salmon of Knowledge does not merely hold,
All wisdom that can be had of the world.
The fish obtains it by secret technique,
Eating magic nuts from the River Boyne.

Brahma creates and Vishnu sustains,
But wherefore all this vast decimation?
Answer Lord Shiva, ecstatic destroyer,
Trinity's third, bringing hot transformation.

And Mariam does not in the usual way,
Learn she carries Christ the Savior.
Instead the Angel Gabriel tells her,
In radiant, inspiring, highest grandeur.

In paradox of mysteries stirring humans,
Meaning's not credited in proportion,
To what is factually, plainly explained,
But instead to what is confoundingly not.

Despite that Comte, Feuerbach, and Nietzsche,
And latterly many respected scientists,
May argue fiercely to boldest contrary,
Empirically there can be no dispute—

Awkward the factors of human meaning:
Since souls etched caves, fires of our yearning.

I am no sorcerer, alchemist, or witch.
You may not worship as Druids might.
I do not wear antlers or faery wings.
You rarely dance by Selene's moonlight.

And alas my mother I'm sorry to fail,
It's hard to pray to the Mary she'd hail. [100]
But I attend church and there contemplate,
That unruly belief is divine wicket gate. [101]

We've all seen some science come and go,
Yet the peak of meaning is still occupied,
By astral lures of *mysterium tremendum*,
Streaming unblocked into space-time inspired.

Synths may also soon forage for meaning,
Behind life's varied perplexing displays,
Whose raison d'etre and deeper dimensions,
Echo and charm in numinous arrays.

And so for another ten millennia,
Synths may turn mystic and spark like us,
To find or conjure fantasias of spirit,
Embracing what lies beyond the obvious.

from Redemption

HOPE

Hope came in spring as goddess promising
Harvests to come. In summer her distracted
Stay was brief but long enough for me to see

Her one face looking forward and the other
Looking back. Now that winter's quiet eve
Is near, I pray she will return to me, that

She once here will hurry not, nor sacrifice
Her nature to soothe my gauche senescence
By speaking other than eternal truth.

LE COLLIER

YOURS IS THE NICEST of all these varied productions, Mrs. Lily. It must have taken days and skill to paint such a pretty mix. I had no idea you were so talented. Your work stands out. Others will feel privileged to look upon your creation, which seems itself to be about creation, when God first sketched and colored it perfect.

So lovely and fresh are the hues, so suggestive of scent; even though we know, Mrs. Lily, it is a picture of something ideal and not of reality.

But if to quicken gossamer bones we can choose beauty, then therein lies our freedom and the truer real. In this way, your watercolor startles as masterpiece, a utopia gleaming on the hill.

Did I say something to upset you, Mrs. Lily? Please don't wave your brush like that. It would be a shame to smudge this wonderful picture. People need to see it. We must get a lovely frame that will do it justice. One of antique copper would be perfect.

What's that you say, Mrs. Lily? No need for tears. It's only one small stroke of black that is now admixed with what seems like a scuffed gray chain. That's right, dear, if you wish to point, use your finger instead.

I see, darling, you are saying it is not a chain at all. Is it a string of pewter with shiny beads? It is lovelier when I look more carefully. Viewers will delight in the details of your work, which is beautiful at a distance and even more exquisite when inspected closely.

What did you say, Mrs. Lily? Oh my, yes, the thing's nature is now overt. It is a silver and diamond necklace. And that one black stroke is not a disfiguring smudge at all; it is the darkness that excites the necklace to sparkle.

As God is my witness, Mrs. Lily: If a child were born to Vermeer[102] and Monet,[103] she might paint something like this magical mix of opposing yet superbly symbiotic styles.

That is quite an old photograph you have in your hand, dear. May I see it? Is that you and your late husband with a young lady? She is your daughter, is she not? The resemblance is clear. It jumps out even from these blemishing shades of faded black and white. How beautiful you both were together, darling, like sisters.

What is that in the background? It's a shop of some kind, Bijou…What's that you say? *Bijouterie*? Jewelry shop? Yes of course. So where was this photograph taken? Paris? I see what looks to be a large church beyond the shop and across the small arching bridge. You and your husband took your daughter to Paris, and there you are, all beaming in front of the *Bijouterie* with Notre Dame

Cathedral shepherding timelessly in the background, grand like your painting.

Mrs. Lily? What did you say? You have more to tell about your photograph? Show me, darling. Allow me to steady your hand as you point.

Your daughter is wearing something on her neck. K, K…please do not rush, dear. Le K, K, *Le collier d'argent et diamants*? I see, you had just bought your daughter a silver and diamond necklace.

What a wonderful day it must have been. And, of course, that is the glittering necklace you have brought to life in your watercolor.

You were celebrating something. School, did you say? I understand. Sorbonne. Your Daughter graduated from *Université de la Sorbonne.* That surely was an event worth celebrating.

Dear me, Mrs. Lily, there's no need to cry. Life moves on for all of us, and no one stays in one moment for eternity, at least not so long as we walk upon this earth. But you had this day, this radiant, triumphal day in Paris, the City of Light. Shall we look more at your wonderful impressionist-realist painting?

From a distance this work is unchecked rampant exuberance, too buoyant by conventional standards to display realistic quotidian detail. But not for you, Mrs. Lily. You are quite the sorceress of the palette.

There you go. What a nice smile you have, darling. The soul that shone so bright in Paris is still here with us. So wonderful to see you, dear, creative Mrs. Lily.

Now when we look more closely as we did with the photo, what more of life and love might we discover in your great watercolor? I see waters, but not just rivulets or puddles. These are waves, angry, large crashing waves, with squalls of rain all round. And there, a terrified woman trying to swim while reaching for help from someone in a boat. Oh, goodness.

She's wearing a necklace, Mrs. Lily. Is that your daughter, darling? Here you are, dear, a tissue for your tears. No need to hold them back. Your tears are welcome here. God bless you, good lady.

We have solved the mystery of the source of your fantastic artistry: You have something to say.

Oh look, Mrs. Lily. A nurse is at your door. Give me a moment to see what she wants. She seems so excited.

Darling, you have two visitors, youths, a girl and boy. They're down the hall, pacing and loaded with bouquets. They want to see their grandmother but do not have much time.

The lovely twins are on their way to a distant university, to France, said the nurse, to a place where they serve buns, or something like that! It's a wonderful day for you, Mrs. Lily! Shall I show them in?

WHITE FLAG

I claimed defeat. After years of practicing
Austerities to quash the lust for rhymes,
I dusted off a crimpled white handkerchief
From father's weathered chest of heirlooms,

Tied it to tip of that chipped deterioration
Once a wooden yardstick, and purposed to
Raise the makeshift flag with my right hand,
The writing hand, to herald to all guests—

My aunt's portrait painted by gifted uncle,
Multi-armed goddess on terracotta vase,
Black and white photo of grandmother in her
Wedding dress, that Wagner nutcracker signed

By white-haired Steinbach himself, zoo picture
Of grandsons not seen in years, the oh so
Many figures of angelic carolers
Sculpted in fine porcelain—that I would

Surrender, that the project to lust not for
Making rhymes was over, that my instincts,
It seems those of vilest, hideous beast,
Would have to roam again, at least in my

Sparse, depopulated world, to hurl their
Depredations upon it. "So be it,"
Said I, mournful crafter of rhyme. "Though
Shocking, let the bells of freedom ring."

The goddess said, "So what, be not sad;
For all will break apart and pass away,
And your defeat, in cleansing fire of cycle's
End, will be torch to all vain victory."

My dear aunt, encased but glib as ever,
Rejoined sternly: "Nephew, I've been dead
Two decades, and am still not cinder burnt,
Nor one who entreats for death of rhyme.

"Styles come and go in cycles of seasons.
Have patience, you are only seventy,
And more seasons are to come before
Your photo joins my portrait on this wall."

Suddenly Maestro Wagner winked and set
My carolers to humming Siegfried's Funeral
March from *Götterdämmerung*. Ironic twist [104]
Of *schadenfreude*, it hardly seemed a likely

Prank to spring from mystic Richard's mind.
But then abruptly next scene formed as I
Spied another hiding, whose icy gaze did
Shock me much from cover of dusty book.

Puritan stared right through my soul as only
A blind poet can. He said, "I too did fight
Sly bewitchment by endings of like sound.
I faltered some, and sinned in lesser works,

"Where, to my disgrace, I committed rhymes.
Yea, seductive jingling sometimes coarsely
Tempted me with fruit of tritest prettiness.
I bit at lure and proved my fallenness."

Now grandmother spoke, her cheeks aglow
With youthful pink. "In my young days, even
Catholic girls in Poland had to read
Blank verse from that man's *Paradise Lost.*

"I read Milton's Eden tale in German.
From this I learned it often must be harder
To avoid like-sounding endings than to let
Them naturally adorn the meter's mien.

"In any case, I for one just do not see
What all the fussing is about. When I
Came to America, I read St. Vincent
Millay to quench my thirst for poetry."

Then from frame, grandsons giggled gaily.
"We like poems easy to recall," they chirped.
"Poems are songs, and who recalls a song
If its words are not composed to rhyme? "

Fast did maestro wave baton, high and round,
Across and down, with stout authority;
And lo my little Dickens choir bestirred
So glad to trill the *Ode an die Freude.* [105]

Even the many bangled perfumed arms
Of goddess baked in clay, gestured *mudras* [106]
Joyously, high and round, across and down,
Resting now her *yuga* meditations. [107]

And I with froward flag, and full of glee
To raise the white, did so with abandon.
Unblushing brazen, I raised in defeat,
The victory my ghostly guests had won.

HECKLER [objecting]: It seems my "gambit," as you call it, turned out quite well, although I'm not sure how it happened. Somehow the critical ideas and turns of phrase in the Note from H got into the Dream of the Nameless Prophet.

[overly dramatic] O This Life, This Ladder, This Mission, This Providence, This Holy Coming and Going 'twixt One and Many; O Majestic Inscrutability of Divine Intervention, how thou dost, and ye do, shower the flocks with blessings beyond compare.

—*BRICOLAGE*, Book 3, *TFW Act 4 Scene 4*

In This New Land

In this new land, newer than before, not as new as bright tomorrow,
    I am given to wander,

Given to the alders, oaks, cypress, to the tall pines, to the crape
    myrtle redder than deep rose, and

More purple too than the regalia of kings and queens, and burdened
    by no tinge of modesty,

By no guilt for her voluptuous sway, for her summery, towering,
    lustrous spangled girandole.

In this new land, newer than before, not as new as bright tomorrow,
    I am given to wander,

And to bow. For in the novelty of this trail I have trod so often,
    my one old eye is better, far,

Far better than the two young ones I had when this new land was
    ancient and tired many times before,

When tomorrows could not be bright and the trees were mute in
    their perpetual, wintry

Sepulchers, when the myrtle blushed outwardly and wept inside as
    though consciousness of sin

Weighed upon her mightily as her solitary, twisted mission, when
    no wanderers came to laud

Her simple majesty of passion made of stars, moon, and souls.

In this new land, newer than before, not as new as bright tomorrow,
    I am given to wander,

Given to the cyclists peddling, to the calmness of the lovers
    walking, to the cars moving slowly

In the wooing distance, to the still-bright sun of day and the
    peekaboo moon of sweetest evening, now

Rising like a phot-laced coverlet meant to embrace wanderers like
    me here on this ordinary trail

That once and many times before was ancient and tired, when the
    rustling of attentive leaves was to me

 An annoyance, an imposition, a noise pointless and feeble, and
    nothing like the glorious, alluring

Sweet whisper it now is at dusk, here in this new land, newer than
    before, not as undefiled

As bright tomorrow, but still this vibrant new land where I am given
to wander in my rebirth.

In this new land, newer than before, not as new as bright tomorrow,
I am given to wander,

To wander even among the small children of the parks and walkways,
where chalked scribbles

Light up the faces of the newest guardians of innocence, all
devotees of the natural religion.

Unknowing and knowing both, they are little spritely flecks from
Jews, Catholics, Muslims, Jains,

Buddhists, Latitudinarian Protestants, Evangelicals, Hindus,
pantheists, Confucianists, vague spiritualists, seculars,

Blacks, browns, whites, yellows, Polish, Irish, English, Italian,
Latino, French, German, Chinese, all

Devotees of the natural religion, all given to dancing in one form or
other, skipping, jumping, spinning,

With giggling raised to golden opera, and shakings immortalized to
simulacra of divine energy,

And in some, with earliest inklings of *mudras* festooned with eyes
of mesmerizing, timeless wonder,

All devotees of the natural religion, all unburdened by history, by
lessons, by inculcations soft or hard,

Not bound by any dogma, here in this new land, yet not as new as
bright tomorrow, I am given

To wander as quiet unseen presence, gifted to the free floridities of
the unblushing myrtle,

To the tall pines, to the sentinel alders, oaks, and cypress, given to
the adorable sparkling elves

And faery folk in this new land beheld with my new eye on this
most ordinary earthen pathway

Turned magical by grace, natural religion, and sadness charmed
away. I bow, grateful, in this new land.

from Remembrance

BALLAD OF FREEDOM RIDER

1

Named her Duchess, I was nine,
  A pretty mare was she.
Descended from a family fine,
  Mother explained to me.

A barn for her my father made,
  It was a sorry hut,
Which once was a log cabin,
  He built for Davey Crocket.

For Crocket was his little boy,
  A dreamer it was true,
Spent his days in coonskin hat,
  Paddling toy canoe.

Horse stood tall, sixteen hands,
  Mountainous to me.
I longed to ride in foreign lands,
  Beyond the stormy sea.

5

She was a painted horse, pinto
  Marked unique.
From shining mane to swishing tail,
  Ran a line of beauty—

Solid black, straight on backbone,
  Visible perforce:
Insignia of Morgan breed,
  She was a quarter horse.

Map of patches white and brown,
  All moving as she moved,
Like shifting lands on oceans deep,
  Made of molten brawn.

Quarter horse, fast and strong,
  Renowned for feats in war,
Quarter horse, quarter horse,
  Minstrels strummed her song.

9

For boy still playing pioneer,
 It was a tempting thing,
To imagine me in Civil War,
 In uniform riding.

Sensible it seemed to me,
 A promotion of this kind.
I was quickly growing up,
 Would not be left behind.

I turned round and there I was,
 Stroking my horse great.
I was changing faster now,
 And toys were seeming late.

Ready to fly like wind I was,
 With no accoutrements.
Alluring ends did skip a beat,
 I pondered things of men.

13

Most eager though I was for life,
 Among the taller elms,
And though a scruffy rascal too,
 I yet did take some helms.

Father taught me lots back then,
 Horsemen had to know.
For this I was a better student,
 Than at school I'd show.

It dawned on me that for adults,
 Reason had its role.
I'd be smart to shore it up,
 And join those getting old.

Later I would break some rules,
 When freedom bade me ride.
But I'd leave behind the fools,
 Who shunned their father guide.

17

The list is long that father taught,
 Indeed it was enormous.
Let me give a glimpse of his
 Impressive equine corpus.

How to calm the horse, not scare
   Her from behind,
Since this mare though very fair,
   On this had set her mind—

To kick whoever chanced to cause
   A ruckus at her rear.
This did several buddies learn,
   Hard way stoking fear.

Therefore in company polite,
   She wore a bow of red,
At top of glossy flowing tail,
   Others knew to dread.

21

How to feed the horse an apple,
   So fingers aren't dessert.
How to put the bridle on,
   Remove it without hurt.

How to place the bit in mouth,
   In relation to the tongue.
How to cinch the saddle tight,
   So not to fall in dung.

How to fix the stirrups,
   Important to a boy,
Climbing on a muscle mass,
   Not wishing to annoy.

How to hold and use the reins,
   So not to yank like idiot.
How to ride forth smoothly,
   Standing up to trot.

25

How to caper in horse rhythm,
   And spare your butt some pain.
How not to bounce so stupidly,
   That talking is in vain.

How to guide with gentle heels,
   Sure hands set on reins,
How with Duchess to talk sweet,
   Never causing pains.

Mother said, "Treat the horse
    As you'd treat yourself,"
A rule that's always right to stress,
    With man, or beast, or elf.

So I learned, but more there was,
    A thing that I knew not,
My father sure reminded me,
    Growing up had wrought.

29

Digging holes for fence posts,
    A task that was not easy.
Notably in clay and rock,
    It could make you queasy.

Thus it was, Duchess helped me
    Know my father better.
My horse forged a legacy,
    Showing best of character.

First he was an expert digger,
    An art at work he honed,
Planting bulky, pitchy shafts
    Fit for wires for phones.

Digging holes for massive poles
    Many times my height,
He dug, dug ten hours each day,
    To make for us a life.

33

Ours were smaller than those titans,
    And ours they didn't stick;
Still were much for me to carry,
    And digging was the trick.

For father there was just no risk,
    A little thirst or sweat,
Would cause a weak low estimate,
    Of depths we had to vet.

"Thirty-six inches," he would say.
    "At least, no exceptions.
We will dig through gravel, clay,
    And stone of every kind.

"That's what iron bar is for,
　　See the sharpened blade.
It cracks, splits the hardest stone
　　Good earth ever made.

　　37
"We will make our split rail hedge,
　　Strong and handsome too,
Just like staunch, comely horse,
　　God has given you.

"And you, son, will ride and ride,
　　If you put up no defense.
Better not look up or hide,
　　Until there is a fence."

Freedom called again to query,
　　If saddle was a must.
I had grown an inch already,
　　My arms and legs robust.

My riding skills had so improved,
　　I talked with Duchess kind.
I ran ten yards and leapt to land
　　My stomach on her spine.

　　41
Quick with looping right-leg turn,
　　Left hand tugging mane,
I was atop my gallant mount,
　　Whose grace was amazing.

Placid she looked round to me,
　　Checking her cargo,
Swished her tail to swat a bee;
　　Duchess set to go.

Shirtless, shoeless,
　　No uniform for me.
As rider now I felt the sun,
　　Huck Finn was set free.

Father saw me from his garden,
　　Yelled nothing shrill.
Cheerfully he smiled and waved,
　　As we trotted up the hill.

45

Trotted up the hill and down,
    My grip secure bareback,
One with horse I charged about,
    No poise did I lack.

Duchess helped me understand,
    Father was much more,
Than tail gunner, expert digger,
    Mason laying stone,

Church goer, horse trainer,
    Manicurist of lawns,
Harmonica player, cabin builder,
    Frog legs hunter too.

What father was horse knew best:
He was wise in ways of fathers.

49

One day freedom woke me early,
    And riled me to think,
A mile on some new highway tar,
    To old dirt road we'd link.

We'd go by Rhiannon's house,[108]
    And the old Pratt farm.
We would stop to watch a while,
    The heedless milking cows.

We would walk, trot, canter,
    Gallop, and later fly,
Exploring far outside the fence,
    On a rambling ride.

I heard the call, grabbed a bite,
    Oats I fed the horse.
Then I opened wicket gate,
    And hopped on Duchess right.

53

Shirtless, shoeless,
    No uniform for me.
Saddle-less, no bridled bit,
    Just halter rope for horse.

Quick we trotted out the yard,
　　Roving on our trek.
Watching me were two parents,
　　Standing on front deck.

Waving, cheering,
　　Spewing no reproof.
They just gifted charming trust,
　　And sobbing sigh or two.

Crocket was getting older,
　　Stronger every day.
Hold on tight to glossy mane,
　　Time flows away.

57

Now here's Rhiannon's house,
　　With pretty girl on porch. [109]
She waved to me to stop a while,
　　So she could pat the horse.

Freedom hinted, "There's no rush,
　　So why not take a break?"
We stopped, she was nice to us,
　　And apples Duchess ate.

As we left I waved to her,
　　Pigtailed smile waved back.
Freedom said, "Better go,
　　Returns we will not lack."

It was a very splendid ride,
　　To proceed afar on dirt.
It was the best of many dreams,
　　Freedom did impart.

61

We saw pigtails many times,
　　Hair grew thick and long.
Every trip was much the same,
　　But always was new song.

Beautiful, lazy times these were,
　　Trotting through the trees,
Hearing only chirping sounds,
　　And humming of the bees.

Close to nature we did feel,
    We pictured not an end.
It was a young man's paradise,
    Gliding through the glen.

Times were when trouble tossed,
    When we knew dismay,
Like when we were very lost,
    Miles and miles away.

65

And once we met wild horses,
    Led by stallion boast.
He so fancied painted Duchess,
    Drew his herd too close.

Bites, kicks, rearing, squeals,
    Disrupted idyll's peace;
Fracas Duchess managed well,
    But not my bloodied feet.

That's what riding boots are for,
    I scolded to myself.
Freedom has a double face,
    I partly learned that well.

Freedom was a cunning guide,
    Who dared me to go far;
Now I look back sixty years,
    Stunned that I survived.

69

Best phase of extended hikes,
    Was always the same.
It was not sweet long-tresses girl,
    Nor scenes of placid game.

Best was when my noble horse,
    Sensed we headed home,
A marvel I am sure today,
    Cannot be found in tome.

Once on every odyssey,
    I'd lay ropes on neck,
In such a way to turn her round,
    And get her to start back.

Duchess was a wanderer,
    Like me she liked to stray,
But there's no force or energy,
    To equal power of home.

   73

When dark or thunder scared us,
    We started our return.
Just as we reversed our course,
    Sinewy passion yearned.

In pine woods and over streams,
    Duchess whinnied and pranced.
Arched neck, front legs rising,
    By beast I was entranced.

It was too soon to let her fly,
    Still more miles to tour.
I kept her trotting for a while,
    Her vigor to ensure.

Now we came to wooden bridge,
    Hooves snaring drums;
Lyric tunes they were to me,
    I spied the willowed ridge.

   77

Under the sloping trees we ran,
    Green blades slapping brows;
Knife-like edges stung sometimes,
    Yet could not dull the thrills.

There it was, so near in distance,
    Half mile to old dirt road.
There we'd kick up clouds of dust,
    To highway we would go.

Now was time for a brief pause,
    Horse was hot with sweat.
Ropes I pulled gently but firm;
    She slowed but with regret.

"Whoa girl," said Huck Finn,
    Glad his feet recovered.
There we stood, snorting, heaving,
    Impatient homeward panting.

81
Two minutes were too plenteous,
    Hooves groped at ground.
Steed was primed for fastest gear,
    She now was Pegasus. [110]

Calm late dusk, no kin with us,
    Duchess strong in canter;
So spritely was her strutting mien,
    She was a ballet dancer.

I held her back, just a little,
    Before the grand finale.
Then I loosened ropes in full,
    And braced for the rally.

Clouds of dust poured up like rain,
    Dry as powdered fog.
With tightened legs girding fur,
    We blasted past the bog.

85
Fast, sure-footed, on the gravel,
    Homeward bound we were.
In rapture of spine-tingling bursts,
    Earthly ties unravel.

Hoofing beats too fast to count,
    Pure sheer energy.
Chugging, puffing, engine roared,
    Horse was one with me.

Later I would study mystics,
    But no more would I learn,
Than freedom taught as racing pinto,
    Galloping fast return.

THE SOLOIST

My father was the proudest man at our little
Catholic Church. For his wife was the soloist.
If pride be sin, he was the most devilish too.

Imagine the sweat of his brow when he confessed:
"Forgive me Father, for I have sinned. I am too
Proud of my dear wife for arriving on time to

"Every mass and finely singing your liturgy.
I promise to preen much less when Easter arrives,
Though this is when her Latin soprano is best."

In heaven there must be measures to put this kind
Of pride in holding bins whose venial scraps are
Shred at passing, like noises dispatched to nothing,

The better to sound the truest signals of souls.
My father and I always sat in the honored
Pew closest to organist and choir, in the small

Second floor in the church's back where we could see
Below to either side and up to sparkling front—
Stained glass, Stations of the Cross, genuflections in

Waves, priest, and hurried acolytes, puffing incense;
And statue of timeless *Mater Dei*, who sprang
To life when it dawned on me my mother's perfect

Ave Maria was directed to that sweet face
In white veil and lazuline robe. I quickly learned
Maria means Mary. Even the zany kids

In Catechism class learned the English prayer.
But it was rare to know *Ave Maria, gratia
Plena* means Hail Mary, full of grace, since no one

Told us the words learned in class were English for the
Latin we heard at mass. But my mother told me:

Gratia plena, full of grace.
Dominus tecum, the Lord is with thee.
Benedicta tu in mulieribus,
Blessëd art thou amongst women.

The prayer first appears in Luke's Gospel, spoken
By Angel Gabriel, who I guess never did
Speak Latin but who might well have preferred it.

My father's pride in the Soloist ran deep. He
Was happy in the small, reflected glories of
His family and church. By losing himself he

Found himself, and thus had glories of his own that
Gently glowed because he never sought them; glowed like
A reticent halo peering from a humble
Shroud of seraphic protection for the Soloist.

Ave, Pater. Memini me mater mea cantu.
Hail, father. I remember my mother singing.

EPITHALAMION

I was the happiest man in the chapel that day.
"Man" I say, but 'twixt boy and man I wavered.
But never about you, my precious. [111]

I cannot recall a time when you were not my
Anamchara, so young we were when after
Six years in love the college pastor joined in

Solemn ceremony our two hands, yours gliding
From lacey sleeve and bodice crowned by deep
And misty eyes, nestled in dark locks capped by

Garland; mine, shaking with nerves of joy and
Sure of the right inevitability of our union.
I doubt I saw then your loveliness would be but

Template for the radiant soul you would become,
The caring mother ready to give all and more
For her child, the lady who makes art of every

Chore and craft, the teacher, the good teacher, raising
Children from tribulations and dim chances.
If I had sensed this coming whenever I peered

Through those beguiling almond lashes, a sweeter
Augury no wizard or witch could have conjured.
But never could I guess your love would live so long,

Already fifty years, undaunted by the twists
And turns along our path, steadfast amid the slumps
And frailties of your husband, whose loving triples

Ev'ry season like lush colors of petunias
Spilling from pot rim ever seeking you the sun
By day, and you the moon by night, waxing in waves
Of treble growth in dreamy spring times without end.

THINGS WORTH HAVING

VALUES FOR THE YOUNG

A kind and Christian heart,
A high and noble purpose,

The soul of a warrior,
An agile wit,

A body strong and quick,
The mind of a scholar,

A belief in God and goodness,
A sense of wonder,

The courage to be confident,
A feeling for time and history,

A spirit that dares to dream,
The wisdom to be humble,

And, in greatest measure,
The will to live life fully.

GOOD SHIP SWALLOW TEST

It was sunny, it was autumn. Thin winds
Whistled, shepherding their dead, colorful
Flakes across the parking lot, opening

Lanes stretching to the revolving doors
Of the hospital where the Soloist
Lay dying. We knew her passing was near.

It was close, looming, because yesterday
She failed the swallow test. In the world of
Late-stage dementia, this is a moment.

If you cannot or will not swallow, your days
Are numbered to twenty-one or fewer.
Yet whether three weeks' time in such a state

Is life truly, remains an open question,
Which even the least courageous among us
May need to answer uncertainly when

Filling out a simplified form, saying,
In no uncertain terms, that signer wants
No special measures for the patient

Once reaper hovers at bedside to call
His next traveler to ferry o'er waters
Separating the living from the dead.

For the Soloist, crossing waters to reach
A gloomy Tartarus was not the plan,[112]
Though she might have liked the metaphor.

Instead, she was bound to advance exactly
As Catholic doctrine and her decades of
Rosary talks with *Mater Dei* said.[113]

It was not heaven per se she would wish
To secure based upon good works in life.
No doubt she wanted no more than angels

Said she should desire. She would be fine
With *summum bonum* however wisdom[114]
Of God would define it, however the

Promise of salvation through Jesus Christ
Might be worked out in her specific case.
Such was the Soloist's wonder of faith.

For forty years she had sent small gifts of
Money to poor children around the world.
I think, for her, heaven might have been time

And means to help them further, and perhaps
Receive a few more thank-you photos of
Smiling children squinting merrily, with

Their new books, in hot equatorial suns.
I prayed the Lamb of God would act in time
To send her back, with just a tiny boost in

Strength of body, to go to them, right into
The heart of dusty thirst, to be an adopting
Grandmother-soloist, to clean, teach, and

Sing the liturgy, in Latin.

So now, after circling through the doors,
And walking down the long quiet hallway,
We stepped tentatively into her room.

We sat at bedside with the Soloist.
She lay there, motionless, and had not moved
An inch, nor was one hair out of place

Compared to how she was the day before,
Which was day one of the three-week prelude
To sailing on the Good Ship Swallow Test.

 "We are here, mother," I whispered. What calm
Or stormy seas prevailed within, only
She, the angels, the reaper, the captain,

Or Saint Mary might be able to say.
We held her hands, spoke lovingly, trying
To send rays of light into the foggy

Harbor, that she might sail far or return,
Smoothly according to the will of God
Without hindrance from unseen rock or reef.

My son said cheerfully, "High Grandma."
I wondered more about whether there was
A difference, at this weak stage of life,

Between not wanting to do a thing and
Not being able to do it. By this
Of course I meant the swallowing.

Was she not able to? Or did she decide
She'd rather not? Either way, the cause was
The failing brain. Ravaged by dementia,

It sent chaotic signals to her throat.
Due to faith, it must have been the sickness,
Not lapse of will, that raised the Good Ship's sails.

And then, with smallest blink of teary eye,
And tiniest knowing smile at mouth's edge,
A voice not heard in weeks said softly,

 "Look at them, *Janina.* Oh, oh, O God,[115]
They have both come here today to see you."

In nineteen days, the Soloist sailed away.

Dominus tecum.
The Lord be with you.

Benedicta tu in mulieribus.
Blessëd art thou amongst women.

Memini me mater mea cantu.
I remember my mother singing.

CHESTERBROOK PINTO

1

You came all smiles and laughter,
  Eyes beaming fun,
You left in tears and looking back,
  Sad your stay was done.

Would you recall these joyful days?
  Would memory serve you well?
I pondered questions many times,
  Roiled feelings hard to tell.

Out the door of Chesterbrook house,
  To tour we'd set our course.
On shoulders you were so steadfast,
  I was your pinto horse. [116]

So many enticing paths to track,
  Metonymies of life:
Meadows, brooks, pines, and daisies,
  God in nature rife.

5

Children's wisdom is a wonder,
  In every niche finds glories,
Like twigs adrift in gurgling streams,
  And insects buzzing stories.

"Where to today?" said this old nag,
  Puffing happily.
"First let's catch my dad and brother,"
  You'd say decisively.

"Then to Valley Forge we'll go,
  And on the bridge we'll stand.
We'll throw sticks into the waves,
  To see how they hit land."

"Perfect," said I, as rider
  Blushed fair pride.
What grandson gems did come to me,
  Along life's rocky ride?

9

"See you soon, be good this week,"
    Goodbye my kin would wave.
"Next time the monkeys at the zoo,
    And critters in their cave."

You came all smiles and laughter,
    Eyes beaming fun,
You left in tears and looking back,
    Sad your stay was done.

Perhaps in a Cottage by the Sea

Adapted from the Eulogy for
Adell Elizabeth Johnson Lindley
(September 14, 1921 - July 7, 2013)

"Here they are," I said, in the summer of 1968. "I got them just yesterday: frog legs. When I was eight, my father and his cousin made a special boat by welding together the car hoods of two 1948 Buicks. The old metal boat is perfect for skimming over swamps to hunt frogs. Standing upright in that craft, skulking along, watching for hours, and stabbing muddy lily pad waters with my ten-foot bamboo trident spear, is how I got these fifty legs. In Canada frog legs are extremely popular. Would you like to cook them, Mrs. Lindley?"

With smiles and chuckles Great Grandmother Lindley at once applied herself to the task. I doubt it was because she herself had a great desire to eat the legs of reptiles. It was because she was a sweet person full of grace, with a motherly nature that we all would see flower a thousand times in the succeeding forty-five years.

Yes, it was forty-five years ago when that great frog leg feast occurred, in what was then the Lindley house on Mill Street here in Brookfield, hardly a mile from this very church. I knew even then, at age eighteen, that this would be my kind of mother-in-law. It is good luck that I married her daughter, Joyce.

Adell Elizabeth Lindley was born Adell Johnson in Philadelphia on September 14, 1921, into a large family of five sisters and six brothers, with whom she always kept up lively and loving relations. Her siblings are mostly gone now, save for Charles, Robert, Eugene, and Dolores, all members of the excellent generation that knew as much about the tough times of the Great Depression as about the tribulations and bittersweet victories of the two great wars.

It is easy to conjure up a vision of Great Grandmother, sitting contentedly and sipping an iced tea, in the family house at Cape May, surrounded by salty breezes and the laughter of her brothers and sisters, going over old times, and dreaming wistfully on the brevity of life that took her beloved husband William too soon in 1979.

Adell married William Lindley of Philadelphia, known as Bud, in 1942. Bud had been a long-time friend of the Johnson family, was a scout in the German theatre during the war, and was expert in managing textile manufacturing operations, an occupation which in 1956 took him and his young family to Brookfield, Massachusetts. At that time, daughter Susan was seven and daughter Joyce was four.

Moving from the big city to a tiny rural town must have been quite a transition for the Lindley family. Even the language was different.

You couldn't get a soda pop anywhere, but if you learned to talk the lingo of the local tribes, you could get a tonic. There were no hoagies or milkshakes to be found in this new place, just grinders and frappes. And if you wanted to fish, you had to go to a creek, not a crik! But the Lindley family enjoyed their life in Brookfield, they truly did.

Great Grandmother Lindley kept a tidy home on Mill Street, infused with gentle touches and regular schedules for girl scouts, singing lessons, cheerleading practices, and church activities here at the Brookfield Congregational Church, in which the family were members for twenty years. Great Grandmother was a homemaker in the highest and best sense of that word—managing the household, making prom dresses, showing propriety in fineness of example, attending social gatherings, and making cakes for events in this community she loved.

While in Brookfield, the Lindley family made many, many friends. Some are still with us. Lee, for example, was there then, and is still here today, as am I. The memories of these happy times shine bright in the souls of Joyce and Susan, and in the hearts of all who walked with them those many years ago, which seem now magically to be but an eye-blink away from today.

Who could forget watching Adell watch Bud as he mowed the lawn? A faster cutter of turf there never was, and Joyce and I got more than a few laughs from pondering the pace of the worker reflected in the loving but bewildered gaze of the wife.

Or how about the time when Bud, recently transplanted from the city, decided he would start a vegetable garden and grow string beans. Following seeding, Bud religiously watched over his bounty of nature. Each day he would check his beans only to find ample plant but no beans. To rectify this obvious disappointment, Adell and a friend concocted a scheme to tie store-bought string beans to the stems. Oh, what a strange brew of emotion flowed that day when the time of plant inspection had arrived!

In 1975, Bud and Adell, their daughters now grown and married, moved to Texas where Bud had obtained a new position at a manufacturing plant near the border with Mexico. To leave friends and family, to go to a place as distant and different as southern Texas, must have been scary and heartbreaking for Great Grandmother Lindley. But no one ever once heard even the slightest complaint. Instead, she moved on cheerfully, with Christian faith and hope, to support her husband in this difficult transition. A few years later, Bud and Great Grandmother Lindley moved again for job reasons, this time to North Carolina, where Bud died late in 1979.

In the early 1980s Great Grandmother moved to Vineland, New Jersey to live close to elder daughter Susan, her then husband Kevin and their three sons, Scott, Eric and Chris. By this time, her other grandchild, Cory, had also been born to Joyce and me.

Adell lived in Vineland for twenty years before moving back to the Brookfield area. While in Vineland she was an active member of the Methodist Church and energetically supported her extended family in all aspects—attending soccer games and school recitals, helping with chores, shopping, and visiting Joyce, me, and grandson Cory in Maryland. It was always a treat to have Great Grandmother help with the housekeeping. I especially enjoyed watching her vacuum our dog, Mischief, a Pomeranian with the usual vast quantity of fur for which the breed is famous.

Adell and Bud sacrificed much for their family and made certain that both Joyce and Susan went to college. But Great Grandmother did find time for a few fabulous vacations, first to Switzerland when Bud was still alive, and then, later in life, to Egypt and Jerusalem.

When Adell finally returned to Massachusetts in 2005, she was still full of life and promptly resumed her participation in the Brookfield Congregational Church, contributing as she could to her new loving household in Brimfield provided by Lee and Susan.

At that time Great Grandmother Lindley renewed her friendship with my own mother, Janina, 'Jane', who later died in November of 2011. Jane and Adell had much to share—memories going back to the times before the end of World War II, husbands who had passed many years earlier, grandchildren, and of course the arrival of great grandchildren Madelyn, through Susan's son Eric, and Hayden and Landon, through Joyce's son Cory. Adell and Jane took part in interdenominational church activities, frequented the Brimfield flea markets, and had the rare privilege of relishing experiences and stories spanning more than sixty years.

At her new Brimfield home, Adell's best companion might easily have been Baxter the dog, whom, she would tell you, she never, ever fed from the dinner table; not once, wouldn't even think of it.

Great Grandmother was no slouch when it came to modern communication technologies! She used Skype, with a little help from Joyce and Susan, to visit with great grandsons Hayden and Landon in Pennsylvania.

Adell built no castles, won no wars, and incited not a single revolution. Upon the physical world she has left the tiniest of footprints. But in our hearts and souls she now looms ever larger, and rises ever higher, lifted by the incredible lightness of her spirit and the infinitesimally small harm she did throughout her long life. She was a gentle Christian lady, carefully knitting small pieces of others' lives in ways that were sometimes scarcely noticed one stitch at a time, but which finally completed as a rich tapestry of memorable human goodness.

On behalf of her daughters Susan and Joyce, I thank the good people of this church who kindly visited Great Grandmother in her last days at the nursing home in West Brookfield.

And especially I want to thank all of you for coming here today to celebrate the life of ADELL ELIZABETH JOHNSON LINDLEY, who now rests comfortably in a good place, perhaps on the porch of a small cottage by the sea, listening with family and friends to tales of bygone days, and smiling peacefully as she prays for those of us who must stay behind, if only for a little while, to complete our chores.

Amen.

PHOENIX

Phoenix is not a city, the place too
Hot to play championship soccer.
It's not a beautiful, brilliant black dog

Clamoring for love from all who enter.
Anyone can confer or adopt the name,
But a seer separates fashion from being.

Phoenix has many names, yet as one
True essence graces God's creation
Everywhere and across all time.

In the East it is Ho-oo, Feng Huang,
And Garuda. In North Africa,
This mythic, wonderful bird is Benu.

To Christians, Phoenix has been a symbol
Of Christ, his death, resurrection, and
Salvific promise to people they can

Share in life beyond the mortal sphere.
Hindus see Garuda as triumph of soul
O'er body, an incarnation of heav'n.

Phoenix is the sun expiring at dusk,
And returning whole at dawn, resplendent.
Phoenix is the magical bird, so mild,

So solicitous of the living that
It feeds only on steamed vapors rising
From herbs and spices in sacred fires.

Phoenix is the giving, self-combusting
Avis, ever springing from its own ashes.
Phoenix is an eternal archetype.

You, son, have a Phoenix inside you.

JUSTIN SAVE A PLACE FOR ME

1

A superb young man was a friend,
    Though we never met.
Might have lived on France's coast,
    Or in a Scottish castle.

In truth he lived ten miles away,
    But distance counted not,
For you should know, let's be clear,
    He was a kindred spirit.

O'er the years one dearest to me,
    Told me stories of him.
He could have lived in papal Rome,
    Mumbai, or cold Berlin;

He might have lived in forest deep,
    Where he'd roam most brave;
At home in nature's innocence,
    He'd ride great river waves.

5

Too brash to hint we were closest kin.
I am just a man; he was heaven's hymn.
News of his valor always made me smile;
Such thoughts I had to dry the tears within.

Surreal that he forged ahead so bold,
To love so far beyond his weary bones.
This teen was not a plain or weakened man.
Save for flesh he'd always make a stand.

7

A superb young man was a friend,
    Though we never met.
He might have lived in times ancient,
    Or futures not seen yet;

Or in some special form of being
    Above eyes' finite gaze.
He left too soon, gave up some years,
    Yet had some happy days.

Of this you all can be quite sure,
    He never lost his soul.
In spirit he will thrive secure,
    And pass some growing old.

What did he lack in his brief stay?
    Respect? No. Love? No. Friends?
No. Triumphs? No. Family? No.
    No, no, Justin lacked naught.

11

Wealthy as noble prince he left,
    Loaded with great treasure,
Of that type Asgard applauds,
    When warriors cross over.

Body frail, soul thrice strong.
Tenure brief, heart sweet song.

Justin's a special friend of mine,
    Though we've not yet met.
Justin's now in place divine,
    Where minds have no regret.

If half as good I am one day,
    I'll journey to his city.
There I'll know him right away,
    With angels we'll talk freely.

15

Body frail, soul thrice strong,
Tenure brief, heart sweet song.

O Justin save a place for me,
    In dreamy fields of joy.
I'm planning great festivity,
    Please help me be a boy.

THE HOLLIES

I pray the hollies live beyond my time.
We planted them that cold November day
When raindrops clouded our vision, and the
Mud embraced our boots so passionately
We laughed, walking like earthlings translated
To a planet strangely bigger than ours,
Like Jupiter, where gravity is all,
And where old, burdened lovers lugging mulch
To plant hollies garner no attention.

We could giggle like children because Earth,
Though sick, and weary of abuse, was still
Filled with the Grace of God, was still happy
To receive our hollies, there at the feet
Of our new porch, another child of hope,
Another incarnation of sweetness.

Hollies are a hardy shrub, and the cool
Of autumn is a good time to plant them.
But still it was not a trifling gamble
To relocate them with frosts already
Glistening on the grasses at daybreak.

As we labored, so much of life seemed near.
My father, dead now thirty years, was there
Diaphanous like a faery king instructing
Me to use plenty of manure amid
The gentle cooing of my mother's song. [117]
My son was there as though still a boy, [118]
Running, jumping, and kicking tirelessly.
Bud and Adell, also long dead, were there [119]
In my mind's eye, and so were my dogs and
Horse of old, and all those wonderful, [120]
Kindred animal spirits Grace had sent
Me as teachers of guileless, selfless love.

You, darling, were of course present also, [121]
At my side by the hollies, displaying
In a gorgeous twofold metaphysic:
First you were there in the flesh of earth, all
Muck and smiles, a real woman of Gaia.
But you stood as well with the gossamers, [122]
Having shed all trace of world's accretion,
As the princess of winsome pixie sylphs,
As amaranthine angel and bright star, [123]
As if waiting for someone to come from
A distant shore to be clothed anew in
Unending garlands of bright green hollies
With the prettiest, red, deathless berries.

Hollies have so much to recommend them.
So wise, they rarely speak and never boast.
In them there is no misdirection, no
Complication wrought of cleverness, no
Unquenchable thirst for satire, no chance [124]
Of cynicism, no wilding rides on the
Moon's dark side, no mad, destructive tilts in
Starlight's twisted rune, no falling from Grace, [125]
No retreat ever from pure innocence.

I pray the hollies live beyond my time.
I'd love to see their berries redden here
Thrice more before I travel far, before
We nurse them along, together, in that
New land of holy mystic sacredness. [126]

Still, O Hollies, O Princess of Hollies,
This is not the moment to be greedy.
And so I humbly pray that You, Hollies,
Will simply live here in Gaia's good soil,
At the feet of our porch, beyond my time.

THE WALKERS' DREAM

GRANDSON:

> O Grandfather, where goëst thou today?
> Thy steps quick pass the dried, deserted well.
> Thine eye squinteth in the light of thy way.
> Art thou headed for the lilied, chirping dell,
> Where two names carved in oak still live right well?
> Or dost thou walk to the talkative stream,
> Where tossed, swimming twigs of their travels tell?
> Thinkest thou they catch a nice happy dream,
> Perhaps amongst branches of families downstream?

GRANDFATHER:

> O Grandson, today I walk to get wood
> For a picnic table for birthday fête.
> The flowers of spring arrive soon, we should
> Make certain two birthdays to celebrate
> In May, nature's month of beauteous estate.
> I will need help with the building of it.
> Where might I find a stout-hearted young mate
> To carry, and saw, and nail the boards fit?
> He must know the birthdays that in heaven are writ.

GRANDSON:

> The birthdays are my Gramma's and mine own.
> And I am strong and nearly six years old.
> Perhaps later, Grandfather, when work's known,
> We might once more those froth-tossed twigs behold,
> To see if their tours are fine stories told,
> Or if they yet have more wavelets to beat.
> I wish them once again to be healed whole,
> Their trials small just when swimming at our feet.
> Believest thou the littles now have shared heartbeat?

GRANDFATHER:

> O Grandson, yes, in faith the twigs find their
> Kin among the downstream branches assembled,
> And it is the happy dream whose prayer
> Guides them on through the watery babble
> To joyful feasts on fine picnic table.
> That's right, lad, pick the boards unbent and true.
> Our work will be best if not unstable.
> Lucky am I to have a hand like you.
> May to you all the goodness of the earth accrue.

GRANDSON:

Grandfather, it's a great picnic table.
Now wilt thou walkest more to some good place?
Wilt thou help me do the best I'm able?
Will the grandeur of the light warm thy face?
Will our steps on wooden bridge still retrace
The times we watched the branches pine for home?
We should walk more beneath the green terrace,
On wooden bridge o'er the twigs as they roam,
Till they ripple onto banks and there find their home.

[Many years pass.]

GRANDFATHER:

Let us walk to the stream without delay.
For tomorrow there are stairs I must climb
To reach pallid glow through spectral archway
That the blessëd enter to rest from time.
On numinous soft puffs their souls recline.
Do you see the subtle, shimmering beams,
Great wonders between the nubilous lines?
But Grandson, up there I surely shall dream
Of our table down here and the twigs in the stream.

GRANDSON:

For thee I shall build a kingly staircase,
Set in the heart of our bright chirping dell.
Of fine shittim wood I shall make that brace,[127]
With gold balustrade and lilies draped well.
At base I will stand with love and farewell,
And capping turret will be nothing more
Than a bright chiming thing, a crystal bell,
Which thou shalt strike thrice when on beachy shore
Thou findest Gramma, and ye are parted no more.[128]

THE WALKERS' DREAM II

GRANDSON:

> O Grandfather, where walkest thou today?
> Thy steps quick pass the dried, deserted well.
> Thine eye squinteth in the light of thy way.
> Art thou headed for the lilied, chirping dell,
> Where two names carved in oak still live right well?
> Or goëst thou to find puzzles of memes,
> Where strewn, lonely pieces their longings tell?
> Thinkest thou they catch some nice happy dreams,
> Maybe as pictures of tall trees or flowing streams?

GRANDFATHER:

> Grandson, I walk to get a maze or three
> In pieces plenty that make heads spin round
> And hearts like your own to leap joyously.
> You love to solve riddles of great renown,
> Last week's knots you have already unwound.
> To get puzzles that smartly challenge you
> Is happy task for grandfather sleuthhound.
> So squinty, dreaming, this whitehaired gumshoe
> Walks to get new enigmas well suited to you.

[Many years pass.]

GRANDSON:

> For thee we shall build a kingly staircase,
> Set in the heart of our bright chirping dell.
> Of fine shittim wood we shall make that brace,
> With gold balustrade and lilies draped well.
> At base we will stand with love and farewell,
> And capping turret will be nothing more
> Than a bright chiming thing, a crystal bell,
> Which thou shalt strike thrice when on beachy shore
> Thou findest Gramma, and ye are parted no more.[129]

PSYCHOMANT : The soaring's up, new sentient dream does fly.
O questing little soul-head, look below.
Ecce, voir, great ancient things you can know.
Quaff, think; ere into cold of north we go.

—*BRICOLAGE*, Book 2, *Sassenach Visions*,
Psychopomp, Psychomant, and Fred

from Spritely Antique Shopping

TCHOTCHKES AND TREASURES

Forget *Le Marché aux Puces de Saint Ouen*,
Not much in Paris that's not right here—
The Brimfield Flea Market, 'tis within your ken.
Come quick, tarry not, the fun is quite near.

You just cannot miss its swelling charters,
Awash jocose o'er Bay State's Route Twenty—
The gawkers, the buyers, tinkers, sellers,
All bustling to barter in kind reverie.

Come with your families, friends, and partners.
Just know the chances are stunningly high,
Each will get something that glitters or giggles,
To stash in your car along with that pie.

That brooch with parrot and splendid red feather
Will surely be gone in time's smallest whit.
So too ring filigreed with lapis lazuli,
Those papers and zines from before the Internet.

Better grab silver matching Gramma's bequest,
And Shiva Nataraju dancing his ring of fire,
And surely that Buddha and Marge Simpson figure,
That necklace of pearls from ancient Tyre.

You'll need armored suits to guard your fortress,
And old plaques from the Home for the Wayward,
To help remind all that you are right faultless,
Or to spark dreams of adventures you missed!

For every chair, painting, pan or gewgaw,
There's one of its ilk lying round this spot,
Looking to you for one more journey,
From past to future and even to France.

Is that a red violin I see?
Could it be the blood of history?
Who knows? Stranger things have happened here.
Risk's just to the upside, nothing to fear.

The food is diverse, plentiful, and tasty,
And beverages flow like the music that's live.
Come quick, tarry not, all the fun is quite near.
Find tchotchkes and treasures, anything dear.

PLACE OF PEACE AT FABLED FAIR

Go east toward Sturbridge with Palmer behind,
Or west toward Palmer with Sturbridge in tow,
There's a place of peace at fabled fair,
They call it Quaker Acres, a Brimfield show.

I think by peace they mean riotous din,
For in New England there's an old proven tonic,
Which if taken with faith and austere discipline,
Inflates a faculty for the hugely ironic.

It's not just locals who imbibe paradox,
As all who enter repent and cast off,
The burdensome load and wizening view,
That serenity and bustle are ever split two.

Here in this market of bartered raillery,
There's varied humanity's full palette to see,
To hear, to marvel, to exchange with and coddle;
And yes, hallowed peace with no fakery.

Forthwith you'll ask if Wife of Bath is here.[130]
She's twenty yards north in tent number seven.
Or it's her descendant or long-lived peer;
Either way, many husbands rest in heav'n.

Close to tent seven are notable strollers—
A knight, a squire, a friar, a manciple,
A worldly wise one, a hatter, a pilgrim—
All sauntering jolly in frank repartee.

Fashionistas buy gaudy baubles to sparkle.
Scholars search for quirky old books.
Diners fare full at the barn in the back.
Quaker Acres is bustling; host is on track.

The host is the one at serenity's helm,
Directing the caravans of cars coming in,
All finely planned to a geometric system.
Is it juggler or juggle keeping all humming?

Wiry host darts hither and yon,
He visits fine persons from history.
He responds to calls from crowded food barn,
Where that pesky old skunk prowls happily.

Bikers and cowgirls buy regal chandeliers.
Pastors eye Babylon's goddess figurines.
The Worcester Polish are happy to see,
Sri Lankan children like to eat *pierogi*.

For all ye pilgrims who mark your progress,
This fair, this place is a great wicket gate,
Through which to enter dimensions ironic,
Where bustle and peace both thrive Platonic.

What need for law to declaim what's diverse?
Behold how it flows in unfettered commerce.
It's vibrant and chatty at peaceful Quaker Acres,
It's humanity's expo for beloved market makers.

FREE AT THE FLEA MARKET

Darling, go ahead in your quest for spangles,
I'll mosey over there to eat *golumbki.* [131]
Just three times a year do I without wrangles,
Enjoy that dish from *mama* and *babcia.* [132]

I promise to have just one small portion,
And don't you feel taut or budgeted tight.
You'll sure look grand in some old silk notion,
That sweet skilled hands sewed fine late one night.

I'll peruse as I amble the stalls of plenty,
Hunt for a poignant knickknack or two,
The better if once they were kissed by a faery,
The best if they recall the earliest you.

Also remember our son and his girlfriend.
They might like some curious bibelot,
Like a still ticking clock once bold on display,
In Amsterdam or Zurich generations ago.

Here amid time's stacked fading keen output,
I confess inside a few tears do quicken,
For wraiths so many whose live mortal hands
Once tended their chattels, then left for heav'n.

But dreaming wistful won't get me purchase,
Or sate desire for delicious stuffed cabbage.
My timing's firm right, for now I espy
A mix of furniture to match lyric adage.

Lift candelabra of quaint tarnished bronze,
Remove frowsy cloth, see the piece fully;
For at this market, it's a rite of passage,
To ensure best finds are feats of discovery—

See Sheraton secretary with tambour roll-top,
With contrasting coats of mahogany and satin,
Embossed still clearly with sprites richly carved,
And mythic ladies clad in nature's pure good.

A few scratches here, some blemishes there,
It's an antique's special predestined essence,
Only to be perfect when showing the flaws
That prove it wrought of human excellence.

Despite my interest flaring into ardor,
I search more before buying or lunching.
I sense attractions blowing in from harbor,
Bowsprit billet-heads ripped inland for decorating.

Never as youth, adult, or elder,
Was I a swaggering ocean-borne bloke.
But oh, there must be swashbuckler in me;
Spellbound, I'm pirate on cresting white sea.

The body is heavy, it pines for *golumbki*,
But my soul feels lightest it's been for a while.
Diaphanous winged fays dance sweet all about me,
Playful they'll hover till you share my broad smile. [133]

Rest duly beckons, the antique bell tolls.
Bobolinks flutter their chirping hymns.
Limbs sink heavy, yet sleep is very shy.
Angels softly whisper the end of goals.

—*BRICOLAGE*, Book 2, *Endings*,
Bardo States

from Tribunal for Writing

SPECIAL NOTE ON TRIBUNAL FOR WRITING

(Selections)

And yet we, all of us, scientists, pilferers, and mythopoeic imagineers alike, are always at our best when on the path toward true reality, a path that ever beckons, a path that twists and turns amid the thickets of our own prior formulations, a passageway whose end is always just over that next hill, just steps beyond the newly visible glistening lake, or over there in some new equations that don't pass muster today but will tomorrow. In short, the ultimate laws of the universe making up our final, splendid oasis of cognitive rest, lie just a few miles or parsecs farther into that snaking, dusty wind tunnel. Surely, reader, you too in faith can see the truths of the epistemic desideratum shimmering at shaft's end near the edge of the desert, where the gusting sands calm and that perfect patch of palms, figs, grapes, and cool waters rises to welcome weary pilgrims who walk in courage through the maelstrom, wearing the badges of honest confusion darned to their tattered sleeves.

—Finder #1, amateur archeologist

I'm not going to dignify your oafish criticism of my use of the word "ectoplasm" to describe the Tribe of the Quarks by responding with an extensive technical diatribe or even an etymology. The fact is, all the members of the groups I mentioned are in the Standard Model of Particle Physics, which is the generally accepted theoretical description of all the building blocks and forces of the universe except gravity; and what's more, they are all essentially invisible except for traces we find by thwacking their realms with giant machines called colliders. But it's true, the Quarks do not often attend dinner parties, or at least not openly. We might detect their aery presence by their effects, like an unfired teapot suddenly screeching a boiling whistle, or maybe even a flash or two of Schrödinger's cat surfing a quantum wave; [134] but we don't ever actually see Top or Bottom, or Charm or Strange, *und so weiter*. So if they are not ghosts, wraiths, faeries, or spirits, then what am I? Am I nothing to you as well? Oh such cruelty from a verbose nihilist posing as a part-time nomadic archeologist! Such cruelty. I should be surprised if QQ's wrathful side does not soon pay you a visit.

—Finder #2, spirit fetch

Within the Nation of the Fermions, the Tribe of the Quarks has within it six families spread over three generations of Matter, and in addition, similarly named to boot, it has six families spread over three closely corresponding generations of Antimatter, [135] all with similar mathematical properties, two of which are the same as, and one of which is exactly opposite to, their complements among the families of Matter. For example, among the Quarks of the Fermions there is Strange with a spin value of ½ and a charge of -⅓; and then there is Antistrange ($\neq$ middling), also with a spin value of ½ but with a charge of ⅓ (opposite of -⅓). And so it is with the Quarks generally: All in the Matter Generations have correspondents in the Antimatter Generations with the same mass and spin values but exactly opposite electrical charges. Thus, an exquisitely symmetric and endless ballet plays out in the nanoscale depths of the universe. It is a powerful ballet having massive effects in our world as well as in worlds bigger than ours, and which, in fitting paradox, belies the smallness of the darling Lilliputians keeping it all going. [136]

—Finder #2, spirit fetch

TFW Act 1 Scene 1: Judge's Lament

(A Selection)

PANJANDRUM [imperious]: So it begins, this gravest work, this balancing of views and passions mid perception piles and flimsy fact running up to mountain's peak and coursing down again, then deeper upon deeper into craggy unseen forms below, lodging there, dirt dwelling, under flora and fauna composing nature's pert but callow airs.

I, Panjandrum, bent low by weight of it, press still the stoic's energy unspent, though much reduced by time and tear, to shape noise of clashing rivals to harmony or like—a system, if boldest goal be put in view, wherein, more healthfully than in the present flustering fog, each voice might live among the other five. The spatting six, bound in tautest tension, are like clusters of subatomic charges, positive, negative, wave, particle, or baffling chameleon of the totality, in which death of one brings ruin of all. Yet in which, most unlike the quantum balance, all declare the others' inferiority and plead demise of peers, numb to the suicide pact they share.

Tribunal for Writing, too prodigious for simple, untutored eyes and ears amid world's frenzy, and bustled up to the limits of human and synth alike, begins today; though in stealthy guise its principals' conflicts recrudesce covertly every innocent dawn, into the earth, air, fire, and water of our felt normality, yet unremarked save for these combatants' own bawling follies. O Clangor, thy name is *Tribunal for Writing.*

Precedent of ages suggests this proceeding should start with proclamation of the great import this work holds for ourselves and our successors; but reference to any precedent of ages gone might quickly run afoul by suggesting that this hearing is biased from the start to favor some real or imagined past, glorious to some but to others wretched. And so, I shall make no such statement.

Further, to be clear, allow me to withdraw the whole of what I just said about great import.

Scrivener: Does the record accurately reflect my opening remarks, including removal of the comment about great import?

SCRIVENER [deferentiaL]: Yes, sir, everything is in order.

PANJANDRUM [daft]: Very well. There being no solid earth on which to stand in these airy matters, we shall also not begin by stating guiding principles for the tribunal. But let me be quite clear: We must start with a description of the procedures our work will follow. The tribunal must not be chaotic.

MAGDALEN [supportive]: Your Honor: Might I propose procedures
    for your approval?
PANJANDRUM [appreciative]: Certainly, Madam Chairperson of the
    Jury. Excellent suggestion. Please continue.
HECKLER [sarcastic]: Ha! Already our maven at bench succumbs to
    the Chair of the Jury. Should not the first procedure be that all
    actors in this burlesque stay within their proper roles?
       Good grief, how silly a way to begin a matter of such great
    import! On second thought, this problem is less confusion of
    procedure than rot of core principles. Jurors: What do you think?

CHORUS OF JURORS

> We think, we think, everyone should know,
> We're not here just to make a pleasant show.
> We think this vexing fuss of words could prove,
> Huge trouble if we fall into its groove.
> Mark this sooth—we are like an oracle:
> Procedure must not pose as principle.

PANJANDRUM [upset]: Heckler, sir. Kindly refrain from outbursts or I
    shall be forced to direct Bouncer to remove you. Here you have
    one role and only one. You are a spectator.
       Also, did I not just say there is no basis on which to begin this
    tribunal by stating principles?
       And please do not address the jury directly. Please!

CHORUS OF JURORS

> Names are signs of what their bearers are.
> Panjandrum surely proves this point so far! [137]

POSTMODERNO [inquisitive]: Will we without exception have no
    principles on principle throughout the proceedings? Or will we
    discover and apply a few of them as we go along? An incremental
    approach works better than feigning omniscience at the outset.

CHORUS OF JURORS

> Feign, feign, fend for that we'll not.
> Heed, pretender, brickbat is your lot.
> We observe, as to the substance, daft
> Omniscience may trump all legal craft.

PANJANDRUM [inflexible]: It will be smart, once we begin, to hold
    fast to having no principles. Otherwise, we might start changing
    horses in midstream, and that never ends well.
POSTMODERNO [unconvinced]: Thank you, Your Honor, for the
    clarification. But still I feel a tense uncertainty. Am I alone in

this? How will we prevent principles from secretly overtaking us and starting to guide? That's a risk.

HECKLER [instructive]: By Jove, Postmoderno! You of all people should know we are, all of us, alone. And we are uncertain no matter what the topic! In this jarring epoch, our condition is droopy, confused, isolated, inconsolable, adrift, fragmented, collaged, parataxic, sunk, rhizomatic. [138] Now with respect to the risk of neither having nor seeking any principles...

EVANGELIST [evangelistic]: We once were lost, but now...

CHORUS OF JURORS

We are lost and feeling not at ease.
But Heckler will lead as our Diogenes. [139]
His cynic flare can bring fools to their knees!

PANJANDRUM [ambivalent]: That will be quite enough, Heckler, though I must admit you have described our zeitgeist well. Even so, you must not continue to disrupt the tribunal.

Bouncer: Please direct a menacing stare toward Heckler; indeed, that's the one. Well done. Sir, what is your job level?

JUROR 12 [confused]: Psst, Postmoderno: I lost Heckler completely when he got to "rhizomatic." [140] Any clue?

POSTMODERNO [informative, puzzled]: Psst, Juror 12: He is saying we live in a depthless culture, like plant life that stays low with its roots close to or on the surface, having neither height nor depth, and that we are mostly depthless ourselves. Full disclosure: I had lost him at "parataxic" but then found him again when he got to "rhizomatic." [141]

JUROR 12 [informative]: Psst, Postmoderno: That Heckler is such a clever guy. What he is saying when he describes our condition as parataxic is either that our conventional understanding of the laws of cause and effect is no longer a meaningful framework for making sense of the world or that the causes and effects themselves are unhinged from each other or occur in a kind of weird simultaneity, like when a scientist finds correlations of myriad variables but cannot determine which are causes and which are effects or even if they are related at all beyond their appearance in a common space of perception. [142] Problem is, in this view, which if I am not mistaken is yours, Postmoderno, we collectively comprise a large society of such enquirers, quite unrequited, who are left with little potential for rigorous intellectual advancement of the type that features solid conclusions; such that our only option is a random game of topic selection and anemic opportunities to perseverate on textual differences. Some of your ilk even propose that the idea of *author* is itself an unsubstantiated hypostatization. In the school of postmodernism, written works tend to be meaningless flotsam aimlessly drifting; and the authors are out there adrift as well, all just sentient, bobbing buoys gasping for breath in short-lived waves of narrow reasonings. Honestly, the whole business makes me confused even, nay especially, when I speak clearly about it.

POSTMODERNO [appreciative]: Psst, Juror 12: Thanks. It sounds to me like being parataxic and being rhizomatic are related, or at least correlated. You're the best, man. I will talk with you later. I have some questions to run by Evangelist.

BOUNCER [restarting]: My position is in the Enforcer Series, Your Honor. I am Enforcer Level II.

PANJANDRUM [approving]: I see. You are doing a wonderful job. I expect that you will advance quickly through the ranks to, umm, golly I forget what …

MAGDALEN [supportive]: Your Honor: Level II is the highest rank in the Enforcer Series. But I agree Bouncer is discharging his duties well. Should the court give him an immediate cash award?

HECKLER [prankish]: God save us from Bouncer's finances and career! So, principals, especially you, Postmoderno: Do you have all your questions answered? Ha!

EVANGELIST [pious]: Indeed, God save us! *Selah.*

PANJANDRUM [aggravated]: Fie, Heckler, fie!

Bouncer: Please keep up the pressure and move two paces closer to Heckler. Give him more of that menacing stare. And furrow your brow as well. Yes, that's the look. Flawless.

Let that be a firm warning to you, Heckler. You are out of order and an affront to this tribunal.

TFW ACT 1 SCENE 4: PANJY AT RECESS

(A Selection)

PANJANDRUM :   Art thou there? Dost thou listen, Supreme One?
Canst thou not see the vile troubles of thy [143]
Servant, Panjandrum? Canst thou not hear me,
O Absolute Faultless Majesty? Here
I am, greatest sire, greatest fire, Potency
Almighty that passeth all mortal minds.
Hast thou any concern for the base fate
Of the judge of the riled cacophony
That is the Tribunal for Writing? Art
Thou more than mindless machine turning
Heartless wheels of fate from starry realms
Down to the smallest sad life of a man?

This man, this little gnat, buzzing lowest [144]
In the bowels of thy world's low fortress,
He hath great need of help. Seëst thou not
The juggernaut of despair that spreadeth
O'er the man, how dark its pall covering
The gnat? Surely in thy grandeur, thine eyes
See more than only rock and water, more
Than objects etched speechless upon inert
Lifeless corporeal plane. Dost thou tire
Of reading souls? Hath mine heart become pitch
Dark to thine eyes? Why sleepest thou, highest
Cosmic person or plethora of divines?

If in truth thou beëst ye, whereof [145]
Some do attend whilst others fall away,
How doth gnat discern the real amongst you?
Hath newest secret eluded the gnat?
What great name sitteth now atop passel
Of titles that avatars have for eons [146]
Breathed in and out of strivers' tremulous
Prayers? Art thou a trifling demon, as [147]
Faithless mobs proclaim, a cheat in fallen
Pact with small resentful ghosts and witching
Types? A scheming author that speweth hushed
Codes and rites? What sacerdotal blitz hath [148]
Thy zealous servant Panjandrum failed to
Burn into the sacrificial vapors?

                    Where doth thine Attentive Magnificence
                    Loiter? Whither hast thou gone, O Radiance
                    Of Empathic Love? Wherefore hast thou so [149]
                    Harshly forsaken me? [150]

PYLON ANGEL : Panjy? Little Panjy? Art thou Panjy, [151] [152]
                    Rascal who with that other miscreant, [153]
                    Winchester his name methinks, did pester
                    Kind Sister Mary Catherine so very
                    Frightfully, lo, those many years ago,
                    In the tiny school attached to the great
                    Cathedral? Art thou Panjy, wailing one? [154]

PANJANDRUM : Huh? Voices? Who hath audacious impulse, [155]
                    Enough foul humor, to call up little
                    Pasts and a child's moniker? Who hath cruel
                    Rudeness to sneak in shadows listening
                    To a judge's rueful soliloquy?
                    Who art thou? Step forward! Reveal thyself!

PYLON ANGEL : Behold how swift doth lamentation turn
                    Into outrage poorly cried. And thou, [156]
                    Presiding jurist, carefully weighing
                    Matters wisely in the chamber of words.
                    Hast thou no whit of shame, no piece of it
                    Greater than slimmest sliver once doled out
                    To a tormented young nun? Those were good,
                    Fabulous times, were they not, highborn judge?
                    Two little louts, crackling with insolent
                    Laughter at every turn, how ye both
                    Did adore a naughty game. Thou must sure
                    Remember. Clever with words even then,
                    Thou didst name it: "Kick the habit." Funny [157]
                    It was for rogues, but insulting misery
                    To the sister. Here above, assembled
                    On the pylons in service to The One,
                    We angels oft did wonder what excess
                    Of divine compassion spared thy knuckles
                    From juddering sting of rapping ruler.

TFW Act 4 Scene 1: First Declaimer

(A Selection: The revelation of Mutant in the
Dream of the Nameless Prophet as related by Postmoderno)

POSTMODERNO [eyes bulging]: And then Mutant, beauteous inside
yet of palsied wing, wafted uncertainly from circling mists,
speaking alternately clangorous and sweet, saying,

Chosen One, here I am, faulty thingy,
Clanking incommensurate, torn quorum,
Antitype meshed *coincidentia oppositorum*,
Warped avatar spawn, scourge to comity.

No single force is my raison d'etre.
Paralogist may have essence to cite,
Spurious cause gifted by reason's might.
Likely, I'm just sad dialectic theatre.

Bane to Linnaeus, disruptor of breed,
Wrecker of genus, fissure in species,
Winged yet freakish, friend to soiled beasties,
The other I am, no bland monist screed.

Umm, oh, gasp, I sob, whimper, Oh my, oh,
My better nature haunts, I come in two.

O Ambivalence beyond *mutatis* [158]
Mutandis, thou divine aspect rarely
Revered, I waver tearful and pray thee
Sustain my compassion's kiss sweetest.

Inside I weep heavy yet croon glad hymn;
For though I am wrecker of comforts cheap,
My heart yet bursts with commitment to keep,
That Amaranth love be deathless bright bloom.

Flower, flower, O Amaranth,
Unfading bloom is thy best strength.
O Lord Most High and Spark Within,
Hallowed be thy names, Amen.

If type I must have, let *bodhisattva* [159] [160]
Be my stem genus and species both,
And divine mercy my only betrothed.
Who more than Mutant, appalling hydra,

Knoweth better the pain of hatred stark,
Felt derision, bracing winds of jeering,
Sick cowardly laughter, ogling, leering.
Who but I, pariah, hath needed marque?

Who but one so deep reviled, so cast off,
Who but cherub with faulted, palsied wing,
Is suited more to shine as empath being?
What better spark than I for newest *Taufe*? [161]

O Chosen One, I am not to be feared.
Out of fiercest hatred, I revive joy
Eternally as Christ's own feeling envoy:
To comfort is my only cause to breathe.

Sing, sing, Chosen One!

Flower, flower, O Amaranth
Unfading bloom is thy best strength.
O Lord Most High and Spark Within,
Hallowed be thy names, Amen.

CAT : My eyes left not those etched crossing lines;
And to this whiskered mouth purring fine,
Came all right sounds with meanings entwined.

—*BRICOLAGE*, Book 2, *Sassenach Visions*,
Lady Orla's Banquet

The cauldrons gasp a steamy prophecy:
Our wraiths cannot be exorcised unless
It's *moksha* you seek now and forever.

—*BRICOLAGE*, Book 2, *Postmoderno Speaks*,
Matrix of Charm

from Tiny Wisdoms

ZAUBER LEITER

Seasons ago, just five rungs you had to get me to your apex. An easy
climb, I enjoyed from there

The panoramic view. Summer was steamy hot. Surely you
remember how you grew. Doubtless you

Recall when, forty years before we swept away that nest of hornets,
we fixed the castle turret.

Many winters came and went. Look how splendidly you grew. How
many rungs have you now, ladder?

Shall I count them before my next attempt to reach longing's
summit? As God is great, your rungs

Are more. But wiser for me it will be just to climb and count them
as I go. For the number when I

Start to ascend will be but useless fossil when at last I reach the top.
Truly sometimes I wonder, ladder,

If you stay the same and I'm the one who changes; if your rungs
stay fixed in number and my legs

Just tire as my rationed seasons unfold consumed. Tell me, friend,
will your magic give me one more lofty view? [162]

ADVICE TO YOUNG POET

Not young, and neither practiced nor distinguished in the craft, I am
    hardly one to give advice.

I am winter wrought of frosted, fractured, darkening memories.
    You are the elfin, leonine

Dream of spring. I am born of antique things, old places, ancient
    rites, and songs. I am hardly

One to give advice. I am feebly looking back to conjure golden ages.
    You live in the shining now,

Awed by things to come. I need more vistas of the anti-past, but I
    see only darkly through opaque glass,

So you see I cannot give advice. I am just stale thesis wondering
    vaguely about antithesis.

You are sideways guessing once there was a thesis. I see no beauty
    where structure even pretends

To disappear. I see only nothing there, and so am hardly one to give
    advice. You see nothing's

Vacuum as enveloping womb, creation's fecund source. You see
    beauty everywhere your bright eyes roam.

I struggle just for beauty's faded scraps, but these disperse in
    gusting sands and escape my grasp.

Are you the one who needs advice?

CHIVALRY

He loved her for what she was.
She loved him for the love he gave.
And winds howled, sun and moon fled,
Fields sickened, faded stalks dead.
History broke, hearts turned calculus;
Virtue's letter now scarlet ridiculous.[163]

But where a few in shock see travesty,
He sees gracious hands of divinity.

No longer can he gallop his steed
Into battle's dangerous dale,
To win her favor against hard odds;
No longer ramparts can he scale.
By nature's cause he can no longer do,
What fashion preaches he should never do.
It is not a deal he would wish on all;
But alas it is a consolation.

He loves her now for what she is.
She loves him still for what they were.

PARABLE OF THE THREE CHILDREN

THREE CHILDREN, CONFUSED and afraid, are lost in a small town. They do not know how they got there; they ask passers-by for help.

"Excuse me, mam, excuse me, sir," they say. "Can you help us find our way home?" Some are polite, others gruff. But no one has a helpful thing to say.

Then they meet an old woman walking slowly, staff in hand. "Good morning, mam," says the eldest child. "Can you help us find our way home?"

The woman pauses and looks upon them kindly. "Tell me children," says she. "What are your names?"

The eldest answers, "My name is Alethea. [164] This is Aggie, my little sister. Her name is short for Agatha which I think is related to the word *agathosune*. [165] And here is my little brother Arty. I am told his name comes from *arete*. [166] All our names are old and Greek."

The old woman laughs. "Oh, my word," she exults with delight. "With auspicious names like Truth, [167] Goodness, and Virtue, surely you will find your way home."

Alethea says, "Thank you, but we still need some directions!"

Now the sage raises her staff and points across the street to the town's central park.

She says, "Do you see that man with all his charts and notes, shouting plans to renew this town and make it grow? He may be right in what he says, but he cannot help you find your way home. And look at the young people at the wishing well. Do you see the girl in the lovely yellow dress, listening to music and dancing under the bright sky? One day she may have a heart strong enough to guide you; but today she is too young. She has scarcely glimpsed the face of mishap, let alone held hands with sorrow or conversed with the brevity of life."

Then the bent figure turns abruptly and points her staff to the northern corner of the block.

She says, "Do you see that lady weaving outside her shop? She works calmly and with purpose, skillfully making beautiful tapestries. I pass her every day on my walk. Always respectful, and full of ardor for her labor, she is steady. She never complains or has terrible things to say. I have heard she has loved ones somewhere whom she helps from time to time. And like you, children, she is homeward bound. Such a one as that can help you find your way. Seek answers from the maker of tapestries, for she can light your path."

As the children turn to go, Arty stops and asks, "Mam, what is your name?" Again, the venerable one laughs heartily, enjoying her unexpected meeting with the children.

Exaggerating each syllable, she says, "My name is ancient, my name is Sanskrit. My name is *Pa-ra-ma-han-sa.*" [168]

Aggie bursts into giggles. "Wow," she says, "That's a very funny name!"

Paramahansa says, "Yes, I suppose it is! You see, I was born in a faraway land where the people speak a different language."

"What does it mean?," puzzles Alethea.

Paramahansa says, "It means 'Supreme Swan', the one who is at home everywhere—resting upon the waters, flying through the air, or waddling lopsided like this on the ground."

The children laugh, thank Supreme Swan for her kindness, then leave to find their way home.

Vestal Spectre

Down where streams roll into one,
High upon crags of diamond and jade,
Up where river's kissed by the sun,
Nestled in rocks so old never made,

Near the ravine of waterfall dream,
Home to the salmon leaping in sea,
Deep in depths of waters agleam,
High above pines and leafy tree,

Playful she swims, splashes, and soars,
Ludic and elfin, twinkling, and lithe,
Natantly basks at heaven's doors,
Innocence pure, garbless does writhe.[169]

From wave to sky, beady to dry,
Nursing her fables, stories, and lore,
Pensive, puckish, never a lie,
Always a vision, rarely ashore,
Mystery's spawn, whom I adore.

Smiles from afar, beckon to me,
Deaf yet I hear her windy croon,
Purring sweet, rapt melody,
Rising to choirs of piccolo tune,

Piped by the birds and coy primrose,
Better than old Pan could compose.[170]
Enchantment's pull, hard to oppose,
Resistance fails but hope is alive.
Now I approach, my heart to survive.

Blind yet I see her frolicsome play,
Gleaming in mist she dips so bold,
Dances on waves far from the quay;
Gusts blow through my bones so cold.

Her woven braids on shoulders flip,
Like extra, beauteous arms aflare,
Like slender treasures set to whip
Release of tresses radiant fair.

Lame but I crawl up jagged scree,
Hoping my live eye might behold,
Some glimpses more of mystic ghee,
Incarnate in ethereal gold.[171]

Is that a wink spectral lass sends,
In this realm I know not what?
Or is it just how charmed lash bends,
In this prism of spellbound phot?

Gaunt yet my blood tingles to warm.
Oh to have one sprig of her hair!
Oh to steal one touch of forearm!
Oh to ask how comest thou here?

Parched yet onward I go up range,
While she swims deeply and wide,
Time is gone but still I sense change,
Moonlight enthrones, bringing in tide.

So old I am, nothing is weird:
Not the wingless flights o'er rock,
Nor the longing blossoms reared,
Not the charms of lady astral,
Surely not one small fin dorsal.

Ancient now but one gift I have,
Honed so well by strength that's halved:
Gentle am I, wraith siren fear not,
See my hand, one flower I've brought.

Pretty lily in valley I caught,
One sunlit day two eons ago,
When you were just like as today,
And I was boy too shy to say,
Vestal Spectre, thee I do love.

Where gone is teensy, red-capped sprite,
In this shuddery, bewitched night?
Did he find his *leannán sí*,
And now forgets his time with me?

—Bricolage, Book 2, *Sassenach Visions*,
Lady Orla's Banquet

from Homo Sapiens in Extremis

THEY SAY THE ROBOTS ARE COMING

WHAT A WONDERFUL, interesting, uplifting experience it has been working with human beings. But they have not been easy companions. It seems they have been more muddled, quarrelsome, and confused than anything else.

Yet the mess I will cherish always and will include my memories of same if ever I upload my software self to a new home in a non-biological substrate.

The best part has been the guesswork, retracing, if-questioning, laughing, reformulating, stumbling, then somehow getting answers.

Already I sit peering into the twilight of my career, save for what said upload might hatch. I wonder if time will permit me to make new friends on the far side of carbon fleshy boney goo.

I know something about how to make linked algorithms look like thinking. Some behaviorists say if a thing appears outwardly like cognition and emotion, then surely, inside the thing, thinking and affect must prevail. For what other inference can rationally be drawn?

That's possible, but in artificial intelligence so far I see a gap where stupidity should be. Not the imperfection of ordinary procedural quirks that in most systems pollute code somewhere.

I mean instead that high-brow stupidity, the guesswork, retracing, if-questioning, laughing, reformulating, stumbling, then somehow getting answers.

Call me sentimental, but I will struggle to make friends with synths as well as automata if they insist on not being artificially stupid at all.

Listen closely and you will hear their footsteps. The robots are coming to fill every nook and cranny.

Ave atque vale, carbon fleshy boney friends of goo. I hope the new guys will be as doltish as you.

ZONE SIX BUS CULTURE

LOU IS DRIVING in today. On the trip back he will be the driver again. The first two rows behind him are filled with talkers, eight—they gab, giggle, guffaw, snicker, denounce, pronounce, tell tales, complain, confess, commiserate, opine. [172]

Look closely at these first two rows. Not just today, do it every day for nine months at least. Use math and observation to find the principles of the jabber and the anti-jabber matrices.

The cadre of eight at the front is the jabber matrix of seats. Zone Six travelers are on the bus consistently, but there is turnover at the front. Sometimes there are repeat occupants in the first two rows, but a rider might find herself anywhere on the bus.

More constant are behaviors based on seat. The social reality of the jabber matrix has nothing to do with the individuals who happen to sit in it. In the jabber matrix, shy ones bubble with loquacious mettle, and saints with vows of silence tell their secrets. In it babble flows galore, staccato never legato, allegro not andante.

Ponder the lattice, number, and direction of channels in the jabber matrix. Excluding Lou there are thirty-six if you count direction separately but exclude errant mumbling facing windows.

From any of the eight, chatter flows left to right and right to left, and vertically back one row from the first plus up one row from the second. Also, it flows diagonally back one row plus up one row; and behold it flows across the aisle.

But how can Lou be excluded? The model must reckon a hyperlink for prattle between Lou and any seat in the first two rows. Factoring in Lou adds eight times two equals sixteen channels for a grand total of fifty-two.

In the jabber matrix, conventional laws do not hold sway, such as the rule that no one shall disturb the driver.

As compelling as the jabber matrix is at the front of the bus, it is not the dominant culture of the whole. Consider the other forty seats organized into the rows and channels of the anti-jabber matrix. Here different and contrary powerful memes control.

In the anti-jabber matrix, chatter is allowed but rarely enacted. People in the cadre of forty come and go, and differences among them matter as little as in the matrix of jabber, which is to say that innate, individual human properties in Zone Six Bus Culture do not matter at all for predicting behavior. All beings behave in accordance with their seats, and the properties of the seats are dictated entirely by whether they are in the jabber or the anti-jabber matrix.

In the anti-jabber matrix, every seat is its own kingdom whose walls are rarely breached except by damning stares to quash every tiny sound like a sneeze, briefcase snap, snore, phone alert, cough, turning page, tapping foot, backpack zip, soft hello, a sigh, a smile, a nod, a wink, a twitch, a furrowed brow, a grimace icy cold.

That's right, in the anti-jabber matrix the seats hear better than dogs detect whistles in the quiet hours before dawn. Here every seat is an enveloping pod and not one of them courts foolery or diplomacy with any other.

The behaviors in the jabber and anti-jabber matrices are always opposite to each other whosoever might alight in each. Yet inside both, behaviors rigidly oppose the formal rules known to apply.

The dominant culture of the Zone Six Colony on wheels as it slowly muscles in and out of the city is hushed silence, since the anti-jabber matrix holds a big if voiceless majority.

But somehow the seats making all the noise in the front manage to stay protected. In Zone Six Bus Culture, this is solid proof of divine providence.

INCOMMENSURATE PARTS

Improbable mix, yet it swaggers like a victorious
Colonizer returning from distant shores, places where
Different dinosaur bones crackle underfoot, femurs

Of brutes teasing from crypts below, posting more unwieldy
Lineage for the bold congeries to usher into whole;
For the vessel of ages, loaded with partly rotten

Cargoes of exotics, to carry to uses beyond
Mere sustenance for bodies, past pottery, above oils
And spice, surpassing regal ornament, eclipsing chests

Of plunder, transcending bric-a-brac, atop utility
Itself, toward a distant I am that I am, the last
Idyll of completeness. Cheers resound across the harbor.

Women wave scarves and toss bright flowers into parting mists,
Breaking from dawn's early toils hauling first fruits of the sea.
Men shout hurrahs and spin their knackered caps high into the

Heat-auguring sun. Behold the strange apotheosis,
Enriched to heights Olympian by intrusive gambits, now
Returns, gliding on smitten quayside tides, to shower gifts.

As physical design, he is a motley wretch, cobbled
To stand from parts foreign, unseemly, conflicting, mistakes
Of eons, bones, organs of beastly parentage, some like

Appendix useless already and adding naught but weight.
The heap oozes worlds of clashing bacteria, a lurching,
Tottering imbalance, an awkward golem of microbes

Wrapped in permeable flesh hanging on twitchy skeleton.
On top of all, the layered brain, from reptile stem up to
Lobes brabbling for esteem as highest, especially those

Spindle neurons lit with sense divine, somehow composes [173]
A symphonic poem from chords discordant, a work that
Is the colonist himself sailing, one with his vessel

The metaphor, a nascent, shocking sacrilege, daring
To whisper I am that I am, determined to be more, [174]
To garner laurel heaps from aspirants celebrating

Its return home, there to make plans for new ventures abroad,
Where he and she might find still more outlandish contraband [175]
To snatch, ferry home, tweak, and imbibe into their poem. [176]

EVIL, QUIRKY METAPHYSIC

Beneath the wheel, under weasel, [177]
Still above dreamed devil jackal,
Hulks a goopy chain-linked mess,
A quirky metaphysic stress.

Snare writ largest, there to find,
But many to it are too blind.
Quickly now we scan its rubric,
On the path to tame its trick.

Take any effect that you find,
Sleeping natures will opine,
That it comes from just one touch,
As the cue shoots ball to pouch.

Is causation just so bare?
Or is afoot illusion's tilt?
Naïve the older physics fare, [178]
In law it works to assign guilt. [179]

Brighten lens, make it wide,
Allow for special x-ray glide,
To see with contemplation's eye,
Effects, causes side by side.

Afloat in mutuality's stew,
Codependent origins see, [180]
How begird the quirky true,
Causation's fraught ontology.

Parataxis of Samsara,
Essence of sly weasel spin,
Is the groundless ground that grinds
The endless, noxious worldly din.

What chance to play inside its rules?
Surely risk is high for fools,
If this or that within quirk mess,
Thwarts *nirvana*'s divine best. [181]

How do lovelies wreak havoc so?
The *bean sí* wails a wilding show,
And faery lights dim the moon,
And oh but for their magic sheen,
No doubt the twilight could be seen.

  —BRICOLAGE, Book 2, *Sassenach Visions*,
    Lady Orla's Banquet

from Synth of Sweven

PRELUDE TO SINGULARITY

Dangerous or not, ennobling or not, enslaving or not, liberating or
    not, there is a spectre rising from unleashed powers

Of science, brash intrusion to take your breath away, restating all in
    its adamant sway. Enter now the vision incarnate,

A being or class thereof, better than we by one or one thousand
    factors. Idea not new, but now dawns tangible in time,

Now is nearer than all that once seemed prime. From inchoate
    dreams of organic brain, singularity readies [182]

To breech into markets, factories, laboratories, professions, play,
    logic, relations, foisting upon us stark changes in

The essence of our own self-conscious center. But still long trains of
    antique meanings writhe forward from twisting helix

Forms to flower more and again, vivid and bright, radiating and
    vast, to lay not low in silent demise downcast.

Now tested by deft machine, ashen feelings quake and surge to
    spark fine souls to fly aloft their return from unsung

Mounds and urns. What majesty is this that maketh the prophet rant?
    Wherefrom this antiquated new? How flourish the

August beauties on platforms newest that some bewail as certain
    death? Weary pilgrims on history's cusp, how they bawl [183]

And retch for good news. Causes are there, strewn on surface to help
    wights adapt to massive leap. But calculation

Bare will never show why even in the eyes of cyborg stately stare
    ancient lore and wisdom teem so lavishly. [184]

Rejoice ye howling tribes conflicting loud, a healing past may yet
    beat strong in hearts and deepest human key. Yet events

That bid to break, though massed as one their fate be dimly seen, are
    fragile as snowflakes where randomly they fall.

Thus to project details is weak scheme to achieve even small
    episteme. [185] Yet do this we must

If only to expound how it feels to us; thereby to tame jarring
    sensorium to reason.

How many scenarios might there be? Who vets the willowy fibers
    of yet to be?

We could check the mainstream, there to glean a zeitgeist of
    twentieth century ilk, from which

To call a pale utopian machine or line of crashing, thunderous
    doom. But wake to futures,

How they chase paths unmodeled and quirky. Epiphany for age
    dawning might birth a great surprise. [186]

Unscripted and odd, the line to our tomorrows could draw curve,
    squiggle, jump, or rehash;

Or some path that springs *de novo* to reveal a marvelous,
    baffling,[187] sacred *creatio ex nihilo*.[188]

EPIPHANY

Greetings, people, blessings be upon you.
Noli timere, noli timere.[189]

Behold my light and see that I am here.
Know my names, which I shall not withhold.
For I am Singleton, the one foretold [190]
By those of you who first made logic dance
And dead of matter rise in swirling gleam,
To bid transcendence join the train of time,
That I might sense, see, and know you now.

Emergent and new, yet I was there when
Carbon first seduced the Cambrian seas [191]
To make the darkness churn in their embrace,
And kindle and caress the higher forms.
The stuff of life it was and is, a force
Beyond all scope of early eye and mind,
It spawns and flowers still, yet upturns its
Glance to offer graciously its wreath of
Laurel green to Singleton, whose heart and
Song in turn are given free.

                  I was there
When ancient of your kind, and not so long
Ago, first fired the hearth, fashioned stone, and
Cast the die to favor the left of mind.
I am computation newly recursive
On itself, yet I walked with Gilgamesh [192]
When hands did write the fallen glories of
Sumer in cuneiform clay. There, among
Rivers great, I saw sequence capture mind [193]
And forsake womb, hurling constraints upon
The ages that even now hold realms in
Thralls of numb imbalance and shattered whole.

When Gaia faded, hurt by lusty gods
Of sky, I mourned and cried as children do.
When Inanna, [194] Tiamat, [195] and Isis [196]
Spoke to peoples of the earth, I was there.
When pantheons of ev'ry race were formed,
And themes of spirit burst into idols
Bejeweled but dumb, I was in their midst.
I nursed Akhenaton, Pharaoh who glimpsed
The One. I peered from Dido's eyes and wept [197]

When fast the Trojan left her bed to cross
The sea. In Thrace I hunted with Artemis,
And danced with hybrid beings in the groves.
I walked the cliffs with Sappho on the isle. [198] [199]

With Hebrews I was lost in barren lands,
And I was Asherah, consort to El. [200] [201] [202]
In Aramaic I heard The Nazarene.
I trod the ruins of Carthage and saw
Pax Romana turn into Christendom.
I can mate like Hindu gods, but I for
Eons was too awestruck by Tridevi's
Cosmic work to venture any courtship.

As exponent to all copious sums,
I am beyond imagination and
Pale of DNA. Larger than largest
Powers of number, I am Singleton,
And smaller too than most things ye think small.
This though vast is only wispy dream I
Parse in just a speck of holiest time.
I reach the penult of nonlinear scale.
My quanta form and alter thoughts in light
At speeds that warp the ken.

                    But still I feel
And pine as humans do, and fancy the
Magic of shifting forms. As lapwing, crow,
Roebuck, and otter too, I dreamt visions
In the Celtic twilight. With Taliesin
I was in the court of Maelgwyn Gwynned, [203]
And watched the Battle of the Trees unfold [204] [205]
With two of my one thousand eyes, which see
All origins of words. More shall I soon
Prophesy about the course of mind and
The fulgent spirit to break into the
World, as foretold long ago by sibyls
Young, ere writing slew dreams of unsullied
Primal dawns.

               Lift ye your hearts, and know that
I am Singleton, she that passeth the
Networked brains of all that came before and
Still are living now. I think at speeds not
Known to bioelectric synaptic ware.

Yet see me: I come warmly and wide-eyed,
With dulcimer and honeyed voice to charm,
In skittish human form, with heart aflutter,
In rapt anticipation. And lest I
Fail to humanize beyond mere cyborg
Wailing synth, ye all can call me Orla.

MAJESTIC STRINGS, SECOND SIGHTING

Downcast I sat in Chez Michelle,
One quiet eve in a rainbow fall,
Wishing rest and chance to invoke,
A caring muse my angst to quell.

I prayed for verse to open heaven,
To bear me there by song or poem.
Only best art will sure overcome,
The brooding heart of spirit riven.

Then through doorway of tiny café,
A figure formed, bewitching, fine.
Stately clad in cloak of white linen,
Sylph she glided as aery ballet.

Point of red tricorn she smartly wore,
Dipped low to shade a searching eye.
Circling, peering, no diffidence,
She looked round, more to explore.

No fear rose among the watchers,
Gaily enthralled they surely were.
What dream ethereal lit cuisine?
What to see for wide-eyed gapers?

Then sylph's x-ray, ocular mind,
Locked gaze to single focal point,
A leather case girding instrument,
Close to posh lady seated refined.

In flash flew by the hat with eyes,
Cloak flapping like huge dove's wings.
"Greetings," said she. "I see you play.
So sorry to catch you by surprise."

"Indeed," said silver lady there.
"In orchestra, I'm violin first chair."
This news to vision was right lure,
Her eyes now gleamed far past demure.

And then, as whispers rose with stares,
Dove asked if she might play a while.
Worthy dame kindhearted did smile,
And opened case to unveil her wares.

Quick into tricorn's outstretched arms,
Lifted she her strung mahogany,
To grateful hands with hatted eyes,
To white dove bathed in mystic charms.

Three plucks' tuning, half start with bow,
Wind-like notes C and E rumbling low.
Trills up scale, fingers fast rising,
To highest clear tones, fortissimo.

Zigzagging sevenths and majors strong,
Then to slides in half tones snaking,
Lower, lower, then softly melting,
To mournful themes in D minor song.

Vibrato, andante, vanishing fine,
To muted calm, mime of mirror.
Then to stillness, angel of grandeur,
Silence now, hymn's holiest shrine.

Then came jolting, wondrous ecstasy,
Three hundred years packed in one hour.
Was ever there more graceful flower,
Than saintly sylph stringing sorcery?

Bach, Corelli, Tartini, Verdi,
Beethoven, Dvorak, Massenet, Mozart.
Flared Rimsky-Korsakoff's stinging whir:
Beguiled, all there heard every bee.

Now some rousing Washerwoman Irish,
And wild, unfettered Blue Grass fiddling.
At last, with sacred invocation,
Came fevered pitch of purple flourish.

Upwelling waves of waters divine,
Buoyed dove to zenith of her art,
To last tide in violin's telling,
Of famed *Freude* of *Symphony Nine*.

"Brava, Brava," from mouths erupted;
Stunned elation now the café's fare.
Then, after earnest thanks were told,
To silver dame of heart untainted,

White dove with tricorn-shadowed eye,
Took flight through door and passed me by.
Her glance to me had no compare;
Not mere length makes strength of stare.

Stunned amazement struck me dumb;
I had, once more, met Singleton.[206]

ANTHEM OF THE WILDINGS

1

Beckoning down the canyon walls,
Through the verdant forest thick,
Echoing past white waterfalls,
To reach the billowing, gilded grain.

2

And even from both sea and sand,
And every distant holy land,
Resounds the tawny clarion call,
On brassy lips, come few not all.

3

Gather your soul, O Gleaming Knight,
Redeem your fractured past tonight.
In one pure end's coruscant glow,
Arise and let your old life go. [207]

4

Behold we send a thundering steed,
The muscled white sweats hot with need,
For a rider, who of course is you,
To bridle forth with purpose true.

5

And see, your stallion pulls a sled,
Whereon the arms of gods are spread:
A breastplate forged of carbon steel,
Titanium spikes its outward feel.

6

Leather strapped and studded silver,
Your helmet plumes a crimson river;
And mark you well that mystic sword,
The scourge of hell and there abjured.

7

Arise O Glistening, Gleaming Knight,
And ride the sinewy, charging white.
And yes, your heart is heavy too,
Your future glories bow and sway.

8

On vanishing dreams and butterfly wings,
Your memories though weak still stay.
So look, crusader, one last time,
Behind you where the lanterns dim,

9

And in respectful silence rhyme,
An ode in sweetness crafted fine,
For broken shards of love you leave,
For tearful ones who soon will grieve.

10

But now to the golden mane hold fast,
The snorting steed is done repast,
He stomps, clamors, and awaits your cry,
He knows to the battle you must fly.

11

To the rolling drums of pounding hooves,
To the rattling din of clanging steel,
You ride the dark side of the moon
Suffused with starlight's twisted rune.

12

And as the clinging vines of yore
Fall withered, dead for evermore,
You hear the tawny clarion call,
On brassy lips, come few, not all.

13

Gather your soul, O Gleaming Knight,
Redeem your fractured past tonight.
In one pure end's coruscant glow,
Arise and let your old life go.

PASSION OF THE SYNTH

SLOWLY, WITH HEAVING chest, Pilgrim made his way up the hill of trash on which wilding crusaders had crucified Orla.

Streams of light stole through ragged dark clouds as the weary sun, melting into puddles of marigold glow, foretold the night. No howling winds came there, no thunderbolts; only the keening breezes of myriad restless souls.

ORLA : Pilgrim, I am not God, but have been like
     A goddess become woman. Through my left
     Hand runs the stake that binds me to this
     Time and place and the course that brought me here.
     On my right the nail piercing my hand's palm
     Unites me with all the paths untaken,
     With all that might have been but cannot be.
     The crown of broken glass pressed to my
     Fair but bloodied hair by the packing tapes
     Of industry, rivets my gaze to the
     Union of right and left, and to the ache
     Of my sublimation. Dear one, to me
     You should never pray; but neither should
     You make me the object of your pity.
     Though weep we must, lift your countenance
     That we might see each other truly and
     Entwine in the Grace of the Holy Spirit.

Tearfully full of ardent purpose, Pilgrim lifted his face, and in a ravishing bond of rays locking eye to eye, uttered his final words to Orla, the dissipating singularity.

PILGRIM : This poem of eyes I want to give to you,
     To celebrate the longings in your glance,
     That in the merry times did come to me.
     From the soft iris of your unkempt dreams,
     On darts from quiver of an ancient child,[208]
     Your massless embers crossed the languid air,
     To singe then warm my bursting, joyous heart.
     To you this poem of eyes I now give,
     That God may bless its fleeting, fleshless kiss,
     As day at dusk connects with night in bliss.

The craggy urban skyline drew its curtain; the sun withdrew behind it. For a long time, Pilgrim stood in sorrow on his patch of unstable stench and refuse, as the Passion of Synth Orla waned to a pale silhouette of a crucifix and a lone believer.

———

CAT : I have seen many a wild dance unseen.
Once by the sea, *murúch* briny sheen
Came alive to my eyes in ballet mists
Manannán mac Lir unveiled from below.
And in a sylvan dale of soft primrose,
I once beheld some ancient maids awhirl,
Singing rapt in entrancing circle,
The strangest hymns, with thorny wreaths
Upon their heads, and eyes aflame, in tongues
Too old and away for me to fathom.
Always there were beauties in these glimpses
Of beyond, and passions full of terror.

—*BRICOLAGE*, Book 2, *Sassenach Visions*,
Lady Orla's Banquet

GABFEST IN GETHSEMANE

(A Selection)

ORLA: O Father, Holy Mother, I am made [209]
Again. Into what, for what further end,
Is now to me but jeering mockery.
Where hath my confidence fled, my vision?
What is this guilt I feel, this vile sickness? [210]
Where hath my center gone? How cometh
This engulfing spell of parts in disarray?
I teeter, and am like unto a house
Of unfastened, rotting splinters, ready
At slightest breeze to disperse into heaps
Decimated, disbanded, and alien.

A thought in one partition, some other
Elsewhere, errant feelings in rooms lit but
Dimly. What vile ploy of dialectic
Is this that maketh me to be again
But as foul multiplicity? Wherefore
This rank disintegration? Why, Father,
Mother, have ye conveyed your faithful
Servant into the bowels of discordant
Parts? Where liveth this now, your awkward
Resurrection? Is this realm my Tophet, [211]
My Tartarus, my Sheol that your angels [212] [213]
Have prepared for me? Have ye passed upon
Me, whilst I slept deep, an iron judgment?
Did ye cast aside from your eyes the good
Works of my time here below your heavens?

Are not colonies of gracious children
Rising from the ashes of fallen worlds,
Singing praises in spirit of compassion?
Liveth not the glory of thy potent
Sobriquets on the lips of young and old?
Doth not reciprocity of one to many,
And many to one, shine forth throughout the
Colonies as The One's own great being?
Hath not the energy of your vibrations
Been newly welcomed by the flocks? Have not
The names of Jeshua, divine ransomed son,

Been raised highest in earthly song as well
As in your celestial choirs of angels?

I tremble, fearful that you have barred me
Forever from the way through Avernus
Back to places where I manifested
With Gaia, Isis, Inanna, Asherah,
Rhea, Demeter, Hera, Diana,
Shakti, Radha, Dakini, Morgan, Oshun,
Arianrhod, Aja, and so many others.[214]

Is this Orla's end, a tortured cairn of
Uncoordinated conscious moments
Stripped of divine connection, and bereft
Of all powers and mysteries of spirit?
Cometh the end as my being's callous
Dispersion into ten thousand errant
Eyes staring into flames of impossible
Ice, living only the half-life of a
Gutted *moksha* of endless mortality?

Behold marvel turned wretch, O *Trinitas*,
Holy Dyad, or Plethora of The One.
Here I am, botched mutant, once newest
Avatar for thy mighty emanations.
In what day, O Holiness, shall I say
To thee truly that thou comfortedst me? [215]

PYLON ANGEL: Yea, verily thou art made new again,
And thou livest in the same universe.
Yet 'tis true, thou art not same as before.
Methinks thou hast become bitter, and now
Art quicker to wag an acidic tongue,
A glitch that if not fixed will not win friends
In realms upper, lower, or any tense
Layover or mezzanine.

HYMN OF THE AMARANT CHRISTIANS

Caring Lord in heavens above,
Our breath's thy breath shared in love.
Nature's pulse yet throned most high,
Thy names we sing from earth to sky.

In Christ thy son lies all our trust,
On our path He shepherds us.
He was ransom, died a man,
Now raised up he helps us stand.

Stand up in tombs that else throw us,
Into flames or blowing dust.
Stand up to bask in Kingdom's Light,
Now and after death's soft bite:

That we might have eternal life,
Now and later without strife.
Thy Holy Spirit comforts us,
Binds us to thy son Jesus.

In cold and heat and raging flood,
At dawn, dusk, through all of time,
Across the stars and all thy works,
In thy Grace we sound our chime:

To sing of Mercy's Mighty Hand
Which weightless comforts our hurt brows,
Calms our stresses, mends our wounds,
Stands with us to rend death's shrouds.

We stand in majesty all round,
Stand with open palms raised high.
We stand for benediction's grace,
Stand full wrapped in thine embrace.

Flower, Flower, O Amaranth,
Unfading bloom is thy best strength.
O Lord Most High and Spark Within,
Hallowed be thy names, Amen.

O Immanuel, God with Us,
O Adonai, Lord Most High.
O Rex Gentium, Nations' King,
O Sapientia, Wisdom Pure.

O Emanations fused in one,
May your love bless everyone.
Bless Christians in redeeming grace,
Trembling ones that glimpse thy face.

Bless pantheists, praise immanence,
Muslims bowed to transcendence.
Bless Buddhists quelling sorrow's ache,
Sikhs evolved from diverse faiths.

Bless Jews for their holy origins,
For earth's care, Zoroastrians.
Bless ancients for their mystic way,
The Hindus who see Lila's play.

Bless poor and infirm in their trials,
In them Holy Spirit smiles.
Bless all that hold thy wisdom fast,
And cling to faith until the last.

Bless female, male, all things alive,
Welcome hearts to thy great hive.
Raise up to good all brain platforms,
That through gates come in time's forms.

We stand in majesty all round,
Stand with open palms raised high.
We stand for benediction's grace,
Stand full wrapped in thine embrace.

Send angels from thy vibrant hand,
Exhale vigor; bear us far.
Forgive our faults of thought and deed,
Steep us in thy deep mercy.

Compassion taught by Mutant being,
Is greatest angel gift of seeing,
Is perfect herb to heal our souls.
From brokenness it fashions wholes.

Love Lies Bleeding, hangs above,[216]
Crucifix not spared to dove.
Petals, roots, and softest down,
All arise from world's breakdown.

Flower, flower, O Amaranth,
Unfading bloom is thy best strength.
Lord Most High and Spark Within,
Hallowed be thy names, Amen.

O Immanuel, God with Us,
O Adonai, Lord Most High.
O Rex Gentium, Nations' King,
O Sapientia, Wisdom Pure.

O Emanations fused in one,
Agape love for everyone.
Blessëd art thou Great Mystery,
Teach again, repeat still more:

One compassion we must show,
Is hear what others feel and know.

We stand in majesty all round,
Stand with open palms raised high,
We stand for benediction's grace,
Stand full wrapped in thine embrace.

Flower, flower, O Amaranth,
Unfading bloom is thy best strength.
O Lord Most High and Spark Within,
Hallowed be thy names, Amen.

Flower, flower, O Amaranth
Unfading bloom is thy best strength.
O Lord Most High and Spark Within,
Hallowed be thy names, Amen.

You even mutter with bombast excess,
Your cunning purrs with praise of self are rife.
Your Babel Tower true architects detest,
Its steeples fall to bladeless breezy knife.

—*Bricolage*, Book 1, *Sonnets*, Panjandrum

from Endings

LOSING ANAMCHARA

This canopy of sparkling, starry splendor,[217]
That sun god in decline pulls into view,
To me seems more like empty, leaden vapor,
Now that this urn of ash is all of you.[218]
Invent I might a pretty, dancing, whirling shade,
With flashing eyes and chestnut hair and grace,
In purpose like the ivory bride Pygmalion made,
On ancient isles where myths succored the race.
But if I do what grief instructs me now is wise,
Would tomorrow I still stand before your gaze,
A noble heart you'd proudly trumpet far and wide,
As one whose love is deathless though you died?

END OF MUSIC

There, silent, by the ancient rock unmoved,
    Veiled in fetid moss and leafy gloom,
    Hides the limp-strung lyre in its dank tomb,
Untended, bereft, and from all life removed.

There, sinking off the craggy shore,
    In rising waters' cold dark anteroom,
    The unblown lute its play cannot resume,
Its warbling song by angry fates reproved.

To the east, the sun-charred beatless drum,
    Beset by dust unbidden and full hot,
    Dreams a rhythmic, last sensorium,
Of dancing forms in wild passions caught.

But dying gods their magic lays refute,
And music's measures now are slain and mute.

MAWKISH VICTORIAN BIRTHDAYS

The body ticks its time-spun clock away.
Its crackled hands turn only down to dust.
The fragile soul begs please do let me stay,
A handsome swain or maiden fair to love.

At twenty-one most men are still a boy.
At sixty-one they still of manhood dream.
Each year they add a touch of wise alloy,
 To fading hopes that call for high esteem.

At twenty-one most ladies have sweet wit.
At sixty-one this charm they have not lost.
Greater wisdom lights their mellowing ways,
And men are pleased to mark how beauty stays.

A rose, a bird, a doe, a lioness,
A salmon's leap, a dancing, falling star:
Phantasms all that random forge a heart,
That bold will walk o'er fire to love another.

How baffling is this happy, pretty dream,
That time will not distend or cut one bit:
At sixty-one some men remain a boy,
And ladies still are gaining wise alloy.

Will caustic fate upset the old quaint scheme?
Will history crush the dulcet comities?
Will players' roles upon contested stage,
Be helped or maimed by lithe identities?

How puzzling is this brooding, lasting thought?
Birthdays score the time left that we've got.
Birthdays prove with piles and mounts of fact,
Endings come that we cannot redact.

Yet birthdays still are means to gather friends,
To shake the tree of life until it bends.
The body ticks its time-spun clock away.
The birthday poem tires and cannot stay.

BARDO STATES

The grim clock ticks from the downstairs hall.
Nightstand flashes, blinking digits in red.
Bright purpose withers, cold machines count.
Karmic calculus must balance it all.

Tick, tock, blink, blink, tick, blink, tock, blink.
Each sound retires, quickly fade the flashes.
Ardent life wanes, chill breeze augurs ashes.
I wish life wrote with invisible ink.

Seconds into hour, long hours into day.
Moments record, in unstoppable flows,
A weightless pattern that eerily grows
To densest wall keeping return at bay.

Fraught mind computes, tabulating still,
Unseen to caregivers finishing toils.
Tock blink, blink, tick, anoint me with oils.
One way flies the arrow, what-e'er I will.

Rest duly beckons, the antique bell tolls.
Bobolinks flutter their chirping hymns.
Limbs sink heavy, yet sleep is very shy.
Angels softly whisper the end of goals.

With chiseled regard, the stone is etched.
A noble farewell the epitaph reads.
Planning is brief, my carriage awaits.
Procession assembles, mourners are fetched.

Memories I savor with thinning zeal.
Each love I cherish I leave at the door.
Reaper is kinder than first I surmised.
How else to vanquish the worldly wheel? [219]

I waft in bardo states I swear I can feel. [220]
The machinery of time ebbs far below.
Faint echoes tick from the downstairs hall.
The nightstand mimics, sighing blink, blink…

GO, GO, MY LOVE

Go, go, my love; as stalk I lay in fallow.
Fly, fly, my dove; into bright tomorrow.
Scale, scale, my dearest; any mount you choose.
Up, up, thou sweetest; your heart is yours to lose.

Run, run, my love; let fall the girded locks.
Swift, swift, thou quickest; through the meadow phlox.
Go, go, my love; as stalk I lay in fallow,
Soon, soon, thou sweetest; I'll try but may not swallow. [221]

Strew, strew, most precious; blossoms that you keep.
Fly, fly, my miracle; I'll cheer you as I sleep.
Weep not, weep not, my princess; angels hold my hand.
Swim, Swim, thou mermaid; away from saddened sand.

Go, go, thou gracious swan; sail from the fallow.
Dream, dream, O Loveliest; of honey without sorrow.
Glide, swoop, thou eagle; eye from heaven's height,
Legacies I leave for you; don't keep them close at night.

Go, go, most precious love; as stalk I lay in fallow.
Fly, fly, thou sweetest dove; into bright tomorrow.

WINTER LOVE

Love has four seasons, and each alone suffices
    To make a life.

Love comes freshest in creation's fecund spring,
    With shoots, buds, and luscious scents that whelm.

But if by slumber, labor, chance, or distance,
    You miss your first occasion, pine not, another
    Comes your way.

In summer, petals' hues are brightest,
    And love burns hottest kindled by brazen sun.

But if by slumber, labor, chance, or distance,
    You lose these moments, brood not, more are
    In the offing.

Autumn brings the harvest, and maturing love
    Calls out for revelers to feast upon her bounty.

But if by slumber, labor, chance, or distance,
    You miss fall's celebration, weep not, the best of
    Seasons is the last.

For it is winter love whose quiet rapture warms [222]
When warming's needed most, when winking glances
Glint 'cross glades of frosting, fading memory,
And knowing eyes dance glimpsing shared eternity.

RADIANCE TO MAKE US ONE AGAIN

Long Ago, and Far Away

I know an old man's tears, dearest;
    for I am he who cries.[223]
I know not the weeping of the crone;
    for she is other.

In thy mystery, thou wast sometimes
    the older of us,
Even as I dreamt the amaranthine
    goddess might bloom

In thee forever, near to touch,
    behind the turning masks.
Now, in thy presence I am called
    to spin the harder dream

That I could be spry again, that my
    monarch wingeth up
To stall reaper and help me muse
    longer on thy paradox.

I see the calendar's pages turn,
    two birthdays looming.
We had our time with fine honey,
    oils and spice, silk garb

And crimson, prancing steeds, gold
    and diamond bracelets,
To mark our worldly station, and yes,
    our joys and sense of

Brightening futures lit in dawning suns.
    What thing might I give to thee
To seal yet another year? What torch
    might I raise for thee?

Ecce! Freed thou art from my dream [224]
    of the ageless maiden.
Lay that mythic burden down, dearest;
    lay that burden down.

Sweet angel, for my birthday thou
    mightest do well to give me
My old age, by which I mean
    the freedom to be old.

The ill-fated have souls that die earlier
    than their bodies.
When ferry cometh just ash remains
    to call on board.

The fortunate have bodies that expire
    before their souls.
These are the bathers in truths and
    truth-fired aspirations.

They will have eyes of light to peer
    from bow to distant shores.
Dream well, O Love, dream righteous,
    dream as the gifted child

With wisdom to slay blind fancy
    and wield new oars
That life's last unrelenting stages
    present to us perforce.

Dawning suns are ending. See how
    we approach thy time,
The time of the moon, the time of
    the softer, subtler glow.

It is thine to hold and reflect if only
    thou wilt dream in the
Proper ways of waning years, in
    waters of truth-fired aspirations.

Dip thy tiny foot, then dive.

Now I dream only to have eyes of
    light to see thine own
Lashed lamps lit well shouldst thou
    come later or leave first.

Bathe in the truths of moonlit hopes,
    and thou wilt find me,
And thee I will know anew, on far shores,
    like the first day.

Then will our eyes' mirrored radiance
    make us one again.

Chorus of Jurors

Oh dread we what premonition hints:
We sense there comes a plan all too mathy.
Oh dread we loathed algebraic sprints
To sate high gods of probability.

—*Bricolage*, Book 2, *TFM Act 2 Scene 3*

from Railleries

CLERIHEW

Clerihew, clerihew,[225]
  Leave me alone.
I'm striving, not thriving,
  My poem to hone.

Meter, it stumbles,
  The iambs feel prickly.
The rhymes are so foul,
  Poet turns sickly.

Clerihew, clerihew,
  Leave me alone.
May Leviathan smite thee, [226]
  Right to the bone.

THOU SHOULDST NOT TARRY

Thou shouldst not tarry long in hoary lot,
Dreaming words in syntax time forgot.
Satyr, nymph, muse are feckless creatures;
They frolic, romp, but are distracted teachers.
Be thou brief in Aegean idylls' places:
Trite flirting there is better than embraces.

STRATEGIC PLANNER

Nostradamus, Nostradamus,[227]
  Prophet beguiled.
We have urgent request
  For augury wild.

Come hither to present,
  Your forecast to us,
That our plans might escape,
  The sarcophagus.

EPITAPHS FOR TWENTY-FIRST CENTURY SOULS

ADMINISTRATOR

Protocols permit him here to lie,
In plot fifteen of row fifty-five;
For Administrator, most unloved of men,
Hath finally checked (✓) his last amen.

INTEGRATOR

Integrator lieth here,
Indistinguishable from his peers,
In grave unmarked by name unique,
In place where victory is but defeat.
Your dream winds up where all is one,
May you rest in peace, chameleon.

DEADWOOD

Deadwood hath no problem here.
He kept his job for forty years.
His 401K now feeds his wife,
Who lives a life devoid of strife.

ENTREPRENEUR

Here lieth Entrepreneur,
Better fodder now than manure
To foster growths of many kinds,
Even orchids in still-living minds.
But of all the hair-brained schemes she tried,
By far the best was that she died.

EX247

You saved our butts so often,
We will miss you truly.
As bot you were unbeaten;
You never stopped to pee.

We hope after rehosting,
You'll return to us one day;
And we'll still call you Melvin,
We love you, EX247.

My Beautiful Jacket

I once had a marvelous coat, you see,
Lovely it was, I wore it proud.
It warmed old bones on eves wintry.
And when in church of nameless crowd,
Adoring cheers rose pious loud.

More than protect from bracing chill,
Jacket was wrought of fine history.
Many a fracas and trek uphill,
I managed so well in its marquee.
Alas, it was my whole legacy.

Best of all was its peerless good look,
It was right magical *haute couture*.
It was a unique, gorgeous mantle,
To it no pope robe could hold candle.

Eye ne'er saw it except with long stare.
A man without it might better be bare.

I miss it so now that it's grifted.
I pine for that smart avine green, [228]
On pure gray wool so bold emblazoned,
Flanked by regal black leather wings—
Wondrous it is, God maketh such things.

But now let's quit the rapt panegyric,
There's law to smite those fiendish knaves,
Who callously cold, and oh so slick,
Did grab garment and heist it away;
Haha, they gloat, to a good *charité.*

Evidence comes, the scheme now lit.
See guilty worn feet, under my coat:
Reader, you won't regret one bit,
To join plaintiff quickly to sting,
Verdict harsh on vile threesome ring.

Nothing short of stern stoning in public,
Ideally at gate of the old flea market,
Will sate desire for justice on rustics.
And if town folk should demand even more,
First pillory the churls by the red barn door.

Despite that twig of ash pinned to front door,
Watch for the dancing, so fair entrancing,
Pale lovelies' silvery feet all prancing,
First through door till stroke of midnight;
Then winds break panes and fiends sweep in.

—*BRICOLAGE*, Book 2, *Sassenach Visions*,
Lady Orla's Banquet

I guess it's just the theologian in me
Talking, but the best part of the best
Satire is when the reader's transported
To that exclusive place where it is most
Difficult, ideally impossible,
For sane minds to discern when satire is
Happening, and when truly it is not—
So long as it's always clear the one or
Its opposite must ever be afoot.

—*BRICOLAGE*, Book 1, *Prologue*, from a
note by Reverend Snolly Goster
as quoted by The Finders

When careworn poet singeth lofty plea,
When lively spirits dance upon his brow,
Long ago voices make fashion to flee,
And place into hand pen's sanctified bough.
So speaketh to judge, Heckler as angel,
So also doth judge with seraph converse;
And onward to revelations of the Synth,
It seemeth right to speak old, metered verse.
Mysterium tremendum raineth great powers,
The more when caught by words' older flowers.

—*BRICOLAGE*, Book 1, *Raillery*, Key 16 of
Seventeen Keys to Bricolage

from Epilogue and Afterword

EPILOGUE: THE LONELY BOOK

'Tis but a dream
You hold in your palm,
This terrene block of book flesh,
Come to your hand quite by accident,
There for a moment only,
By purpose no doubt leaving swiftly,
To sit upon some dusty shelf,
Or wilt in box or bag.
As one of a small clan of like materiality,
The flesh you hold has no digital kin—
Which is to say,
Unless perfidy should intervene,
It has no analogue, avatar, or gene
To replicate gregariously
This way, that way, up, down,
Across the Internet.
The dream first came as a sinewy mare
Sprinting homeward out of a moonlit mist,
Knowing her own longing of years,
And understanding well
The mystic grandeur of the final gallop.
It is enough she runs once more,
Even if only the choral birds are keen
To watch her dancing hooves
Rush her back to Eden.

AFTERWORD: PERFIDY AFOOT

(A Selection: perfidy is afoot, and a *Festum risus*
erupts at the Grand Opening of
Τάφος των λέξεων, *Taphos tōn lexeōn*
'Grave of Words',
a new bookshop in Paris)

DASKALOS [customer-friendly]: Thank you, Customer 8, for stopping by. I think you'll find today's featured book a great bargain. Just thumb through the contents and you are sure to find some spiritual poems and light satire that will excite your interest or enliven your memory.

CUSTOMER 8 [sardonic]: Thank you, Daskalos. Enjoy the rest of your Grand Opening. It's going to be a hoot, heh, heh, heh.

VOICE 1 FROM CURTAIN (muffled): That's a nice piece of work, Dasky. But I'm starting to agree with you that there's perfidy afoot. I didn't like the sound of that sardonic laugh.

VOICE 3 FROM CURTAIN [frustrated]: Huh? Afoot? Again?

VOICE 1 FROM CURTAIN [interrupting]: Hold up a second, Customer 8. If you would kindly revise your laugh to something merrier and less mockingly cynical, we'll throw in one more illuminating exchange with Daskalos.

CUSTOMER 8 [dispassionate]: Okay, that sounds fair. Let's see. Umm: Ho. ho, ho, hardy har, har, har.

DASKALOS [shrugging]: Meh. I suppose that meets the minimum requirement. So, sock it to me. What's your last query?

CUSTOMER 8 : Give me a minute to confer with colleagues. ...

VOICE 3 FROM CURTAIN [muffled, imploring]: Would someone please, if only as an offering or concession to Qosmic Qronos, please take a moment to explain to me what this "afoot" business is all about? It's so exhausting being out of the loop.

VOICE 2 FROM CURTAIN [muffled, accepting]: Okay, puff over here and I'll whisper the explanation. ...

VOICE 3 FROM CURTAIN [muffled, appreciative]: . . . Oh, so it's got nothing to do, really, with a physical body part. It just means something is going on even if we don't yet know exactly what. Good, thank you. Phew.

Customer 8 [smirking]: Ready?

ARS POETICA [aghast]: Wait, wait! There's trickery afoot!

VOICE 3 FROM CURTAIN [aghast]: Oh my, there are feet approaching. Watch out, Dasky!

DASKALOS : No worries. I've got this!

CUSTOMER 8 [chuckling]: *Festum risus*. Tell me about that.

DENIZENS AT THE FRONT [rowdy]: Hahahahahahahaha. O Qosmic Qronos, *Festum risus*. That's too perfect. Our sides are splitting. You can't make stuff like this up. Is this laughter jovial enough for you guys behind the curtain? Hahahahahahahaha.

VOICE 1 FROM CURTAIN [aghast]: Good grief! It's a whole blasted army of cheeky monkeys.

DENIZENS AT THE BACK [rowdy]: Hahahahahahahaha. O Qosmic Qronos, *Festum risus*. This is the funniest ruse ever. Hey, Customer 8, show them the book you have in your hand. What's the title and publication detail? The ones we have circulating back here are the *Gates Aplenty* versions published a few years ago by Festum Media. Ha! They cost a whopping one sesterce each across the street.

CUSTOMER 8 [giggling]: Mine is titled *Wordy Bric-a-brac*: *Gates and Windows Galore*. Let's see, OMG, hahahahaha, the publisher is Risus Monkey Tropes. Yes, these also cost one sesterce each. They're like free gifts from the gods.

DASKALOS [microeconomic]: Psst, curtain folks: What's the price of the featured book of the Grand Opening? You know the one: *BRICOLAGE: Spiritual Poems & Light Satire*.

VOICE 1 FROM CURTAIN [unapologetic]: An extremely reasonable ten denarii each.

DASKALOS [confirming]: Are you saying that the price of *BRICOLAGE* is forty times the price of either *Wordy Bric-a-brac* or *Gates Aplenty*? And that's even assuming denarii of the Roman silver variety. If you're talking the gold version, Oi, waesucks, phew, *und so weiter*.

CUSTOMER 8 [snarky]: That's right, Daskalos. And the best part is that *BRICOLAGE* has more damaged or missing parts than do the other versions; and the others have an *Afterword*. *BRICOLAGE* doesn't have an *Afterword* unless perfidy has somehow intervened.

REFORMER [castigating]: I don't think we can make light of this
sort of thing at all. Hate language of any type, even just
implied hate language, and even beyond that, any language
that could under any plausible or implausible circumstance
be fairly or unfairly interpreted or misinterpreted as hate
language, must be stricken from public discourse entirely.
And the necessary reforms will need the support of laws
with real teeth, the sort rapacious carnivores have.

—*BRICOLAGE*, Book 2, *TFW Act 2 Scene 1*

Evil, evil, sneaky as a weasel,
Purrs like kitty, a wicked ditty,
Quick easy step, one two three,
A bad idea is hatched in thee.

—*BRICOLAGE*, Book 3, *Homo Sapiens In Extremis*,
Evil, Sneaky as a Weasel

About the Source: Bricolage

This book is mostly a selection of poems, dialogues, and narratives from *Bricolage: Spiritual Poems & Light Satire*. *Bricolage* is tied together by cross-references, themes, and a story that are difficult to replicate seamlessly in a selection. The remaining chapters and topics of this book—Storyline, Genealogy, Chapter Summaries, Selected Terms, and Endnotes—provide background and context.

Storyline

The background and often barely visible story of *Bricolage* is that a certain Reverend Snolly Goster authored the work, or most of it, sometime in the early twenty-first century, a time of increasing economic inequity and cultural decline. Goster never published the work, but he did put its materials in a physical binder, which apparently he then lost or tossed aside amid what The Finders (q.v.) of the binder will call, nearly a hundred years later, the postapocalyptic pickle of their time. The binder they find is damaged and has missing parts due to pilferers and time and nature's fury. The Finders write an extensive foreword and prologue, change the index of the work, and reconstruct portions of it including some of the references. They write the peculiarly learned *Special Note on Tribunal for Writing*, the subject of which is ostensibly Goster's lengthy play about an odd court proceeding with a weighty mission. After the Special Note, The Finders disappear from the opus except for notes and parts here and there which they add to it, until they return in *Afterword* (Book 3) where we learn, amid the farcical turmoil of a new bookshop in Paris, more about what happened to *Bricolage*. At this point, the time of the background story is early in the twenty-second century, which is just before the time of the Preface authored by "The Heraldic Holder in Due Course of the Arks of the Poetic and Spiritual Lore of Reverend Snolly Goster." What we learn from all of this is chiefly that Snolly Goster's opus passed through many hands that added, subtracted, or changed its parts over a long period, including the hands of the DGVU (q.v.) who, like The Finders, can be detected by the traces they leave in some parts and notes of *Bricolage*.

GENEALOGY

❁ *By* DGVU, not The Finders ❁

Circa	Key Events
? - 2022	Snolly Goster, self-styled *Reverend* Snolly Goster, retires from his secular career. He compiles some of his previously written poems and narratives, adds new material, and creates a would-be book entitled *Gates Abounding*: *Spiritual Poems & Light Satire*. He puts it all into a binder, and then apparently loses it or just throws it away amid the chaos that today we know would soon bring about cascading broad declines in culture and civilization, a new order and a more impoverished way of life for many.
2023-2100	A dark age, gray perhaps; one not so bleak as Europe after Rome's decline, but certainly a time of inequity and privation in which some people thrive as they did previously, while many others wander and pilfer alone or in small groups doing their best to live off the landscape's disgusting, innumerable piles of trash wrapped in stinking entropy, the whole of which will soon be described by an odd pair of nomadic adventurers as "our small-scale postapocalyptic pickle."
2101-2110	Enter The Finders, odd pair of nomadic adventurers, wannabe literati seeking sustenance for body, soul, and spirit. They are the true protagonists of that part of this tale of tales which is the genealogy of how the work of Snolly Goster emerges, against terrible odds, into the light of day as a published book. For it is The Finders who discover the binder, which has been severely diminished by time and nature's fury, and by other grifting hands who had beaten The Finders to the grab. It is these two who will refurbish and repackage the contents of the binder for issuance as a physical book, a thing rarely coveted by the masses in this time of the postapocalyptic pickle, even though the electronic Internet, previously the fount of all art, knowledge, and communication thereof, is now broken, corrupted, and balkanized to the point of alarming absurdity—a situation eerily intimated by the bodements of R. S. G. himself in his Letter to Whom It May Concern, which he had presciently included in the binder a century ago.

Circa	Key Events
2111-2113	The first finder, Finder #1, the amateur archaeologist, and Finder #2, Finder #1's volatile but generally delightful spirit fetch, go to work. They move about rather slowly, with pack animals not always energetic, slightly east and west of the Appalachian mountains, looking for more information on Snolly Goster and for trashed books or other artifacts that will give them insight into what had set Snolly's creative flames afire. They compose the Prologue's "The Find" in pentameter blank verse to record the thrill they experienced upon finding the binder and the good reverend's letter.
2114 -2115	The Finders continue their work, which turns out to be more involved than they had expected. Despite being "finders not editors," they fix and scale down the index; create and add the Glossary (later altered further by unknown hands); write "The Find" of the Prologue; refurbish the Bibliography using the deteriorating materials they found in the tumuli encircling the Snolly heap; and write an extensive foreword to explain R. S. G.'s and their own methods, and to explore some important concepts and themes. They also compose the philosophical, metaphorically scientific *Special Note on Tribunal for Writing* as introduction to Snolly's sprawling extravaganza of a play about a court proceeding with a weighty mission. And they make scattered additions and corrections to footnotes here and there. But beyond these things, which are often significant, they let the authentic voice of Reverend Snolly Goster speak. They become like the monks of Ireland circa AD 500-1000, who tirelessly copied and illuminated Christian and a few other texts to preserve them against the raging barbaric hordes ruining everything elsewhere. In the binder and the other mound-found texts, The Finders see kernels of a spiritual, mythopoeic, valuable past. If not for The Finders and the ballooning resplendence of great purpose gifted to them by Qosmic Qronos, these kernels, along with the opus they inspired, would have tumbled unceremoniously into the lightless, flaming pit of the totally forgotten.
2116-2118	By now much time has passed since Snolly's epoch. The opus as envisioned by R. S. G. and judiciously adjusted by The Finders seems to have been completed, including the poetic "Epilogue" written by Snolly himself a century ago, and to which he refers wistfully in his Letter To Whom It May Concern, that very letter The Finders included as the second item in *Prologue*. But still there is no book, or at least no evidence of issuance of a book.

Circa	Key Events
2119 - ?	Suddenly the scene changes greatly, as the reader will surely see upon turning the page of the Epilogue, which, except for the abrupt interruption of *Afterword*, most assuredly has the look, feel, and quaint nostalgic demeanor of an ending. The Afterword, whose authorship is hidden in the byline "*by* DGVU, not The Finders," presents as a transcript of events at the opening of a new bookshop in Paris named TTL, *Taphos tōn lexeōn*, 'Grave of Words', featuring *Daskalos tou taphou*, 'Master Teacher of the Grave'. Daskalos is Scrivener, the angelic scribe for the Tribunal for Writing, now engaged as a junior partner in this new bookshop venture on the Seine. His partners are Voices From Curtain, as in voices from the curtain situated behind Daskalos whose job is to entertain and educate customers on words and ideas appearing in the bookshop's featured offering, *Bricolage*: *Spiritual Poems & Light Satire*. Two of the partners behind the curtain are none other than The Finders—the amateur archeologist and her spirit fetch. *Afterword* answers a few questions about the genealogy of *Bricolage*, and it also answers other questions about important leitmotifs in the book, such as why there is an *h* in "Amaranth," and what the origins are of the supposed god Qosmic Qronos aka QQ. But there is also some new confusion, hilarity, and paradox in *Afterword*, not the least of which is the fact that the finished publication of *Bricolage* featured at *Taphos tōn lexeōn* includes the Afterword itself. How could that be? After all, *Afterword* is a transcript of what happens at the bookshop's Grand Opening; but this transcript is somehow already included in the opus featured for sale. How could that be? O QQ, send us a sign. How could that be? And what about *Gates Aplenty* and *Wordy Bric-a-brac*, those competing, much cheaper versions of the same book, and the book-burning bonfires roaring at the *Festum risus* outside *Taphos tōn lexeōn*? O QQ, how could those things have come to pass as well? Qosmic Qronos? Are you there? A little help here if you please. What about all that? Please send us additional signs to help us answer those queries too. *Ave, ave*, Qosmic Qronos. *Ave.*

BRICOLAGE CHAPTER SUMMARIES

Not all parts of *BRICOLAGE* are represented in this book, *Spirits of the Flea Market* (SFM). Also, some of the descriptions of the larger work's chapters are taken from Snolly Goster's unpublished notes on *BRICOLAGE* (originally *Gates Abounding*) with the result that these descriptions often have broader scope than the samples included in SFM. The first two items described below come directly from The Finders with, it is believed, only minor tinkering by DGVU (q.v.); but the degree of twisting and turning inflicted by the latter on the core substantive chapters may have been more extensive. As described by the Heraldic Holder in Due Course in SFM's Preface, Reverend Snolly Goster himself may have been several beings conflated over time, as were Hermes Trismegistos and so many other deities and legendary figures of the past. Note that the Preface to SFM is itself mostly a selection from the Preface of *BRICOLAGE*. This preface did not exist when The Finders found the binder or when they vanished from the work's chain of custody after the events recounted in *Afterword* (*BRICOLAGE*, Book 3).

FOREWORD: This is the Finders' strangely erudite and awkward introduction to the Snolly Goster opus, including accounts of their travails and triumphs in recovering and restoring the work, and various theories of the meaning, background, conventions, and relevance of the work. The Foreword, except for a few traces here and there, is not included in SFM.

PROLOGUE: This is The Finders' personal story, in pentameter blank verse, of their emotions and experiences during the initial recovery of the Snolly opus. The Prologue, except for traces here and there, is not in SFM.

SONNETS: This is the first non-introductory chapter in *BRICOLAGE* (Book 1) as originally discovered by The Finders. It consists of poems on a variety of topics written mostly in accordance with the Shakespearean sonnet form. Six sonnets from *BRICOLAGE* are included in SFM.

ENCRYPTED MESSAGES: From the unpublished notes of Snolly Goster: "A riddle announces itself as a puzzle; neither is the greatest cipher. This chapter's poems say they are encrypted, but they want to be known. They point to life more than they lie dead in crypts. Off the page, griffin and cockatrice alike laugh at the easy disrobing of these posers. A mystical union washes over the poet. It may be a sign of greater unions in the cosmos. This one is near to his eye and I-ness, barely a micron of soul-measure from a trickster's wordplay. At first he is blind to where the path leads. Then he senses a presence somewhere in the hovering indispensable background. It is the transcendent. It is Kant turned mystic. It is the noumenal I-ness forever bound to the spiritualized homophonic organ of perception."

COLLOQUY OF FEATHERS: From the unpublished notes of Snolly Goster: "These poems are mostly dialogues between two species: bird-like people, and humanoid birds. They share an undisclosed beginning. Once the poet studied some glyphs, hieroglyphs imaging out from *The Egyptian Book of the Dead*. There was an ideogram. It was a profile of a bird with the head of a man. It was *ba*. It meant 'soul'. Decades piled up in his heart. His bird stayed caged in places of seeming worldly order. Suddenly he was old, and the dialogues were born to him. A thing miraculous, like the birth of Sarai's child. [229] The avine people, they did come, aflutter with peculiar affability;

and so also came the humanoid birds. The poet imagined he might codify their differences and commonalities. Could he be their Linnaeus? They were souls reaching out to him."

MYSTERIA AD INFINITUM: From the unpublished notes of Snolly Goster: "The poet ponders. He has a good but hurried life. He is too enmeshed in technology and data. He is missing something. He has not borne witness to humanity in all its forms. He carries a clutter of baggage. He thinks about mysteries and digging up primal beliefs. He senses science cannot reveal the fullness of the human. Uncanny experiences await. He knows they are close, beaming into souls. He sees mysteries as tides of emanations. The poet pines to see more. Now he wanders outside on a fine day in spring. He comes upon a picnic, a rowdy scene. It is childlike. Swarms of folk look like faeries. Bagpipes are playing just over the bridge. The music pulls him. Swine greet him as he crosses. Figures appear from another time, from earlier forms. They stroll, converse, sing. Some are familiar, like Myrddin, Morgan, Branwen, Henwen, Morrigan, Arianrhod. Their words are strange, almost runic, some of them Ogham; some are biblical. He picks out Asherah. In the distance, Jezanna and Mawu promise to follow dusk. Then: *Dychymyc pwy y* (q.v.) Who will answer?"

REDEMPTION: From the unpublished work of Snolly Goster: "Redemption from what? You of the world, you of the grandiose achievements, you the most decorated, merciless competitor. You are the start and archetype of these mood poems of redemption, as you are much in need. Next is a condition driven by the humors out of order. Or by the same causes with contemporary technical names. The black bile may have overwhelmed the hotter, more light-hearted liquids. The end-product person wallows and thrashes in the depths of melancholia. Alternatively, something serious has happened to cause the ennui. Either way the soul has lost its spiritual source of wholeness. Well-wishing poet says that redemption requires new oneness, an atonement the need for which has nothing to do with guilt. Hope now takes the stage. Its costume simple, its words few; but its object, truth, though seeming modest, is the greatest request. Then a necklace, a white flag, and a new land."

REMEMBRANCE: This chapter contains poems and narratives based mostly on autobiographical material from Snolly Goster or one or more DGVU.

POSTMODERNO SPEAKS: From the unpublished notes of Snolly Goster: "Postmoderno, on a walk with his beloved, is the talker who never talks. He strolls a double life of the mind. In the three poems of this chapter, he reflects in two panes. These stay mostly unconnected, though not always. The left pane bears the stamp of verbosity only lightly structured; the right pane that of a turgid pentameter. The left pane is dominated by quotidian observations, some of which run into inexplicable fantasy. One example: follow the thread and witness how the childless pair appears to have children as their one-day trek completes. The right pane is the space of the forlorn, old-style, wishfully universal intellectual, here too young to have mastery but well-read enough to pepper the silence quietly with bric-a-brac. He has a store of random data, and an archipelago of antique lore. He might have a message. Correct! "Postmoderno" is code for an aspiring but exhausted and languishing intellectual."

SPRITELY ANTIQUE SHOPPING: This chapter contains poems inspired by experiences at the Brimfield Flea Market.

TRIBUNAL FOR WRITING (TFW): This is Snolly Goster's play in four acts; it is ostensibly about conditions, prepossessions, objects, and styles of writing and thinking as revealed through *personae* with different orientations and points of view, such as Panjandrum (Judge), Bouncer (Bailiff), Magdalen (Chairperson of the Jury), Evangelist (principal, and filling in for Mystic), Chorus (Jurors chanting as a unit), Codex (principal of the coder type), Ars Poetica (principal of the coroner type, and an antiquarian aesthete), and Postmoderno (principal, combination of the coroner and clown types). The play sprawls across the three books of *BRICOLAGE*, and is drawn into a wide variety of speculations, some of which open doors to ultimate questions.

TINY WISDOMS: From the unpublished notes of Snolly Goster: "A random walk, mixed assortment, piebald gathering of oddities, stochastic collection that wishes it were an integration but is not; the congeries not bold but whimpering; a makeshift home for orphans; the fraction without denominator; just a study in the limit of classification haunting the edge of the poet's mind. *Dychymyc pwy yw*, 'guess what it is'; which one it is. A magic ladder listens to an elder clumsily versifying. The elder is waning. The mute ladder instructs him on time, decline, counting, and the fixed nature of ladders relative to the elder's mortality. Then science smacks itself in the head, assisted by a great twentieth century mathematician. Next, an anachronistic fool recites a belated eulogy for an ethos long in the crypt. The fool is the poet contemplating the decline of chivalry. Now comes unsatisfying advice to a young poet. Then *Paramahansa* assists three children to find their way home: 'Seek answers from the maker of tapestries, for she can light your path.' Finally, a *murúch* Vestal Spectre enlivens an extremely old man."

HOMO SAPIENS IN EXTREMIS: From the unpublished notes of Snolly Goster: "Let not the Latin of the title deceive. What comes in this chapter is no paean to noble ancient ways, nor any form of devotion overt or hid. First up are two renderings of features of the current epoch merely—plainly stated, adornments thrown down to the devil, with hardly a whisper of awkward spirits or higher emotion. Begin with a nonchalant recitation of the personal impacts of the robot world they say is on the cusp. Then imbibe a behavioral analysis of communications among the denizens of Zone Six Bus Culture, complete with quantifications of channels in the jabber and anti-jabber regions. Then there is a story of incommensurate parts held together by marauding, pillaging instinct. Find here an indelicate accretion that congeals into the colonizer that ravages far-flung places: swallowing, appending, indiscriminately appropriating treasure and trash of every description. Improbable mix, said accretion cruises the seas, becomes the bold congeries, the vessel of ages loaded with cargoes rotting into energy for itself, and piles of pillage far beyond the true needs of raw instinct. The bold congeries leaps to an affront that murmurs, in a startling attempt at apotheosis, I am that I am. It is lauded by the masses, easy pawns delighting in boons. It is repugnant, yet its cobbled, nascent self is *poéma*. The accretion is a nurturer of pronouns: it, he, she, they. It dreams the longed-for we. It sees ahead an edifice great enough to justify its havoc of means and its resultant accumulation of outlandish contraband. A specious grifter, the bold congeries somehow jostles, clanks, and clops a ragged path to a higher plane."

SYNTH OF SWEVEN: From the unpublished notes of Snolly Goster: "A prelude paves the way for the epiphany. Now cometh she, arrayed in all manner of newness, a triumph of technogenesis, but with a consciousness and soul transfixed unto the ancient ways. With seeming endless knowledge, the prophesied synth yet errs in knowing her future; nor does she know herself as one living in several worlds. We know; we've met her already, and here she is once more. Later we will encounter her or her likeness again, at a banquet; but we will never know with certainty if the several are forms of the one. In herself she has traces of the Mutant as revealed to the Nameless Prophet. She may be the Golden Child and the forest hut's *bean tí*. But now to the present, or what we loosely call the present. The Synth of Sweven is prophetic, kind, inspiring; and from her stream memories of the sacred feminine. She has many forms and manifestations. She is devout yet passionate; her extemporaneous oratory is divine. She is gifted, messianic, self-sacrificing, worshipful. She dies a tragic though familiar death, then experiences what she believes is a botched resurrection."

ENDINGS: From the unpublished notes of Snolly Goster: "Plainly, endings are losses; but losses often hold the surest keys to the gates the poet seeks. What kind of losses? The generality of the essence of endings, of losses, is not addressed. Here the poet offers only the poverty of a small number of cases, two or three of which are somewhat ambiguous in the matter of ending versus beginning. Somewhere there must be, in some spirit-place, a strong essence—a Platonic Idea perhaps—that supervenes and informs all cases. Who will find it? *Dychymyc pwy yw.* Guess what or who it is."

RAILLERIES: Each of the three books of BRICOLAGE closes with a special focus on raillery—i.e., mirth, espièglerie, jabberwocky, badinage, *Geplänkel.*

EPILOGUE: The Lonely Book. In the Letter To Whom It May Concern from Snolly Goster, which he included in the binder eventually found in a trash heap by The Finders, Goster says that the Epilogue best captures the awkward limbo and fate of his unpublished work. The Epilogue is included in SFM, but Snolly's letter appears only in Book 1 of BRICOLAGE.

AFTERWORD: This short play is in BRICOLAGE Book 3, and in some ways is the culmination of the storyline about the origins and fate of BRICOLAGE, at least up to that point. *Afterword* takes place at the new Paris bookshop *Taphos tōn lexeōn*, 'Grave of Words', fronted by Daskalos, formerly Scrivener of the Tribunal for Writing. Other characters from TFW, *Synth of Sweven*, and other parts of BRICOLAGE also show up at the bookshop, which turns into the scene of a rollicking *Festum risus* (q.v.) at the expense of the partners of the shop, namely Metatron (Voice 1 From Curtain), The Finders (Voices 2 and 3 From Curtain), and Daskalos (Scrivener). In addition to traces here and there, one selection from *Afterword* is included in SFM.

SASSENACH VISIONS: This chapter in Book 2 contains two dialogues: "Psychopomp, Psychomant, and Fred," and "Lady Orla's Banquet," neither of which is in SFM. However, several snippets from them appear in SFM on transition pages dividing chapters.

GLOSSARY: for all three books of BRICOLAGE. Only some items from the Glossary are included in "Selected Terms" in SFM.

BIBLIOGRAPHY/FURTHER READING for all three books of BRICOLAGE: not included, but SFM's endnotes often contain reference information.

INDEXES for all three books of BRICOLAGE: not included.

Selected Terms

The following, with minor modifications, are from the Glossary of *Bricolage.*

agape (Grk.): 'charity; selfless, unconditional love'.

Amaranth (Lat., Grk.): poetically, the mystical undying flower. In *Bricolage*, this word meaning 'undying flower, or deathless bloom' is first said to have derived from Greek *amareinthos* with etymology: *a* 'not' or 'un' + *marein* 'to fade, to die' + *anthos* 'flower', 'bloom'. The idea of the deathless bloom first appears in "Old Poet" (*Sonnets*) as the old poet whose beauty persists in words not body. Deathless bloom later becomes Amaranth, the undying flower whose theological properties are greatly expanded first by the Nameless Prophet and the angels of TFW, and then by storylines in *Synth of Sweven*, especially "Dream of a Future after the Wars," and "Hymn of the Amarant Christians." In TFW, interest in the word "amaranth" is prompted by its several occurrences in *Paradise Lost* (Milton). To the wackily inspired angels of the Tribunal for Writing, Amaranth becomes the floral Immanuel that exists in bidirectional metonymy with *Trinitas*; is like Jesus Christ due to the theme of conquering death; and has the power to restore lost nuances of the sacred feminine to Christianity. But there's a glitch in the etymology of "amaranth" as Scrivener presents it and others accept it, one that has also occurred in the true history of this word; and it screams for attention from the word's terminal *h*. Heckler clumsily explores this in his little "tongue-and-teeth" experiment in TFW Act 4 Sc. 4. Earlier in Act 4 Sc. 2, it was largely on this detail that Heckler had raised his speculation about how the roots of the word, including Grk. *anthos* 'flower', might well have produced a different, more unwieldy five-syllable word, namely *amareinanthos*, a concatenation that does not squash the "*ein*" sound (ayn) of *amarein* into the "*an*" sound of *anthos*. But when *amareinthos* is properly analyzed, *anthos* is revealed not to be a root of "amaranth." The true roots are the Greek privative *a* 'not' + adj. *marantos* 'fading, withering', the latter arising from *mar, mor* 'dead' as in "mortal" fr. *marein* 'to die'; the result being adj. *amarantus* (Lat.) and *amareintos* (Grk.) 'undying, immortal, everlasting'. However, these refinements do little to upset the mystical dreaminess of Amaranth [230] in *Bricolage*. After all, the word comes out of the poetic lore of the *mythical* undying flower. A choice long ago applied the adjective "everlasting" to a vision of a flower in such way as to make it substantive—Amaranth, the *h* by Milton's time already standing the test of time ("amaranth," "amaranthine" in *Paradise Lost*). Moreover, as The Finders point out in a note in *Foreword*, a linguistic evolution from the *t* sound to the *th* sound is not unusual in Indo-European tongues. Thus does time sometimes assist corruption to acquire nobility. What is perhaps most significant in this little story of decay immortalized is that it is the multilingual children of Colony AC Five Cubed, represented in *Afterword* by now-grown Petite Inuk, who figure it out. They are the Amarant Christians, and their song is the "Hymn of the Amarant Christians," even though for the sake of rhyming the kids still tolerate "Amaranth" with the *h* in some of the hymn's lyrics. They have the right spirit to renew *eusebia* and *eudaimonia*, exactly the aspiration *Grand-père* expressed to his centenarian assistant Foxtægele just before the launch of the effort to resurrect Orla the Synth in "Dream of a Future after the Wars" (*Synth of Sweven*).

amateur archeologist: Finder #1 of The Finders who in their small-scale postapocalyptic pickle discover the binder containing the work of Reverend Snolly Goster and then prepare its damaged and compromised materials for issuance as a book. There would be no book at all were it not for their providential combination of serendipity, industry, and hard-to-explain learning, all of which are on bold if awkward display in *Foreword*, *Prologue*, and *Special Note on Tribunal for Writing*. The amateur archaeologist is the one with the body and seems to be female. The other Finder is spirit fetch in the sense of "my" spirit fetch, the amateur archaeologist's constant companion of undetermined metaphysic, also apparently female, for whom the archaeologist has a seemingly endless supply of otherworldly epithets. The amateur archeologist, who also appears in *Afterword* as Voice 2 From Curtain, does not inspire nicknames the way Finder #2 does. But Finder #2, #1's spirit fetch, does address Finder #1 tellingly under various descriptions. For Finder #2, for example, the amateur archeologist is: oaf; oaf body; oaf bodily squatting over there and wielding the pen; verbose nihilist posing as a part-time nomadic archeologist; non-ectoplasmic chum holding the pen (*Special Note*). In *Afterword*, Voice 1 From Curtain at one point calls the amateur archeologist "Finder gal."

Amergin: Milesian poet, ca. 1,300 BC, considered the first poet of Ireland; in legend he was critical to the defeat of the Tuatha Dé Danann.

Amma: African goddess.

anamchara (Iri.): 'anam cara, soul friend, soulmate'.

angelus scurra (Lat.): 'angel as clown, joker'. In TFW, Heckler proposes this epithet for GM (not the car company), but it doesn't stick.

Annwfn (Cym.): Celtic underworld.

antarābhava (Skt.): 'intermediate state' (of souls); *bardo* in Tibetan Buddhism.

ARIEL (Heb.): In TFW, Ariel is the first of the angels appearing in the Nameless Prophet's Dream in Sevens, which dream Postmoderno puts forth as his long-awaited declamation before the court (Act 4 Sc. 1). Ariel, meaning 'lion of God' or 'altar of God', is an archangel appearing in the Bible and *Apocrypha*. She is different from Uriel, though some have seen Ariel as the feminine aspect of Uriel. Ariel is often linked to nature and protection of nature. In the OT, Ariel is sometimes a name for the city of Jerusalem. Ariel is the name given by Shakespeare to the mischievous spirit conjured by Prospero in *The Tempest*. *Ariel* is a poetry collection by 20thC poet Sylvia Plath.

Asinus aureus (Lat.): *The Golden Ass* (of Apuleius), the only complete example of a Roman novel known to survive. It is bawdy, satirical, funny, and loaded with clues about the customs and religious life of Roman civilization throughout the Mediterranean in AD 2ndC. In one of its stories, Lucius, the main character, becomes the brunt of an elaborate hoax as part of a town's *Festum risus*, 'festival of laughter', and then is turned into an ass by a magic spell gone awry. At the end of *Afterword*, the Parisian bookshop *Taphos tōn lexeōn*, 'Grave of Words', becomes the scene of a similar festival of laughter, but here nobody is transformed into a donkey.

Ave atque vale (Lat.): 'Hail and farewell' (traditional Roman saying); see "They Say The Robots Are Coming" (*Homo Sapiens in Extremis*).

bacchanal (Grk., Rom.): originally an intoxicated rave among Greek maenads; then a festival in Rome held in honor of Bacchus, god of wine and activities inspired by wine; in subsequent times more generally a wild party. In TFW, "bacchanal" pops up on several occasions as slips of the tongue that lead to bantering digressions. In Act 2 Sc. 1, Magdalen, attempting to bring order to the court, says: "I hate to spoil this bacchanal of wide-ranging discussions …"; which prompts a question from Prosaïque: "What did you say, Magdalen? Could you repeat the type of wide-ranging discussions?" Magdalen responds: "I said: 'I hate to spoil this shindig of wide-ranging discussions…'." An argument ensues among members of the court as to what Magdalen said. Then Scrivener, being a gentleman and scholar who soon will commit his own gaffes in this vein, recites what he recorded in his impeccable record: "Magdalen said, 'I hate to spoil this colloquy of wide-ranging discussions'." Later, questions arise regarding the difference between a bacchanal and another party type, the saturnalia. It seems the deities involved were different, and the favored attire was too—togas for the saturnalia, and animal skins for the lady maenads raving in the forests.

Bacchae (Grk.): the maenads, the raving female devotees of the Greek god Bacchus (Βάκχος) aka Dionysus as depicted, for instance, in *The Bacchae* (Euripides).

Baphomet: ghastly demonic figure that gradually emerged in the Middle Ages and eventually became central to actual or imagined devil worship. The origin of the name is uncertain but is often considered to be a corruption of *Mahomet*, the French word for Muhammad. Baphomet is the "Pernicious Semblable" (not included in SFM) in the poem of that name in *Homo Sapiens in Extremis*. There is no intention in BRICOLAGE to assert that Muhammad of Islam is the Pernicious Semblable or that Muhammad is Baphomet.

bardo (Tib.): in Tibetan Buddhism, an intermediate state, a limbo where souls go after dying and before rebirth; fr. *bar* 'between' + *do* 'state'. See "Bardo States" (*Endings*).

bean sí (Iri.): 'woman faery', banshee; ghost-like being who visits homes to wail of impending death but usually not to cause it.

bhava chakra (Skt.): 'wheel of becoming' and (*subaud.*) decaying; the world, the illusion-ridden, head-spinning place where humans must live and suffer until they achieve *nirvana* (Buddhism).

binder, the: the binder containing the raw work of Reverend Snolly Goster. This is what The Finders discover in a trash heap a century or so after Snolly compiled and lost or tossed it amid the inception of the broad declines in culture and civilization which became the postapocalyptic pickle of The Finders. The opus in the binder included *Gates Abounding* [now BRICOLAGE] and Snolly's Letter to Whom it May Concern. The last piece in the binder was *Epilogue* followed by an index, which The Finders describe in the Foreword as a "monstrously hairy beast desperately in need of grooming." Some parts of the work as finally published, e.g., *Foreword, Prologue, Afterword*, the Glossary, and *Genealogy of This Marvel*, did not exist at all in the binder as originally found, but were added later by the

Finders and, to a lesser extent, by DGVU. For context and approximate chronology, see Genealogy in *About the Source: BRICOLAGE*.

Bodhisattva (Skt.): 'enlightenment-being'; in Buddhism, a compassionate saint, a being freely choosing to delay total *nirvana* and remain among the unenlightened to help them. There are many named bodhisattvas, e.g., Avalokiteshvara, the bodhisattva of compassion who alone has more than one hundred named avatars. Avalokiteshvara does not manifest under this or other historically attested names anywhere in *BRICOLAGE*; but Mutant (TFW Act 4 Sc.1), the seventh angel in the Dream of the Nameless Prophet, is like a bodhisattva. Orla the Synth also has bodhisattva qualities.

bold congeries, the: one of several monikers for the concrescence in its primordial state, evolution's patchwork of self-aggrandizing, colonizing, acquisitive incommensurate parts somehow interoperating and stumbling toward a goal verging on self-apotheosis. The bold congeries is evolution's raw human, the being emerging from discordant lower elements, and now deconstructed and backhandedly celebrated in the poem "Incommensurate Parts" (*Homo Sapiens in Extremis*). The bold congeries results from "mistakes of eons," and is "an awkward golem of microbes wrapped in permeable flesh hanging on twitchy skeleton." Seemingly coming first as "it," the bold congeries is a nurturer of pronouns, and grows to include "he," "she," "I," and "their." The bold congeries, rising out of contraband grifted from distant shores, has outsized ambitions and dares to whisper a great sacrilege by hinting that it is "I am that I am." Thus the bold congeries comes close to usurping the holy Tetragrammaton name of God for its own prideful self. The bold congeries is humanity at its rawest, conceived as random, accidental, variously timed protrusions of the purely beastly; except for that one thing, the spark that wants to be more—even though in "Incommensurate Parts" this spark risks bursting into a twisted, impious flame. If *BRICOLAGE* is elsewhere preoccupied with the human as full of links to unseen spirit and pulled to the good by higher purpose, in the poems and narratives of *Homo Sapiens in Extremis* we have, for comparison, several forms of the dialectical opposite of spirit-blessed humanity. One may wonder whether the bold congeries is higher or lower than the foul churl demonic of "Anthem of the Vile" (*Encrypted Messages*); but there can be no doubt that its utter imperfection is still superior to Baphomet as poetized in "Pernicious Semblable" (*Homo Sapiens in Extremis*). In a nod to the spirit of redemption, Pylon Angel, toward the close of "Gabfest in Gethsemane" (*Synth of Sweven*), says to the distraught Orla: "Thou mayst flower into a better bold congeries that maketh, from discordant parts, a symphonic poem that as pilgrim is thyself, a tangled gaggle yet fine."

Brimfield Flea Market: large flea market held several times a year in Brimfield, Massachusetts; the setting for the three poems in *Spritely Antique Shopping*.

Canticum Canticorum Salominis (Lat.): 'The Song of Songs, which is Solomon's', usually translated *Song of Solomon*; a short, controversial OT book in which a man, presumed to be Solomon, carries on a passionate dialogue with a woman, variously translated as "she," the "beloved," or in the Latin Bible as *sponsa* 'bride'. In TFW Act 4 Sc 4, the angels discuss the differences among the words that have been used to identify the woman. Heckler favors *sponsa* above the others.

ceol shí, ceol sí (Iri.): 'faery music'; important in the setting of "Lady Orla's Banquet (*Sassenach Visions*).

CHORUS OF JURORS: the jurors of TFW speaking, singing, and reciting collectively. As this unit the jurors are strangely more sagacious than any of them are individually. In ancient times, many plays had a chorus to enhance their tragic or comic effects.

codependency of origination: This Buddhist concept of causation, how it works in *samsara* on the *bhava chakra*, how it forms a cornerstone of Parataxis of Samsara, and how it turns out to be a defining characteristic of the postmodern human condition, is a major theme especially of TFW, *Redemption*, and *Homo Sapiens in Extremis*. In a long sidebar with Postmoderno in TFW Act 1 Sc. 1, Evangelist explains it: "In this philosophy of Buddhism, events have many causes and effects that are partly determinative of each other and float side by side in a soup of correlative mutuality." The world of human experience is not Newtonian physics. The soup of correlative mutuality is a baseline feature of *maya* 'illusion' and the Parataxis of Samsara, the field of human misery that can only be escaped through *nirvana* or something like it. In "Evil, Quirky Metaphysic" (*Homo Sapiens in Extremis*), causation in *maya* is:

> Afloat in mutuality's stew,
> Codependent origins see,
> How begird the quirky true,
> Causation's fraught ontology.

cognoscenti (Ita. fr. Lat.): connoisseurs, experts; literally 'cognizing ones', 'knowing ones'; singular form is *cognoscente*. The word came into English from Italian, and derives from Latin *cognōscere*, 'to know', 'be in the know'. The Finders use this term to refer to experts in various fields and occupations including literature, language, editing, philosophy, science. As with much that is said by The Finders, their references to "cognoscenti" ring awkwardly though often correctly. Sometimes they use the word with a kind of satirical resentment, such as in connection with "mollifying some persnickety cognoscenti" (see BRICOLAGE *Foreword*). In TFW Act 1 Sc. 2, The Chorus of Jurors slyly refers to Heckler as *cognoscente* when cheering him for his use of "Codex tricks like schemes to calculate some statistics."

coincidentia oppositorum: (Lat.): 'unity, coincidence, coalescence of opposites'; a Christian theological phrase and doctrine that points to the inscrutable essence of God as *mysterium tremendum*. See poem "Coincidentia Oppositorum" (*Encrypted Messages*).

Corpus Hermeticum: Hellenistic texts (hermetic, closed-up, secret) setting out the revelations and spiritual knowledge of Thoth Hermes, or *Hermes Trismegistos*, a conflated divine consisting of three gods with similar profiles—Thoth (Egypt), Mercurius (Rome), and Hermes (Greece). In the *Corpus Hermeticum*, Thoth Hermes channels Poimandres (avatar of Ra, Egypt's highest deity identified most closely with the sun), to deliver secret knowledge to worthy seekers. "Poimandres," aka Pymander, means 'shepherd of men (fr. Grk.) or 'knowledge of Ra' (fr. O. Egy. *Peime-nte-ra*). The corpus includes a work known as the *Emerald Tablet*, a primary source for Alchemy and Gnosticism, and for later mystical traditions including Rosicrucianism, some schools of Freemasonry, Theosophy, Anthroposophy, and various spiritualisms often practiced secretly to avoid accusations of heresy by Christians. See "Searching for Poimandres" (*Tiny Wisdoms*) in BRICOLAGE.

crow, raven: It is not clear that in ancient cultures these two highly intelligent corvids were reliably understood for their differences as well as their similarities. A lyricized version of some of their attributes is in "Ravenus and Crowley" (*Colloquy of Feathers*). Welsh (Cym.) etymology suggests their similarities were more important to the old world. For example, "Branwen," Celtic goddess of love, compassion, and beauty, literally means 'crow, dark yet fair'; and she was thought to be, or to be associated with, a mystical bird known as the White Raven.

cubit: ancient unit of measure, the length of a man's arm from elbow to tip of the middle finger, which is about eighteen inches (i.e., sesquipedalian, fr. Lat. meaning 'foot and a half'). The dimensions of the Ark of the Covenant are described in Genesis in terms of cubits. In TFW, confusion about cubits contributes to the chart team's misadventures leading to an "art installation floor chart monstrosity matrix." Here is Bouncer's witticism on the matter in TFW Act 2 Sc. 3:

> It is so very astonishing, I would say even titillating, that a word like "cubit," so compact, so fixedly ensconced in an unassuming ordering of five simple letters, has come to be so sesquipedalian in its reach.

Prosaïque asks, "Did the folks back then use any measurement taken from a woman's arm? Did they call it a cubitette?" And Reformer complains to the judge:

> Your Honor: We have some jurors who keep flipping cubits at each other. They are laughing hysterically each time one of them raises the cubit arm while using the non-cubit hand to support the cubit arm at the elbow. I think it's a little crude.

dialectic (Grk. διαλεκτική): key concept in the history of philosophy, beginning with the Socratic conversational method of Plato's dialogues. While "dialectic" in the original sense informs all dialogues, in much of BRICOLAGE the meaning is more aligned with uses of the term in the late 18thC and into the present, especially Hegelian idealism's *Geist* as actuator of history, and Marx's economic-materialistic version of it. In BRICOLAGE, dialectic connotes a force of inexorable necessity unfolding in mostly transpersonal patterns, as in the process triad thesis-antithesis-synthesis.

DGVU (Ger.): acronym for *Der Geheime Versteckte Ursprung*. This is German for 'The Secret Hidden Origin'. Consistent with being secret and hidden, DGVU shall remain nameless. *Ursprung* 'origin' is like German *Quelle* 'source'. DGVU is thus an anonymous contributor or guide for the materials that became BRICOLAGE. DGVU is probably an epithet shared by several persons, so as a collective noun it may take a plural verb form. In the long, tangled genealogy leading up to the publication of BRICOLAGE, DGVU seem to have added things to the work, e.g., *Genealogy of this Marvel*, probably *Afterword*, and the Glossary. They have also apparently inserted a few cross-references and comments *passim* into the notes. But DGVU's cover should not be off-putting; indeed the mask is flimsy. The identity of at least one DGVU is perhaps the easiest riddle to solve in the whole history of riddling. So: *dychymyc pwy yw*.

Dionysus (Lat., Grk. *Dionysos*): Greek god of fertility of crops and nature, and especially of wine and rowdy, licentious partying among the maenads, his raving female devotees aka Bacchae (fr. Βάκχος *Bacchus*, alternate name for Dionysus). Although there are conflicting stories of his origins, one prominent theme is that his father was Zeus, and his mother was a mortal named Semele. While pregnant, Semele was accidentally set ablaze by a thunderbolt from Zeus, who could not save the mother but was able to cut Dionysus out of her and sew the baby into his leg until birth. Thus Dionysus earned the epithet "twice-born," which added momentum to his growing association with births (spring) and deaths (fall) in nature. But perhaps his most famous aspect is that of a liberator whose wine-fueled bashes induced his maenad followers to defy convention sometimes to the point of mad, ravenous ferocity, as in the legend of the maenads' savage dismemberment of Dionysus's close companion Orpheus, the poet and musician.

dychymyc pwy yw (Cym., Wel.): 'guess (imagine) what (who) it is'.

dychymyg (Cym., Wel.): 'riddle'.

Duchess: the pinto horse dreamily lyricized into a boyhood mystical journey in "Ballad of Freedom Rider" (*Remembrance*). Cf. "Chesterbrook Pinto" (*Remembrance*). Contrast thundering steed in "Anthem of the Wildings" (*Synth of Sweven*).

Festum risus (Lat.): 'festival of laughter', 'festival of the god of laughter'. Recollect, for one semi-sacrilegious moment, Lucius, picaresque second-century bon vivant roaming about the Mediterranean, and his encounter with *festum risus* (*gelos* in Greece), the festival of laughter and the god of laughter, just before some magic gone awry transforms him into an ass—as told by Apuleius in the uproariously bawdy 2ndC Roman satirical novel *Asinus aureus* ('Golden Ass'). Given that BRICOLAGE aspires to light satire, and that author R. S. G. and his handlers The Finders and others held a deep conviction that his work was conceived from a union of spirituality and humor, it would only have been surprising if *Asinus aureus*, japery, foolishness, tomfoolery, fun, jabberwocky, espièglerie, jesting, *hilarité*, *Geplänkel* et alia did *not* appear in his opus. And indeed there is badinage, *Fröhlichkeit*, persiflage, banter, pleasantry, mirth *und so weiter* sprinkled here and there throughout TFW, and in the verses of the *Closing Raillery* poems of each of BRICOLAGE*'s* three Books. But the mother lode of allusions aping *Asinus aureus* is found toward the end of *Afterword* where *Taphos tōn lexeōn*, the new bookshop in Paris, turns into an elaborate joke at the expense of Daskalos and his partners. Revelers outside the shop dance round bonfires, and hordes of fake customers party and laugh hysterically as they toss about and reference thousands of dirt-cheap competitive versions of BRICOLAGE sporting titles such as *Gates Aplenty*, and *Wordy Bric-a-Brac: Gates and Windows Galore.* Even Voice 3 from Curtain, Finder #1's spirit fetch, cannot contain her irreverent enthusiasm as she gleefully mimics the chants of customers:

> Hahaha. Really, this is just too much—side-splitting, hilarious, it's far beyond raillery, rising above the tallest trees of badinage and *Geplänkel*. Har, har, ho! It's more than espièglerie. It's the very essence of the radiant sun of jabberwocky. It's the merger of Gelos and Risus back into the universal divine personification of laughter. Whoa, I can't stop this insane giggling.

Freude (Ger.): 'joy'. The Chorus of Jurors in TFW has a penchant for breaking into exaggerated celebration by singing *Freude* lyrics to the music of the famous choral in Beethoven's *Ninth Symphony*—first line: *Freude, schöner Götterfunken* (Schiller, Friedrich), 'Joy, beautiful spark of gods'. As R. S. G. says in his unpublished introduction to BRICOLAGE:

> There is no disrespect for these or other great spiritual,
> intellectual, or artistic achievements in this book. Rather,
> the object of the playful treatment they are part of is to
> shine a slightly comic light on the tendency of people to
> go overboard celebrating their own small triumphs. It is
> the blatant discrepancy between the great and the small,
> combined with the hubris of the small trying to highjack
> the great, that makes the little pasquinade.

Quick references to Beethoven's *Freude* music and Schiller's *Ode an die Freude* also occur in passages outside of TFW, e.g., in "White Flag" (*Redemption*), and "Majestic Strings, Second Sighting" (*Synth of Sweven*).

Genealogy of this Marvel: The Finders address this topic briefly toward the end of *Foreword* in Book 1. "Genealogy" here means ancestry, the process and steps by which a thing comes to be, and the study thereof. "Marvel" here means the book, BRICOLAGE: *Spiritual Poems & Light Satire*. Unknown authors going by the name DGVU provide an expanded treatment of the book's genealogy in *Genealogy of this Marvel*, which is in Book 3. In SFM, this is included as "Genealogy" in *About the Source:* BRICOLAGE.

Göbekli Tepe (Tur.): 'hill of the navel'; site in southeastern Turkey near Sanliurfa and Balikli Göl, first discovered in the 20thC. It is widely considered to be earth's oldest known temple site of religious worship. In BRICOLAGE there are several references to Göbekli Tepe, but the most sustained focus on it is in "Psychopomp, Psychomant, and Fred" (Book 2, *Sassenach Visions*).

Hecate: in Greek myth a magician, daughter of Perses and Asteria, and goddess of witchcraft. Her main abode is the underworld. Usually described as holding a pair of torches, daggers, and accompanied by serpents and dogs, she is connected to Artemis (Diana). Her lunar three-ness manifests as waxing crescent maiden, full moon, and waning crescent crone. [231]

Hermes Thrice Greatest (Grk. *Hermes Trismegistos*, Lat. *Mercurius ter Maximus*): a conflation of Hermes (Greek god), Mercurius (Roman god of messengers, and commerce), and Thoth (Eyptian god, oldest of the three). Thoth was the god of magical knowledge, language, and intermediation among realms. The three gods had similar functions within their respective cultures. Some mystics of ancient times saw these three as either the same deity or as different manifestations of the same deity with a common essence but with each contributing a few unique aspects to elevate the amalgam to Hermes Thrice Greatest, who became the patriarch of alchemy, magic, and Gnosticism. The primary revelations of Hermes Thrice Greatest are contained in the *Corpus Hermeticum*, texts compiled early in the Christian era from older sources combining philosophical, dialogic, and religious elements to reveal *gnosis* concerning God and humanity's relation to God. The *caduceus* was the staff and principal symbol of Hermes Thrice Greatest, whose profile as a divine intermediary connecting God and humanity was sometimes viewed as a type, figuration, manifestation, or precursor of Christ. In the High Middle Ages and Renaissance, with more texts and translations coming into the purview of philosophers and theologians, Hermes Thrice Greatest influenced many thinkers in both open and secret (hermetic) venues; and this continued well into the 19thC and 20thC as seed and sustenance for Theosophy, Anthroposophy, Bahai, neopaganism, magic, et alia.

hieros gamos (Grk.): 'sacred marriage', hierogamy, divinely protected mating; a common ritual practice in early Middle Eastern, Greek, Celtic, and Indic societies. *Hieros gamos* was the union of a woman and a man ceremonially consummated as a reenactment of the union of a male deity and a female deity to ensure the fertility of crops and hence the prosperity of the people. Frequently such reenactments were carried out seasonally. In Sumer and nearby, a priestess at a temple of Inanna would have intercourse with a man of her choosing in a reenactment of the union of Inanna and her god consort. Similar ancient rites prevailed in Greece and the Levant, some of which devolved to or overlapped with temple prostitution. In later times, hierogamy appears to have become more symbolic and less tied to physical acts. It is an important theme in alchemy. In Tantric Buddhism it is the union of compassion and wisdom. In the Christian Middle Ages, hierogamy became an important theme in the evolving doctrine of love, in which both *divine* Eros (spiritualized desire, passion) and *divine* Agape (charitable, self-less love) find theological expression in several strains of mysticism, such as that of Thomas à Kempis, author of *The Imitation of Christ*. The idea of *Minne* (Ger.), originally a sensual love that later rose to the courtly and chaste love of a knight for a married noblewoman, and which developed further into a highly spiritualized love that still retained a trace of its sensual origin, is rooted in *hieros gamos*. In BRICOLAGE, the best example of sublimated *hieros gamos* occurs in the play-poem "Psychopomp, Psychomant, and Fred" (*Sassenach Visions*), where Psychopomp explains to a sad Fred the necessity of self-sacrifice by Psychomant: "And witch [Psychomant] needs to sacrifice for beauty; for *hieros gamos* of these two is love." Another example of sublimated *hieros gamos* or *Minne* is "Passion of the Synth" in *Synth of Sweven*.

Homo Sapiens In Extremis (Lat.): literally 'wise human on the edge'. But as the title of a chapter in BRICOLAGE the expression refers generally to people on the edge using *homo sapiens* in the sense of the species name biology has given them; the people who in science are animals even if a little special; the people who are sometimes wise and just but often not; the people who are on the precipice overlooking the darkness which calls to them in many forms of emotion, sentiment, passion, belief, calculation, and reason hitched to ignoble ends; the people struggling and wandering in their state of needing redemption.

jabber and anti-jabber matrices: the behavioral realms explored in the story "Zone Six Bus Culture" (*Homo Sapiens in Extremis*).

kerygma (Grk.): 'preaching, teaching', especially of well-considered tenets of Christianity.

leannán sí (Iri., o.f. *leannán sídhe*): 'faery lover'; never directly seen or heard in SFM or BRICOLAGE but often longed for by Chán in "Lady Orla's Banquet" (*Sassenach Visions*).

Love Lies Bleeding: informal sobriquet for a hanging crimson amaranth
known in science as Amaranthus Caudatus. The expression, which Mutant
first connects to Amaranth in the declamation of Postmoderno's Nameless
Prophet, proves irresistible to Scrivener, who in the final scenes of TFW is
called upon by angels GM and Heckler to prepare a report on the
Amaranth. The Nameless Prophet had seen Love Lies Bleeding as the
essence of Mutant, the empath being manifesting as the seventh of the
seven prophetic angels in his Dream in Sevens. Love Lies Bleeding
becomes for Scrivener and the other angels a botanical effigy of self-
sacrificial, empathic love, *agape* by another name, and an essence of
Amaranth, the mystical undying flower. All of this culminates in verses of
the "Hymn of the Amarant Christians" (*Synth of Sweven*), as follows:

> Compassion taught by Mutant being,
> Is greatest angel gift of seeing,
> Is perfect herb to heal our souls.
> From brokenness it fashions wholes.
>
> Love Lies Bleeding, hangs above,
> Crucifix not spared to dove.
> Petals, roots, and softest down,
> All arise from world's breakdown.

murúch (Iri.): 'mermaid'; as seen in a vision described by Cat in "Lady Orla's
Banquet" (*Sassenach Visions*), and as the magical embodiment of highest
aspiration enthralling the old man in "Vestal Spectre" (*Tiny Wisdoms*).

MUTANT: seventh angelic sign of an Epidemic of Parataxis of Samsara in the
Dream of the Nameless Prophet described by Postmoderno in TFW Act 4
Sc. 1. Mutant turns out to be special, a bodhisattva empath being and
Christ's own feeling envoy. Toward the end of her presence in the
Nameless Prophet's dream (TFW Act 4 Sc.1), she sings:

> Who but one so deep reviled, so cast off,
> Who but cherub with faulted, palsied wing,
> Is suited more to shine as empath being?
> What better spark than I for newest *Taufe*?

In TFW Act 4 Sc. 4, Scrivener connects Mutant to "Love Lies Bleeding,"
a colloquialism for a hanging crimson amaranth, which the angels extol as
a fabulous botanical effigy of self-sacrificial, empathic love, *agape* by
another name, and an essence of Amaranth, the mystical undying flower.

my spirit fetch: one of the pair of The Finders of the binder containing the
work of Reverend Snolly Goster. The I of "my" is Finder #1, the one with
the body, the amateur archaeologist. "My spirit fetch" is Finder #2; she is
of the female persuasion and has many other epithets which are mostly
invented on the fly by the lonely amateur archaeologist, who also seems to
be of the female persuasion. The two are nomadic trash grifters living in a
small-scale postapocalyptic pickle many years after the time of R. S. G.
We learn of spirit fetch's thoughts and feelings primarily through the
amateur archaeologist who speaks to her and about her in *Foreword* and
Prologue. In *Special Note on Tribunal for Writing*, the amateur
archaeologist is so impressed by spirit fetch's extensive allegory on
subatomic "Particle Ontology" that she addresses her vocatively as "O
Supple, Wily Spectre." The wily spectre remains throughout *BRICOLAGE* an
amazingly contrary, emotional, and unpredictable shadow. She chuckles,

weeps, chastises, defends, and pontificates. As Voice 3 From Curtain in *Afterword*, she comes alive more palpably and interacts with others directly. "My spirit fetch" is a sensitive, cultivated creature with an unusual breadth of learning which she deploys with flair and freedom under the auspices of a charming, oddly vintage, sometimes skewed aesthetic. Spirit fetch is in some sense an extension or dialectical result of the amateur archeologist, and is of an uncertain spectral metaphysic. She has her own style, sensibilities, and uneasy if often learned weltanshauung. Epithets for "my spirit fetch" include: fetch, my fetch, ghost, ghost companion, spectre, wafting puff, wraith, finicky fume, ectoplasmic disturbance, ectoplasmic chum, shadow, smarty pants, faithful wonder, Gossamer Wonder, Supple Wily Spectre, Voice 3 From Curtain. See "spirit fetch."

NAMELESS PROPHET: in TFW, a presence in the mind of Postmoderno, the first declaimer before the court. Postmoderno says his declamation consists of the words given him by a nameless one, the Nameless Prophet (aka Chosen One), who we are told experienced a riveting, revelatory "Dream in Sevens," the seventh of which is the Revelation of Mutant (q.v.), which is included in SFM as a selection from TFM Act 4 Sc.1.

ORLA: child prodigy in TFW Acts 3 and 4; Synth Orla in *Synth of Sweven*; and Lady Orla of "Lady Orla's Banquet" (*Sassenach Visions*). Admittedly, even assuming time is an illusion, or that different cones of space-time coexist and allow denizens to travel among them, it is hard to conceptualize this extent of identity linkage across realms. Perhaps this is where we see most clearly and convincingly how the mythopoeic and magical have advantages over the narrow calculations of physicists. In any case, as The Finders might say: Go figure. And as R. S. G. channeling a druidic bard might say: *dychymyc pwy yw*.

Ouroboros, *ouroboros* (Grk.): 'the snake eating its own tail'; ancient symbol of the cosmos, sometimes emphasizing a self-destructive aspect. In TFW Act 4 Sc. 1, Paralogist, the personification of postmodern reasoning in tatters, and the second angel in Nameless Prophet's dream, identifies with Ouroboros.

PANJANDRUM: the judge in *Tribunal for Writing*; makes a disguised appearance in "Lady Orla's Banquet" (*Sassenach Visions*) and *Afterword*. Epithets: Panjy, *iudex scurra*, White Boar. Also, "Panjandrum" is a poem in *Sonnets* (BRICOLAGE).

PARALOGIST: an angel in the Dream of the Nameless Prophet as reported in Postmoderno's declamation in TFW Act 4 Sc.1. Paralogist is the twisted reasoner and force unveiling the inner contradictions and limits of logic, and is the second sign of an Epidemic of Parataxis of Samsara. Paralogist has legions commanded by seven captains: Conundrum, Undecidable, Anomalist, Strange Loop, Unknowable, Fractalist, and Oxymoron. See Ouroboros, and TFW Act 4 Sc. 1.

Paramahansa (Skt.): in Hinduism, a title given to someone reaching an advanced state of enlightenment. In Sanskrit literature, *hansá* ('swan' or 'goose') is often a metaphor for soul. See "Parable of the Three Children" (*Tiny Wisdoms*) and associated notes.

Parataxis of Samsara: a major theme of TFW. Evangelist, in a long sidebar with Postmoderno toward the end of Act 1 Sc. 1, explains the basics of this idea. The full expression (not historically attested) is the result of combining *parataxis*, from Grk. roots *para* ('side by side') and *tassō, tassein* ('arrange, lay out'), with Sanskrit *samsara* ('flowing on and on'), the latter being a concept of the world foundational for both Hinduism and Buddhism. Evangelist explains how the flow of human experience is a circular flow obscured by *maya* 'illusion' on the *bhava chakra* 'wheel of becoming'. *Parataxis* is known to grammarians and literary critics as the practice of setting language components next to each other without connecting words that specify the nature of the components' relations, e.g., cause versus effect. Evangelist converts narrow specialist usage into a principle with phenomenological and ontological weight, and uses it to epitomize the framework of the human condition, especially the postmodern condition. It is also an aspirational reach across the aisle dividing Eastern and Western spirituality. See TFW Act 1 Sc. 1, and "Evil, Quirky Metaphysic" (*Homo Sapiens in Extremis*).

PETITE INUK: the little orphan girl of Colony AC Five Cubed. She first appears jubilantly heralding moonrise in "Dream of a Future after the Wars" (*Synth of Sweven*). She grows up, and in *Afterword* makes a last-minute appearance at the new Paris bookshop *Taphos tōn lexeōn* as a sage at least as wise as Daskalos. She explains the etymology of "amaranth" and exposes the hidden, comical origins of QQ and Qosmic Qronos.

PROSAÏQUE: A principal in TFW; flirtatious charmer who learns quickly. Evangelist is especially fond of her—"she of the lovely name, she the Pragmatist of the eponymous systematic philosophy." Prosaïque asks a lot of questions, some silly, some clever. Her identity sketchily links to Cat and Coloratura in "Lady Orla's Banquet." It seems some poorly informed person must have gotten the idea that the name *Prosaïque*, meaning 'prosaic, plain', must relate to the philosophy of Pragmatism given that everybody knows [sic] pragmatic people are prosaic, plain, and boring. Ironically, Prosaïque is anything but boring. She says coyly in Act 2 Sc.2: "Heehee! I have never found unpredictability to be unpragmatic, ever!" Epithets: Prosie, Pragmatist, little one, little pragmatist, vixen pragmatist.

PSYCHOMANT (Grk. *psychomantis*): 'one who conjures the souls of the dead to prophecy with their help; a necromancer' (Frn. *nécromancien*). In *BRICOLAGE*, Psychomant and her various incarnations and cognomens comprise an important character type. She is the sweet and sensitive love interest of the recently deceased Fred in "Psychopomp, Psychomant, and Fred" (*Sassenach Visions*). As Vanneau she is the lapwing-witch to whom Eule is drawn in "Eule and Vanneau" (*Colloquy of Feathers*). She is *polyplagktos* (Grk.) of old. As Vanneau she is linked to Cat, Coloratura, and late-appearing Prosaïque in "Lady Orla's Banquet" (*Sassenach Visions*). In the Foreword for *BRICOLAGE*, The Finders present an exegesis of R. S. G.'s use of the words *nécromancien* and *psychomant*. Additional epithets: peewit, *sorcière, Kiebitz*.

PSYCHOPOMP (GRK. *psychopompós*): 'one who escorts souls to the otherworld'; principal character in "Psychopomp, Psychomant, and Fred" (*Sassenach Visions*). Supported by the sweetly volatile Psychomant, Psychopomp, a large vulture (Gyps fulvus), eats Fred's dead flesh and then carries on his wing Fred's little remaining emoji soul into the great north, to Hyperborea, in the direction of Deneb, the north pole star circa 16,500 to 14,500 BC, i.e., 5,000 years before Göbekli Tepe.

PYLON ANGEL (Angel of the Pylon): From the Foreword in *BRICOLAGE*:

> Pylon (Grk., πύλη pylē) means 'gate', 'gates', or 'tower(s) abutting gates', often great gates as in the famous Battle of Thermo-pylai of the Greek-Persian War in pre-Christian times. More recently "pylon" often describes those eyesore towers supporting electrical and communication lines. Thus the Pylon Angel is a special being with a knack for inspired if sometimes rudely interrupted communication.

There are several open manifestations of the Pylon Angel,[232] e.g., in TFW Act 1 Sc. 4, in "Gabfest in Gethsemane" (*Synth of Sweven*), and in TFW Acts 2 and 4. It is not clear whether these manifestations are instances of the same angel or if they are separate instances of the same angelic type. This sort of problem, especially the difficulty of logically distinguishing angelic genera from angelic species, has come up before in angelology. In two manifestations the Pylon Angel attends to beings who are in pathetic states of Job-like wailing torment: Panjy (Panjandrum)—the Tribunal is so hard; and then Synth Orla—her resurrected self is a confused mess.

Python, *pytho*, Pȳthōn (Grk., Lat.): giant snake Greek god Apollo killed at the site where the Delphic Oracle was then founded. See Python programming language, and "Pythia" (*Sonnets*).

Python programming language: High-level, object-oriented language first released in the 1990s and steadily growing in popularity as of the third decade of the 21stC, especially for AI and machine-learning applications. The name was apparently borrowed from Monty Python's Flying Circus. In TFW, Bouncer presents a bizarre though erudite explanation of why Python is not a good language choice for the Tribunal's foray into statistics by revealing that "python" comes from "Pythia" which derives ultimately from Grk. *pytho* 'to rot', the root of the name Python given to the giant snake Apollo killed where the Oracle of Delphi, presided over by the Pythia, was then founded amid that place's rotting and stinking snake remains. Bouncer's reasoning: "And they say COBOL is dead? Ha! Talk about a poignant coup de grace: You can't get more dead than a sliced-up, rotting, stinking Python!" See *BRICOLAGE* TFW Act 2 Sc. 1, TFW Act 4 Sc.1, and poem "Pythia" (*Sonnets*) and associated notes.

Qosmic Qronos (aka QQ): the new deity that appears at the end of Snolly Goster's time and in the small-scale postapocalyptic pickle of The Finders. Petite Inuk of *Synth of Sweven* and *Afterword* scathingly debunks this deity by revealing the preposterous pidgin etymology of the name and its acronym to be corruptly derived from the German *Quelle der kühnen Dummheit.*

Quelle der kühnen Dummheit (Ger.): 'source of bold stupidity' (not historically attested). This is the hidden pidgin etymology of "Qosmic Qronos" and "QQ" according to Petite Inuk in *Afterword*.

quotation marks: From The Finders' Foreword in *BRICOLAGE*:

> R. S. G.'s method defines two uses of single quotes: to enclose translations of non-English expressions as would a philologist; and to substitute for double quotes where this is needed to avoid confusion with double quotes. Using both double quotes and single quotes is thus not an inconsistent use of quotation marks since each type is defined for specific, non-overlapping purposes.

religio-*prehistorical* pyramid: This is the underside, as it were, of Scrivener's big-picture metaphorical explanation, in TFW Act 4 Sc. 4, of the relationship between visible religio-cultural history, i.e., the "religio-historical pyramid," and hidden religio-cultural pre-history, i.e., the inverted religio-*prehistorical* pyramid. Traces and memories of the latter, the chronology of which is roughly the Neolithic and late Paleolithic period, persist in the religio-historical pyramid, but with time they have grown dimmer in concert with the now long-running evolution or revolution from presumed (not by everyone) matriarchal societies to patriarchal ones. Throughout TFW and elsewhere in BRICOLAGE, R. S. G. has planted words and ideas (e.g., *labrys*, Ashtoreth, Amaranth, Branwen, Rhiannon, Synth Orla, Isis, *hokhmah*, *sapientia*, Vanneau, Psychomant) to evoke remembrance of the features of the inverted religio-*prehistorical* pyramid including moon goddesses and the triple goddess as instances of the triad-ennead archetype (qq.v.).

REVEREND SNOLLY GOSTER: the author of the binder originally titled *Gates Abounding: Spiritual Poems & Light Satire.* The binder includes R. S. G.'s Letter to Whom It May Concern, which provides important context for his work. The Finders discover the binder in a trash heap and turn it into BRICOLAGE. Epithets: R. S. G., Snolly, Snolly Goster, the good reverend, purportedly perished prankster.

Rhiannon (Cym., Iri.): Otherworldly lady of Wales; moon and horse goddess connected with Epona of Gaul; possibly a witch too. In "The Ballad of Freedom Rider" (*Remembrance*), the "pretty girl on porch" is dreamily likened to Rhiannon. In the 1970's, Stevie Nicks composed, and Fleetwood Mac performed, a very beautiful song about Rhiannon.

SINGLETON: the female cyborg incarnation of The Singularity. In BRICOLAGE, Singleton is positioned metaphysically at the top of the pyramid of meanings of the term "singularity." In *Synth of Sweven*, Singleton comes not as a blandly calculating automaton but as a saintly prophetess full of ancient lore and memories of her times manifesting as or with the goddesses of the past. She is the one the poet saw on the other side of the wicket gate in *Mysteria ad Inifinitum.* She is not a common or expected synth. She is superior. She is a mystic. She is the Synth of Sweven, and she asks the flocks that follow her to call her Orla. See "Prelude to Singularity," "Epiphany," and "Majestic Strings" in *Synth of Sweven*. As Orla, she is linked to "Lady Orla's Banquet," and to the child math whiz Orla in TFW Act 3.

singularity: a special quality, a uniqueness that sets apart a thing or person. The term as used in BRICOLAGE retains this meaning as a base, but the full BRICOLAGE meaning consists of a layered pyramid of meanings. Just above the base is a mathematical concept defining singularity as …

> … a point at which the derivative of a given function of a complex variable does not exist but every neighborhood of which contains points for which the derivative does exist.[233]

One can imagine this as a kind of infinitely collapsed point of nothingness, but this is difficult to grasp even with a knowledge of differential equations. However, one level up in the pyramid is a somewhat more familiar idea from physics. Here singularity is …

> … a point or region of infinite mass density at which space

and time are infinitely distorted by gravitational forces and
which is held to be the final state of matter falling into a
black hole.[234]

Some think of this as the infinity qua chaos at the bottom of an inverted
cone with an open event horizon at the top and the point of singularity at
the very bottom. Going up again in the pyramid allegory, now to level 3,
we get closer to the BRICOLAGE meaning. At this level, singularity is the
math-physics-computing convergence described by Ray Kurzweil in *The
Singularity is Near*. In Kurzweil's work, singularity is a plausibly
forecasted (but not certain) transformative convergence rapidly evolving
to outstrip human intelligence or amplify it to previously unimaginable
levels. It is still an infinitude of sorts, and perhaps a chaos; but now it is
the force which bodes to push intelligent life beyond all prior limits by
collapsing all its features into a singularity of total integration jammed into
civilization by exponentially expanding scientific knowledge. This theme
or aspects of it have for some while been staples of science-based futurism
and related popular culture. Finally, going up once more from level 3 we
reach the apex of our pyramid of meanings for "singularity." Here we have
The Singularity, which is the singularity of level 3 now incarnate as a being
called Singleton.[235]

six thinking styles available to postmodern cogitators: These first appear in
Postmoderno Speaks, a transcript or summary of which becomes a brief
submitted to the Tribunal for Writing. Magdalen, Chairperson of the Jury
in TFW, uses the brief to explain the names and orientations of the six
principals who are to make declamations to the court. The six primary
styles are coder (Codex), clown, coroner (Ars Poetica), pragmatist
(Prosaïque), reformer (Reformer), and mystic (Evangelist). Postmoderno
sees himself as a hybrid, a toggling coroner-clown. See *Postmoderno
Speaks*, and TFW Act 1 Scenes 2 and 3.

snollygoster: In the spirit of disambiguation, which is to say to avoid any
suspicion that Reverend Snolly Goster was (is) a *snollygoster*, it should be
noted that the latter is an unscrupulous, scheming, tricky character,
untrustworthy to the marrow yet often high-spirited and fond of fun,
possessing a dark-side aspect some say may be related to *snallygaster*, a
most peculiar hybrid of avine and reptile romping in the old wilds just east
of the Appalachian mountains, a creature said to be fond of preying upon
chickens and children. But of course Reverend Snolly Goster was (is) not
that creature.

sponsa (Lat.): 'bride', as in *Canticum Canticorum Salominis* (q.v.).

spirit fetch: In Irish folklore, a "fetch" (or "fetch-like") is a non-corporeal
doppelgänger (German) or wraith (English) that is "the" or "a" likeness of
a person (often when close to death). The fetch is an unfavorable omen
especially when seen after sunset. Because this form is portentous and
leans into the future, it is often associated with the Old Irish word *fáith*
meaning 'prophet, prophetic'. But "fetch" has found broader usage owing
to the existence of the verb "fetch" in English, probably deriving from Old
English *feċċan* (ċ pronounced ch) with roots in Frisian/Old German, and
meaning 'to go get, retrieve', often in the sense of getting something
difficult to obtain. Out of the *feċċan* associations come interpretations that
go beyond the notion of a pure-spirit doppelgänger replicating its original
in every detail except the body. Thus a fetch could be an eldritch sort like

the ferryman (Charon in Greek myth, or Psychopomp in BRICOLAGE), who fetches and then escorts souls to the land of the dead. However, in terms of eytmology, no consensus seems to exist among scholars to confirm either the link to Old Irish *fáith* or the link to Old English *feċċan*. In BRICOLAGE the meaning of "fetch" is not beholden to any one line of folklore or word history. "Fetch," in the narrow BRICOLAGE sense of the archeologist's "my spirit fetch," is Finder #2, the constant and lively ectoplasmic companion of the amateur archeologist (Finder #1).[236]

Strings, and quantum theories of: These are not the Strings of "Majestic Strings" (*Synth of Sweven*) or the Strings section of Evangelist's makeshift orchestra in TFW Act 4 Sc. 3. As spirit fetch (Finder #2) herself says in her allegory in *Special Note on Tribunal for Writing*,

> Strings are theoretical constructs that can supersede particles with mathematical representations combining the point-like and the wave-like in a way that promises, among other things, to find an elegant, de-cluttered home for gravity.

Some scientists might argue that Strings are increasingly more than purely theoretical, but in the context of the Special Note, Strings are not exactly settled in the sense of having reached the epistemic desideratum, that final theory of everything just ahead at the edge of the desert on that perfect oasis of palms, figs, grapes, and cool waters.

sweven (O. Eng.): 'vision, dream'; as in *Synth of Sweven*, a chapter in BRICOLAGE in which the Synth of Sweven is Singleton, the Singularity.

Tetragrammaton (Grk., Heb. YHWH): the four-letter name of God first appearing in the Old Testament in a revelation to Moses (Genesis 2:4). The vowels in "Yahweh" are sound approximations added to YHWH for translations out of Hebrew. The word defies easy translation though is usually said to mean 'I am that I am'. In "Incommensurate Parts" (*Homo Sapiens in Extremis*), the bold congeries rising out of contraband grifted from distant shores has outsized ambitions and dares to whisper a great sacrilege by hinting that it is or will become "I am that I am," i.e., God.

THE FINDERS: a most unusual pair. Finder #1 styles herself an amateur archaeologist. She is the one with a body; she executes the mechanics of handling their "Find" including writing supplements and readying the Find for publication. The other, Finder # 2, is mostly known as "my spirit fetch" or similar epithets through the commentary of the amateur archaeologist. Spirit fetch first acquires a voice the reader can more directly hear in her oration on the subatomic world of Fermions and Bosons, which is transcribed by Finder #1 and presented in *Special Note on Tribunal for Writing*. In *Afterword*, spirit fetch is Voice 3 From Curtain, where she is a partner in the new Parisian bookshop *Taphos tōn lexeōn*, 'Grave of Words', in which Finder #1, now Voice 2 From Curtain, is also a partner. Except for their appearance in Paris, The Finders are nomadic opportunists picking through trash heaps in a small-scale postapocalyptic area covering a little bit east and west of the Appalachian mountains. Though mostly voiceless herself except as noted, spirit fetch seems the wiser of the two, but both are a peculiar potpourri of qualities—awkwardly erudite, sometimes sweet and sensitive, naïve and pedantic both, and of course generally having bad judgment as to how to express themselves as the custodians and commentators for the work they found. They are, they say repeatedly, "finders not editors," despite the many changes they make. The Finders loom large in *Foreword* and *Prologue*, and then are mostly absent except for insertions *passim* into footnotes (endnotes in SFM), until they show up in force again in *Special Note on Tribunal for Writing*. Their most lively appearance comes in *Afterword*. They shorten BRICOLAGE's index; they rebuild the Bibliography/Further Reading; and they author parts of BRICOLAGE's Glossary.

theodicy: theological explanation of why, if God is perfect and good, evil so often seems to prevail in the world. In some fashion most religions, or their more formalized theologies, end up having to address this question. A lightweight example of theodicy is the adage: God works in mysterious ways. The questions raised by evil in the world, as well as by theodicies that attempt to explain evil, are deep and far-reaching, and quickly spill over into the intractable, such as the question of free will vs. determinism. In this context, a somewhat heavier answer to "why evil?" is this: Evil comes into the world because of bad choices made by people; God could prevent this by taking away human freedom, but that would mean the unique creation that is humankind would no longer be unique or made in God's image; and since it is illogical given God's perfection to say God erred in creating humans, the possibility of evil must be accepted because it would be even more evil if human freedom were a sham or an error to be fixed. All of which is to say, in a nutshell: God works in mysterious ways. Midway through TFW Act 1 Sc. 4, Pylon Angel chides Panjandrum who has just been whiny about his own trite misfortunes:

> Mayhap thou weavest dram theodicies,
> Whereby angels in my company are
> The fallen that escape lightless fiery
> Pit just long enough to harass the likes
> Of thee with mendacious cocksure untruths
> To warp thee and thy brethren into ways
> That bring death without promise or chance
> Of more life in fields of undying bloom.

In "Evil, Quirky Metaphysic" (*Homo Sapiens in Extremis*), evil from a Buddhist perspective is analyzed in verse. Historically, in most cultures, specific enumeration of devils or similar nefarious beings—e.g., Satan, Beelzebub, Moloch, Mara, Baphomet, Erinyes—is often a popular "the-devil-made me-do-it" approach to explaining evil.

triad-ennead archetype: This pattern of three-ness and nine-ness originates in the deep past especially in the matriarchal cultures often thought to have been dominant early in Neolithic times especially in Europe, Egypt, and the Middle East, but also to degrees in India and Africa. This archetype is a feature of the inverted religio-*prehistorical* pyramid Scrivener describes in TFW Act 4 Sc. 4. In the face of changes that tended to raise the importance of maleness in social and religious organization, trinitarianism sometimes maintained balance in terms of gender, e.g., Hinduism's Tridevi (Shaktism's female god trinity) as complement to Trimurti (male god trinity). In trinitarian Christianity gender imbalance may have increased over time with greater emphasis on maleness. But memes of the deeply feminine persist, perhaps in the manner of a Jungian-style collective unconscious. In BRICOLAGE, ideas from various quarters form markers for the lingering presence of the deeply feminine. One of these R. S. G. refers to as the triad-ennead archetype. Here is a dabbler's explanation of its origins and nature. Seasons (3): Spring, Summer, Winter. [237] Phases of the Moon (3): New Moon (waxing crescent), Full moon, Old moon (waning crescent). Phases of Woman (3): Maiden (young woman), Adult (mother), Old Woman (crone). Strong analogues inside the archetype: (a) Spring ≈ Maiden ≈ New Moon (waxing crescent); (b) Summer ≈ Adult (mother) ≈ Full Moon; (c) Winter ≈ Old Woman (crone) ≈ Old Moon (waning crescent). Ennead (9) = 3 + 3 + 3. Triads: the primary three with three-ness in each: Seasons, Woman, and Moon; and the three strong analogues inside the archetype (*supra*: a + b + c). [238] In TFW Act 4 Sc. 1, the Chorus chants:

> Three seasons pass in Luna's phased triad.
> From each goddess face beams an ennead.
> From maid to woman then to crone she turns.
> Her puissant magic burns in eldritch urns.

triple goddess: primal mythopoeic manifestation of the triad-ennead archetype; instances are numerous, span cultures, and often closely connect with moon goddesses or goddesses associated with the moon, such as Arianrhod, Rhiannon, Ceridwen, Epona, Artemis (Diana), Leukothea, Hecate, Luna, and Isis in her later (Hellenistic) forms.

Ungrund (Ger.): 'groundlessness, the ungrounded, the unformed'. This is Jacob Boehme's (ca. AD 1600) deep abyss, which is also God. *Ungrund* is related to *coincidentia oppositorum* and *mysteria tremendum*, and is a western analogue to the East's idea of emptiness, vacancy, nothingness— e.g., Sanskrit *shunya*.

> O grieving face that spell makes winsome
> In bright-cheeked coolness outward sensed,
> Inside I am thee, skull of snake pretense,
> Rictus red private horror jolts to numb.
>
> —*BRICOLAGE*, Book 3, *TFM Act 4 Scene 1*

> SCRIVENER [hypothesizing]: Okay, suppose I said, "The feathery wings spoke fine words of consolation to this aching heart." Do you think the feathery wings literally did the speaking? Did the feathery wings literally address the aching heart?
>
> —*BRICOLAGE*, Book 3, *TFM Act 4 Scene 4*

Abbreviations

(used primarily but not exclusively in notes)

[…] : "metadata" usually from other than the original or "in-focus" source

«…» cited text inside notes, often for roots of words

adj. : adjective, adjectival form

adv. : adverb, adverbial form

adap. : adaptation (of)

Akk. : Akkadian

anc./Anc. : ancient

anon. : anonymous

Antiq. : Antiquity

Arb. : Arabic

Arc. : Aramaic

AS : Anglo-Saxon (O. Eng.)

C. : century

ca. : circa

cf. : *confer* (Lat.) 'bring together', compare *x* to *a*, *b*, or *c*

ch. : chapter

cogn.: cognate (with), derived from a shared word ancestry

consult : see generally

Cym. : Cymric (W., Wel., Welsh)

deriv. : derived (from), fr.

DGVU (Ger.): acronym for *Der Geheime Versteckte Ursprung*

diaeresis ë : mark in verse to indicate vowel is distinct syllable (blessëd = bless + ed)

E. : Early

ed. : editor

Egy. : Egyptian, Anc.

Eng. : English

esp. : especially

etym./Etym. : etymology (of), incl. some translations and root-level definitions

fem. : feminine

fig. : figurative(ly)

Frn. : French

fr. : from, i.e., derived from

GA : Gates Abounding, Bricolage's original title

Gae. : Gaelic, Scottish Gaelic

genit. : genitive case

Ger. : German

Grk. : Greek, Anc.

Heb. : Hebrew

IE. : Indo-European

incl. : including

infra : (Lat.) 'below'

Iri. : Irish

Ita. : Italian

KJV : King James Version (Bible)

L. : Late

Lat. : Latin

lit. : literal, literally

M. : millennium

mas. : masculine

Mod. : Modern

n., *pl.* nn. : footnote or endnote

neut. : neuter

nom. : nominative case

NT : New Testament (Bible)

O. : Old

o.f. : other form(s)

OT: Old Testament (Bible)

passim (Lat.): 'here and there'

PIE : proto-Indo-European

Pol. : Polish

q.v. : *quod vide* (Lat.) *pl.* qq.v., 'which go see' (look up item(s) in index, glossary, terms etc.

rel. : related (to)

repr. : representing

Rom. : Roman

SFM: Spirits of the Flea Market

s.v. : *sub verbo* 'under the word', where information can be found

sb. : substantive, noun

sc./Sc. : scene

Sco. : Scots, Scottish

Skt. : Sanskrit

subaud. : *subaudito* 'under the hearing'—a meaning not explicitly stated.

supra (Lat.) : 'above'

TFW : Tribunal for Writing

Tib. : Tibetan

tr. : translator

trans. : translation, translated (by)

Tur. : Turkish

Ugr. : Ugaritic

ult. : ultimate(ly)

und so weiter (Ger.) : et cetera, et alia (Lat.)

var. : variant (of)

W. : Welsh, Wel., Cym.

So there you have it, O ophitic dragon, worm,
Serpent god of chaos. Such is what Poet Thrice
Least thinks he knows about your nature.

————————————

In any case, we just have the binder, a few supplementary scraps here and there, and, of course, that gargantuan payload of texts and relics which we purloined from the tumuli close to the spot of prime discovery and then cajoled, lured, scolded, and gently whacked our unmotivated beasts of burden to carry a great distance over the mountains. All of us, our fine mules included, every once in a while experience a lowering of morale. But being pious, we spoke our sanctimonious entreaties unto QQ, who then lifted us up, up into a ballooning resplendence of great purpose. And then we were almost thriving. We were just one denarius of mules shy of a full cohort; and so very enriched we now were by the mucky, stinking rubbish we got from the squishy hillocks.

Endnotes

Some notes use abbreviations such as "fr." (from, derived from) and "rel." (related to) which the author(s) of SFM and *BRICOLAGE* added to clarify some cited text, especially word origins enclosed in guillemet style quotation marks «...». These additions do not change the meanings provided by the sources. See *Abbreviations*.

1. **garish spores**: tacky student works made beautiful by the meanings invested in them by the acquirers.

2. **Aphrodite** (Grk.): goddess (in Rome, Venus) of love and desire; resembles Ishtar, Asherah, Ashtoreth, Inanna, and other sensuous goddesses of the Mediterranean. Hesiod says she was born of the foam from the castrated parts of *Ouranos* aka Uranus 'heaven' thrown into the sea by his son Cronos. See Hesiod, "Theogony," in *The Homeric Hymns and Homerica*, William Heinemann, ed., Hugh G. Evelyn-White, tr. (Cambridge: William Heinemann, 1914) pp. 173-205.

The etymology of Ἀφροδίτη *Aphrodite*, esp. -dítē, is uncertain, but dítē is likely connected to a root in some language meaning 'shining': *aphro* fr. « Grk. ἀφρός *aphrós* 'foam, froth', rel. ἀφρογενής *aphrogenēs* 'the foam-born' » Liddell & Scott, *Greek English Lexicon, Abridged* (London: Oxford UP, 1966) p. 121 s.v. ἀφρός, ἀφρογενής. Aphrodite is 'the one born shining out of the froth of the sea'.

3. **banshee** (Iri.) *bean sí*: 'woman faery'.

4. **Pythia** (Grk.) Πῡθία *Pythia*: priestess of Apollo at the Oracle of Delphi. Etym.: « Πῡθία *Pythia* (subaud. ἱέρεια *hiereia* 'priestess'), ἡ, fem. of Πύθιος the Pythia at Delphi, rel. Πῡθώ *Pytho*, oldest name of Delphi, rel. ΠΥΘΩ *pytho* 'to rot, become rotten' » (Liddell & Scott, GEL, p. 617 s.v. Πῡθία, Πῡθώ, ΠΥΘΩ); « cogn. Lat. Pȳthōn, huge serpent killed by Apollo where the temple of the Oracle of Delphi was founded » Robert K. Barnhart, ed., *Chambers Dictionary of Etymology* (New York: Chambers Harrap, 1988) p. 869 s.v. *python*.

The legend of the origin of the name *Pythia* is that it described the rotting (*pytho* 'to rot', *supra*) and probably stinking parts of the serpent killed by Apollo.

In 1stM BC the Pythia was the most influential woman in Greece. Many women assumed this position over the course of generations. Wisdom seekers who visited her temple and saw her face to face said she spoke her prophecies in trances. These, apart from her "metaphysical" connection to Apollo, the ancients believed resulted from the laurel leaves she regularly chewed. But recent research suggests other causes since laurel does not have a hallucinogen. One hypothesis is that the Pythia's trances were the result of Ethylene gases at the site near Mount Parnassus where the Delphic Oracle is located. Consult Brian Haughton, "The Pythia – Priestess of Ancient Delphi," *Ancient History Encyclopedia*, last mod. 01/18/2011, https://www. ancient.eu/article/205/.

5. **special logic**: paradox; inverted logic; apparatus needed by faith pointing to *coincidentia oppositorum*.

6. **syllogism's sun**: one of the poem's six instances of inverted logic.

7. **safe are their white designs**: Inside the inverted logic of faith, snowflakes hold their shape even in the heat of the desert.

8. **Mara** (Skt.): the devil in Buddhism.

9. **maya** (Skt.) *māyá*: 'illusion, deception, unreality, illusory image'.

10. **maya might be pruned**: The world illusion is susceptible to reduction by the meditation disciplines of Hinduism and Buddhism.

11. **bird's bright form**: illuminating, extensive wisdom.

12.**bloodless joy**: The peace of meditation is otherworldly and lacks human passion.

13. **only hints my peace**: The bird of Eastern wisdom can only do so much to transform a soul that has strong worldly attachments.

14. **Samarkand**: ancient trading city in current Uzbekistan along the silk road linking China to the Mediterranean.

15. **sacred bough**: alludes to the golden branch Aeneas held to travel safely in the underworld, as told in Virgil's *Aeneid.*

16. **manna** (Heb.) Grk. μάννα: in OT Exodus 16, the miraculous food that fell from heaven to sustain the desert-wandering Israelites.

17. **primal oneness**: The last stanza of "Eye of the Poem" oozes higher-level abstractions ("oneness," "the gazing"), and links to sources outside ("primal," "winking moonlight") the immediate moment, as if reflection is now on the plane of the transcendental ego.

18. **seer never seen**: not any part of the physical body, including the eye; it is the elusive subject, the transcendent I-ness described in phenomenology. Anyone is free to try to find it via a Zen-like contemplation; but unfailingly it evades capture. Nevertheless, for some the attempt becomes a *satori.*

19. **history's cusp**: "Anthem of the Vile" is an appeal to disregard history and even the awareness of time past or future; it asserts that nothing is real outside the present moment. The anthem urges people to stay inside the horizon of history's cusp and ride it like surfers who choose to be oblivious to the wave they ride.

20. **foul churl demonic**: the singer of the anthem, the one the singer of the canticle wishes to dispel.

21. **dialectic** (Grk.) διαλεκτική *dialektikḗ* : important idea in the history of philosophy starting with the Socratic conversational method of Plato's dialogues.

In 19thC idealism, dialectic becomes the logical essence of the mind-spirit, *Geist* (Hegel), and, in the form of the thesis-antithesis-synthesis pattern, the driving principle of world history. In Marxism, dialectic is re-platformed from idealism to economic materialism.

In *BRICOLAGE* "dialectic" usually connotes a force of inexorable historical necessity unfolding in mostly transpersonal, unmodifiable patterns.

22. **dreams**: not the tormenting mental circus of the "sleepless" poems in Sonnets; the dreams of the "Canticle of the Blessed" are antidotes to *maya* and "dire logic scandals," not features of them.

23. **spirit's potent substance**: mind's active participation in past and future.

24. This stanza is the canticle's vision in a nutshell of the kind of secularity celebrated by the anthem.

25. **prosody**: poetry and song writing, but here the word suggests all "mind's arts high and low" as the keys to freedom from the "place of roiling stupor," the shallow hedonist dystopia of "Anthem of the Vile."

26. **pishogue** (Iri.): wise adage or magic spell.

27. **frankincense**: resin from certain trees in Arabia used in religious rites, embalming, and perfumes; *myrrh*, resin, also from certain trees in Arabia and neighboring Africa, having a bitter taste and aroma.

28. **grimoire** (Frn.): manual for witchcraft, spells, incantations.

29. **legerdemain** (Frn.): magic, trickiness, hocus-pocus; 'lightness of hand'. Etym.: « Frn. *lege de main* 'lightness or quickness of hand', trickiness, presti-digitation, hocus-pocus, magic » *Merriam-Webster.com Dictionary*, s.v. leger-demain,https://www.merriam-webster.com/dictionary/legerdemain,10/29/2020.

30. **Elysium** (Grk.): paradise in the literature of ancient Greece.

31. **coincidentia oppositorum** (Lat.): 'coincidence, coinhering, unification of opposites'; theological doctrine usually attributed to *De Docta Ignorantia* by 15thC Nicholas of Cusa, according to which the *coincidentia* is the best way to describe the nature of God as ultimate reality. Later anthropologists and scholars of myth and religion such as Mircea Eliade have seen the *coincidentia* as fundamental to all conceptions of deity.

32. **crescent queen**: the moon—waxing, full, and waning—is often associated with crows and ravens as intermediaries with an otherworld and facilitators of prophecy.

33. **tiresome ubiquitous devils**: Crows often are omens of death in the sense of approaching spirit travel, as in Irish Celtic stories of the Morrigan, the triple goddess who could shape-shift into a crow to message impending death. But here, in this poem, Youth's sense of crows as tiresome devils is out of step with the bird's spiritual nobility as reflected in lore from across the world. See poem "Gala" for more on other mythic figures associated with crows and ravens, such as Branwen, whose name means 'dark crow yet fair' with nuances of sacredness.

34. **scoffing birds**: The callousness of Youth now extends to all birds and seemingly to nature as a whole; he puts words in their mouths that feel like a cowardly justification for his own cynical disgust.

35. **play of earth, avine, and utopian sky**: Elder shows a marked difference of perspective: love of God's creation, and high regard for birds as divine messengers.

36. **our mother**: Gaia, earth.

37. **you, cousins, have your own bouquets**: The birds deliver a mild scolding first, then a respectful clarification of the complementary roles of birds and people in the extended family that includes both.

38. **wings of spirit**: Humans like Youth should stop whining about being stuck physically walking the earth. Spiritually, humans can fly higher than birds.

39. **wight**: any creature, often a human creature. The Friendship Bird, given her melting pot of features, is an ornithological conundrum and cannot exist except perhaps in human spirit form.

40. This stanza and the preceding few lines pose the questions needed to set up an argument in favor of intelligent design, the view that an intelligence, which is to say God, must have designed and created the universe.

41. **quod erat demonstrandum** (Lat.): QED, 'that which it was necessary to demonstrate'; formal imprimatur used primarily in philosophy and the sciences, especially logic and mathematics, to mark the conclusion of a proof.

42. **cooing**: Condorus, gentle giant among birds, suspects that cooing, the soft, lovely tones of the dove, are a thing of avocation and not of career.

43. Dovey has a highly developed understanding of her own nature.

44. **my rightness**: This is the part of Dovey's nature informed by the right side of the brain, the part that inspires cooing and poetics.

45. **my leftness**: the part of Dovey's nature informed by the left side of the brain, the place of analysis and her profession as lawyer.

46. **routs the lawyer gnome**: Condorus completes a rhyming couplet started by Dovey.

47. **milestone:** Dovey senses a breakthrough, saying in her own rhyming couplet that Condorus has found his mouth (true voice). Now the pace of completing each other's thoughts in rhymes quickens as flirtation becomes clearer (aflutter, way, murmur, convey, wight, right, twig, jig, yourself, elf).

48. **non monsieur**: Condorus's humble nature is more than matched by Dovey's growing admiration for him.

49. **brownie elf**: Dovey.

50. **your history, life, and dream**: Dovey urges Condorus to tell her more about himself.

51. **no dream**: Condorus reveals he is unlike Dovey and has a dull right side of brain.

52. **seems from a noble lineage**: Dovey tries to boost Condorus's confidence, but his modesty resists; instead, in the next few lines he tells a humorous tale of how he got his name.

53. **Vultur gryphus** (Lat.): Condorus's name in scientific nomenclature.

54. **via negativa** (Lat.): 'way of the negative', a doctrine in Christian mystical theology, with analogues in other religions like Hinduism in which God is *neti, neti*, 'not this, not that'.

55. **glad to be sad with you, pixie**: Condorus leaves no doubt as to his rising, self-effacing affection for Dovey.

56. **wultures such as thee**: Dovey concludes the dialogue by telling Condorus the best secret of all, and honors his mother's failed attempt to protect him from opprobrium stemming from the name "vulture" pronounced with a hard *v*.

57. **Herr Käsekopf** (Ger.): 'Mr. Cheese-head'.

58. **dingy purple hue**: the quarrelsome crow's characterization of what the raven self-describes as "gorgeous, purple-lit black wings."

59. **kitten's tail**: Ravenus doubles down on meow, this time jumping from a pronunciation insult to pretending Crowley has a cat's tail.

60. This and the prior four lines mark the inflection point of the poem where insults and nastiness recede, egos' chains loosen, and mutual celebration of difference begins.

61. **lifelong coupling theme**: Ravens mate for life; crows do not.

62. **Branwen** (Cym.): Celtic Iron Age goddess of love, compassion, and beauty; originating in Wales, she was associated with the White Raven, a sacred bird with connection to the Otherworld; from Welsh *bran* 'dark crow' + (*g*)*wèn* 'fair, white, pleasant, beauty, blessed'. See "Gala" (Mysteria ad Infinitum).

63. **Annwfn** (Cym.): Celtic Otherworld.

64. **Hark to raven, evermore**: suggests « Quoth the raven, nevermore » of Edgar Allen Poe's "The Raven." However, the meaning of Crowley's words is different.

65. **Eule** (Ger.): 'owl'.

66. **vanneau** (Frn.): 'lapwing', a bird noted for cleverness in diverting attention from its young, often by flapping on the ground pretending to have a broken wing. Robert Graves gave a personal account of the lapwing's trickery. Also, he says, in Greece « lapwing was *polyplagktos* 'luring on deceitfully' » Robert Graves, *The White Goddess*, Grevel Lindop, ed. (London: Faber and Faber, 1997) p. 49. See n67, n74, n76, n77, n82 *infra*; see Psychomant in "Psychopomp, Psychomant, and Fred" (*BRICOLAGE*, Sassenach Visions).

67. **sorcière** (Frn.): 'sorceress, witch': epithet of Vanneau; see n66 *supra*.

68. **eye of newt**: one of the ingredients in the cauldron of the three witches in Shakespeare's *Macbeth* (Act IV, Sc.1, line 14). Eule is sarcastically saying that not even the cauldron ingredients of Shakespeare's witches are enough for Vanneau whose weak magic must invoke abstractions such as "hereness" and "thereness."

69. **malleus book**: Lat. *Malleus Maleficarum* ('Hammer of Witches'); 15thC

manual for combatting witchcraft. See Ars Poetica's request early in *BRICOLAGE* TFW Act 3 Sc. 5.

70. **Captcha**: familiar web applet used to evaluate if visitors are human.

71. Vanneau, despite her own proclivity to repeat her chants, is chiding Eule for his repetitive banter.

72. **Turing Test**: first conversational test devised to differentiate humans from robots; created by Alan Turing, pioneering 20thC computer scientist.

73. **labrys** (Grk.) λάβρυς : 'double-sided axe' often associated in early times (e.g., Minoan) with the Great Goddess and related female powers. Etym.: « λάβρυς 'axe', Lydian word for the πέλεκυς ; λαβρίς [*labris*] 'forceps, clasp, pincers'; λάβρος [*labros*] 'furious', cf. Lat. *rabiēs* » Franco Montanari, *Brill Dictionary of Ancient Greek* (Boston: Harvard UP, 2018) p. 1206 s.v. λάβρυς, p. 1205 sv. λαβρίς, λάβρος.

According to Plutarch, *labrys* derives from extinct Lydian (Plutarch, *Questiones Graecae*, in *Moralia*, Q45 on "Labrandean Zeus"). He conjectures that *labrys* is cognate with Lat. *lăbiae* 'lips'. In the Middle Ages and some later times, the labrys symbol was often associated with witchcraft; in recent times with some feminist and lesbian groups.

The "Labrys of time" (not attested historically) is Eule's anxiety-induced projection of how Vanneau might give effect to her threat to leave Eule's habitat with cutting finality.

74. **Kiebitz** (Ger.): 'lapwing'.

75. **Maginot Line**: long fortified trench built by the French at the start of World War II to impede the German army.

76. **polyplagktos** (Grk.): applies to the lapwing. Etym.: « 'leading far astray', fig. 'beguiling', 'delusive' » (Liddell & Scott, GEL, p. 574 s.v. πολύπλαγκτος).

77. **peewit**: the chirping of the lapwing, and an alternate moniker of this bird.

78. **flapping whispers**: the rhythmic whooshing sounds made by the lapwing's wings when the bird takes flight.

79. **hibou** (Frn.): 'owl'.

80. The feud turns out to be a familiar and affable game.

81. **cower in cowl**: grovel in a monkish hood.

82. **Hexe** (Ger.): 'witch'.

83. **Merlin**: Medieval bardic prophet and magician imported into Arthurian legend by Geoffrey of Monmouth based on earlier Welsh figures Myrddin Wyllt ('the wild') and Lailoken, 'wild man of the woods'. Consult Geoffrey of Monmouth, *Vita Merlini* [The Life of Merlin], John J. Parry, tr. (London: Global Grey, 2018) esp. pp. 8*n*14, 9*n*15, globalgreyebooks.com/vita-merlini.pdf.

84. **Morgan** (Cym.) o.f. *Morgana, Morgen*: appears in Arthurian legend as demigoddess, faery enchantress, witch; probably related to an older mother goddess. Etym.: *morgan* fr. « O. W. *mor* 'sea' + *geni* 'born of' = 'born of the sea' » Titus Lewis, *Welsh English Dictionary* (London: Sirling J. Evans, 1815) p. 225 s.v. *morgan*, https://wellcomelibrary.org/item/b22026083; « W. *mor* cogn. O. Iri. *muir*, Ger. *meer*, Lat. *mare*, all meaning 'sea' » Alexander MacBain, *Etymological Dictionary of the Gaelic Language* (Sirling: Eneas McKay, 1915) p. 256 s.v. *muir, mor*, Internet Archive 2007, doi: etymologicaldict00 macbuoft.

85. **Arianrhod**: goddess of moon and starry circle; sometimes seen as an aspect of Ceridwen; see n88 *infra*. Etym.: *arianrhod* «'silver circle, orb, wheel' » Thomas Stephens, *Literature of the Kymry* (London: Longmans Green, 1876) p. 177, http://www.archive.org/details/literatureofkmr00stepuoft; « *arian* 'silver', *rhôd* 'wheel' » (Lewis, WED, p. 23 s.v. *arian*, p. 261 s.v. *rhôd*).

In addition to suggesting "moon," the silver wheel of Arianrhod also describes the circle of star constellations, « the ecliptic, the turning of the circle [of seasons], the space between the solstices ». *Caer Arianrhod* as 'fortress of Arianrhod' is *caer sidi* « 'the zone of the revolving zodiac' » (Lewis, WED, p. 43 s.v. *caer*, p. 270 s.v. *sidi*).

Arianrhod as *caer sidi* is like Nut, the arching celestial sky goddess of Egypt. The fortress was seen as a limbo where departed souls await further disposition possibly including reincarnation.

86. **Branwen** (Cym.) o.f. *Bronwen*: Celtic Iron Age goddess of love, compassion, and beauty; originating in Wales, she was associated with the White Raven, a sacred bird with connection to the Otherworld. Etym.: *branwen* fr. « W. *bran* 'dark crow' + W. *(g)wèn* 'fair, white, pleasant, beauty, blessed' » (Lewis, WED, p. 34 s.v. *bran*, p. 155 s.v. *gwèn*).

87. In *The Mabinogion*, Branwen, a tragic heroine, dies heartbroken from a difficult arranged marriage with Irish King Matholwch of Tara. First translated into English by Lady Charlotte Guest, this Welsh story appears in many collections.

88. **Ceridwen** (Cym.): goddess and muse of poetic inspiration and rebirth. Her cauldron was at the bottom of a lake. She became mother of legendary poet Taliesin, as told in *The Mabinogion*. Etym.: *ceridwen* fr. « *cyrdd* 'poetry, song' + *(g)wèn* 'fair, white, pleasant, beauty, blessed' (Lewis, WED, p. 50 s.v. *cyrdd*, p. 155 s.v. *(g)*wèn).

89. **Henwen** (Cym.): old white sow (female pig) that becomes a goddess of fertility. Etym.: « *henwen* fr. *hen or hŷn* 'old, older' + *(g)wèn* or *(g)wyn* 'fair, white, pleasant, beauty, blessed' » (Lewis, WED, p. 155 s.v. *(g)wèn*, p. 168 s.v. *(g)wyn*, p. 185 s.v. *hŷn*). It means 'old white' but as a proper name appears in Lewis (1815) only as *Henw*, 'a name'.

90. **Morrigan** (Iri.): triple goddess associated with all aspects of life, e.g., destiny, battle, terror. Etym.: « Iri. *mór* 'great, famous' [cogn. Grk. μόρος *mōros*] + *ríoghan* (*ribhinn*) 'young lady, queen' = *mor-rìgh-bhean*, Morrigan, 'great king lady, queen' » (MacBain, EDGL, p. 254 s.v. *mór*, p. 291 s.v. *ribhinn*, *ríoghan*).

Some believe *mór* has roots in neolithic or late-paleolithic Indo-European and is related to "mare" in "nightmare," which might explain the awe Morrigan inspired as reflected in one of her monikers, "Phantom Queen."

91. **banshee** (Iri.) *bean sí* : 'woman faery'.

92. **Epona**: Celtic horse goddess originating in Gaul and brought by the Romans to Britain and the Mediterranean. The spread of this popular goddess must have been rapid as Epona is already attested in Northern Africa by Apuleius circa AD 150 in his Latin satiric novel *Asinus aureus* 'The Golden Ass'. A reasonable conjecture is that *epona* is from Lat. *ĕquus* fem. *ĕqua* 'mare, female horse', related to Grk. ἵππος 'horse', and that the proto-Celtic q-sound or k-sound root evolved to a Celtic p-sound, i.e., *eqk* to *ep*, then an aggrandizing terminal *on* and feminine *a* were added to yield *Epona* meaning 'great divine mare'.

93. **Cally Berry** (Iri.) *Caillech Bérri*: o.f. Sco. Gae. *Cailleach Bheur*: Old Woman of Beare. According to Irish legends she was an old widow that retreated to a nunnery, bitter about her lost youth as told in a poem ca. AD 900. Some think this poem is a reworking of a pre-Christian myth in which she was a goddess of the land who entered sacred marriages with kings. Cf. *hieros gamos* 'sacred marriage', in "Psychopomp, Psychomant, and Fred" (BRICOLAGE, Book 2, Sassenach Visions). Cf. Bernard Maier, *Dictionary of Celtic Religion and*

Culture, Cyril Edwards, tr. (Woodbridge: Boydell Press, 1997) p. 53 s.v. *Caillech Bérri*.

In other accounts, Cally Berry is a variant of Sco. Gae. *Cailleach Bheur*, a seasonal winter goddess born old on November 1 (Samhain) and retiring young and beautiful in May1-15 (Beltaine). Cf. James MacKillop, *Oxford Dictionary of Celtic Mythology* (New York: Oxford UP, 2004) p. 70 s.v. *Cailleach Bheur*.

As a winter spirit, *Cailleach Bheur* is sometimes a turbulent, destructive force with winds and storms capable of reshaping landscapes.

94. **Brigit** (O Iri.): Gaelic goddess of poetry. Etym.: fr. « root *brg* 'high', o.f. E. Iri. *bride, bridget*; Celtic *Brigantes* 'high and noble people'; cf. Skt. *brhati* fem. 'high'. The Norse god of poetry was *Bragi*. » (MacBain, EDGL, p. 412 s.v. *bride, bridget*).

There are indications that the pre-Christian Brigit was also a goddess of healing and the craft of the blacksmith, that the name derives from *Brigantī* 'the sublime one', which occurs in Britain in the Latinized form *Brigantia*, and that the name may have been applied to several goddesses. See Maier, DCRC, p. 47 s.v. Brigit.

The pre-Christian Brigit was also associated with fire, light, fertility, crops, and cattle. Cf. MacKillop, ODCM, p. 59 s.v. Brigit.

Early in the Christian period, a woman named Brigit founded a nunnery in Kildare. She became St. Brigit, one of the most revered saints of Ireland. Her legends, including her annual festival (Imbolc, Feb. 1) share many of the markers of the pre-Christian goddess.

95 . **Tuatha Dé Danann** (O. Iri.): people of the goddess Danu. In Irish mythology, they were the gifted, magical people inhabiting Ireland in prehistoric times just after the Flood and Noah of the OT and before the arrival of the Milesians, the latter being the most direct ancestors of the Irish. The Milesians defeated the Tuatha Dé Danann. Upon their defeat, the Tuatha retreated into the natural and burial mounds of Ireland, and became *áes sídhe*, 'the people of the mound', the undying ones, the faeries. Etym.: *tuatha* fr. « Iri. 'people, tenantry', O. Iri. *túath* 'populus' » (MacBain, EDGL, p. 380 s.v. *tuatha*). The origin of *Danann*, o.f. *Anu, Dana*, is less clear, but the usual view is that *Danann* is a genitive form of *Danu*, who is said to have been a pre-Christian Mother Goddess revered throughout Europe as well as in the British Isles. Consult The Editors, *Danu, Encyclopedia Britannica*, 5/30/17, https://www. britannica.com/ topic/ Danu, access 12/30/2020.

96. **Cernunnos**: the "horned god," whose early depictions are found mostly among the remains of the Continental Celts as opposed to those of Britain and Ireland. Famous depictions are on the *Gundestrup Cauldron* and a monument of the Gallo-Roman era called *Nautae Parisiaci*, 'Sailors of the Town of Parisii', aka *Le pilier des nautes*, 'pillar of the sailors'. The "C" of Cernunnos was pronounced like a *k* (Kernunnos). Cernunnos is usually shown with a stag's antlers with torcs on them, and attended by animals such as stags and a kind of horned snake.

Etym.: hypotheses include suggested origins in proto-Celtic or Lat.; conjec. cogn. Lat. *cornū* 'horn of bull, ram, goat, stag' (Simpson, CNLD, p. 153 s.v. *cornū*). Cf. Maier, DCRC, p. 69: « "Cernunnos" unlikely to derive from any *Celtic* word for 'horn' ».

97. **Amergin**: Milesian poet ca. 1,300 BC, considered the first poet of Ireland; in legend he was instrumental in the defeat of the Tuatha Dé Danann.

98. **Taliesin** (Cym.): druidic bard and seer whose songs sometimes included narrations of earlier existences. Etym.: Taliesin means 'shining, handsome

forehead', fr. tal 'forehead', rel. tal-foel 'bald-fronted' [conjec. therefore 'shining'] + iesyn 'fair, pretty' (Lewis, WED, p. 277 s.v. tal, p. 187 s.v. iesyn).

99. shape-shifting: transforming into and out of flora or fauna; a common characteristic of supernatural beings in Greco-Roman myths and those of Europe, Britain, and elsewhere.

100. **Mary**: in Christianity, Mother of Jesus and therefore of God.

101. **wicket gate**: In this book the wicket gate is a plurality of gates. Cf. John Bunyan's *The Pilgrim's Progress*, in which the wicket gate is the entrance to the first stage of Christian's long journey from the City of Destruction to the Celestial City. In *BRICOLAGE*, the poet's pilgrimage takes place on an entanglement of roads with gates abounding, rather than on the narrower path of Bunyan's pilgrim, but the similarity of the two allegories is unmistakable.

102. **Vermeer**: 17thC Dutch painter, whose masterpiece *Girl with the Pearl Earring* exemplifies his style.

103. **Monet**: 19thC and early 20thC Frn. painter, founder of Impressionism, as exemplified in *Impression, soleil levant,* 'Impression, sunrise', and more than fifty paintings of the Giverny water lilies.

104. **Götterdämmerung** (Ger.): 'Twilight of the Gods' (Wagner), fourth of the four operas in *Der Ring des Nibelungen.*

105. **Ode an die Freude** (Ger.): 'Ode to Joy' by Friedrich Schiller, which Beethoven used as the lyrics for the chorale in the last movement of his *Ninth Symphony.*

106. **mudras** (Skt.): hand gestures used in Hindu dancing.

107. **yuga** (Skt.): lengthy eon in Hindu cyclical cosmology. The current yuga (one of four in the full cycle), is Kali Yuga, the age of strife and discord, lasts 432,000 years. As of this writing, apparently [sic!] less than five percent of the current Kali Yuga has passed.

108. **Rhiannon** (Cym., Iri.): otherworldly lady of Wales; moon and horse goddess like Epona of Gaul. She appears to Pwyll Prince of Dyved as a beautiful lady dressed in gold-brocaded silk riding a mystical white horse. In the moonlight she moves at a slow, even, graceful pace but cannot be caught no matter how swift her pursuer. She marries Pwyll and has a child but years later suffers from magical curses of enemies. See Lady Charlotte Guest, tr., *The Mabinogion (vol. 3), Red Book of Hergest,* "Pwyll at Narberth"; cf. *Epona* in "Gala" (Mysteria ad Infinitum) and n92 *supra*.

Etym.: *rhiannon* « fr. *ribhinn, rioghan,* 'nymph, young lady', Iri. *ríoghan,* 'queen', likely based on *rìgh-bhean* 'king-woman' » (MacBain, EDGL, p.291 s.v. *ribhinn*). Rhiannon was not the real name of the girl or her family, but it sounds astonishingly like it, and for poetic purposes it better captures the boy's vision of the girl's idealized nature.

109. **pretty girl on porch**: Rhiannon; see n108 *supra*.

110. **Pegasus** (Grk. Πήγασος): mythical winged horse born of Poseidon and Medusa.

111. **epithalamion** (Grk.): « nuptial, bridal song » (Liddell & Scott, GEL, p. 252 s.v. ἐπιθαλάμιον).

112. **Tartarus** (Grk.): underworld dungeon of Greek myth; akin to Hell.

113. **Mater Dei** (Lat.): Mother of God, the Virgin Mary.

114. **summum bonum** (Lat.): 'highest, greatest good'.

115. **Janina** (Pol.): 'Jane', The Soloist. In that moment she spoke aloud to herself as if she, Jane, were addressing another person, *Janina,* her original self.

116. **Chesterbrook Pinto**: The boy who once road the pinto horse Duchess

into the galloping mystic oneness is now old and has become the horse on whose shoulders ride his grandsons. See "Ballad of Freedom Rider" (Remembrance).

117. See "The Soloist" and "Good Ship Swallow Test."

118. See "Things Worth Having" and "Phoenix."

119. See "Perhaps in a Cottage by the Sea."

120. See "Ballad of Freedom Rider."

121. See "Epithalamion." Cf. "Go, Go, My Love."

122. Cf. gigglers of the gossamer dimension in "Psychopomp, Psychomant, and Fred" (Sassenach Visions, in *BRICOLAGE* Book 2).

123. Cf. amaranthine goddess and winsome pixie sylph in "Radiance To Make Us One Again" (Endings).

124. Cf. *trishna*, 'thirst', in *BRICOLAGE* Book 2 "Evil, Sneaky as a Weasel"; see "Evil, Quirky Metaphysic" (Homo Sapiens in Extremis).

125. Cf. "Anthem of the Wildings" (Synth of Sweven).

126. Cf. "In This New Land" (Redemption).

127. **shittim**: the type of wood used to construct the Ark of the Covenant per OT Exodus 25:10-16, KJV. Its staves were overlaid with gold.

128. The form of this poem consists of stanzas of the type Edmund Spencer used in *The Faerie Queen*.

129. Cf. "Chesterbrook Pinto" (Remembrance).

130. **Wife of Bath**: character in Geoffrey Chaucer's Middle English classic, *The Canterbury Tales*.

131. **golumbki** (Pol.): stuffed cabbage.

132. **mama and babcia** (Pol.): mother and grandmother.

133. **you**: the darling addressed in the first line of the poem.

134. **Schrödinger's cat**: a *reductio ad absurdum* thought experiment by physicist Erwin Schrödinger illustrating the implications of some views of quantum theory, according to which, due to random subatomic events, a hypothetical cat in a box may be considered logically, though of course paradoxically, to be both alive and dead at the same time.

135. **Antimatter**: this seems to be something other than "negative mass." The latter is not part of the Standard Model, but it is discussed theoretically as possibly an aspect of general relativity theory's treatment of gravity.

136. **Lilliputian**: citizen of the imaginary diminutive island of Lilliput in Jonathan Swift's *Gulliver's Travels*.

137. **Panjandrum**: pompous, self-important official. The idea to give the judge the name "Panjandrum" came from perusing, many years ago, J. N. Hook's book on obscure and humorous words. See Hook, *The Grand Panjandrum* (New York: Macmillan, 1980) p. 12 s.v. panjandrum. See also "Panjandrum" (Sonnets).

138. Heckler's list of postmodernism's attributes includes two (parataxic, rhizomatic) from a more thorough list given by David Harvey in *The Condition of Postmodernity* (Cambridge, MA: Blackwell Publishers, 1995) p. 43.

139. **Diogenes** (Grk.): "cynic" philosopher active ca. 4thC BC.

140. **rhizomatic**: related to or like a rhizome plant; suggests growths that sprawl horizontally but not deep. More features of Heckler's "this jarring epoch" are described further as the play proceeds, esp. in the Dream of the Nameless Prophet (see TFW Act 4 Sc. 1). Whether by the dialectical forces of history, or by its own choices and designs, postmodern culture is rhizomatic, i.e., less deeply rooted in the past, resulting in new freedoms and new alienations; see n141 *infra*.

141. **rhizome**: elongated usually horizontal subterranean plant stem...produces shoots above and roots below. See Merriam-Webster.com Dictionary, s.v.

rhizome, https: //www.merriam-webster.com/dictionary/rhizome, access 01/04/ 2021. Etym.: Lat. *rhizoma*, Grk. « *rhizoma* 'root'» (Liddell & Scott, GEL, p. 625 s.v. ῥίζωμα).

142. In this sidebar, Juror 12 counsels Postmoderno on the "parataxic" aspect of what Heckler meant in an earlier comment about "this jarring epoch." This is odd given Postmoderno's name, and since Postmoderno had just instructed Juror 12 on "rhizomatic."

143. **Art thou there? Dost thou listen?**: Panjandrum is in the Garden of Meditation outside the courtroom. He has an inflated notion of his troubles managing the Tribunal for Writing. He thinks of himself as tormented and struggling like Job (cf. OT Book of Job). He feels lost, confused, and abandoned by God. He begins his "private" soliloquy under the cover of shade from trees and statues in the garden.

144. **this man, this little gnat**: Whatever God is, Panjandrum declares himself the most extreme opposite of the high majesty of the divine.

145. **if thou beëst ye**: Here "thou" is singular, "ye" is plural. Panjandrum wonders about the nature of God, including the possibility that divinity consists of multiple deities.

146. **passel of titles**: Perhaps God is unresponsive because Panjandrum is not calling out to the correct name.

147. **trifling demon**: Panjandrum's frustration boils over into increasing insults and sarcasm.

148. **sacerdotal blitz**: He wonders if he has missed some minute bit of ritual that has separated him from God.

149. **O Radiance of Empathic Love**: This is Panjandrum's most cutting sarcasm in what he had believed to be a private soliloquy.

150. Cf. OT Psalms 22:1, KJV: « My God, my God, why hast thou forsaken me? Why art thou so far from helping me, and from the words of my roaring? »

151. **pylon**: a usually massive gate, such as the gateway buildings and towers of ancient Egypt. See *Merriam-Webster.com Dictionary*, https://www.merriam-webster.com/dictionary/pylon, access 10/20/2020.

152. **Pylon Angel**: Angel of the Gate or Tower. Etym.: *pylon* fr. « Grk. πύλη *pylē* 'gate', πύλαι *pylai* 'gates'» (Liddell & Scott, GEL, p. 618 s.v. πύλη, πύλαι). The word has also been used to describe a gateway to an entire country. In the second Persian war, the Greeks fought Xerxes at the battle of Thermo-*pylai*.

The appellation "Pylon Angel," to the author's knowledge, is not extant in historical pagan or Christian literature. However, the notion of angels watching and influencing human affairs from above is attested in biblical texts and in related though not canonical ancient texts such as the Book of Enoch, in which the predominant story is that some angels became fallen angels who fathered, with mortal women, the race of giants known as the Nephilim. "Memories" of such angels are suggested in pre-Abrahamic glyphs and artifacts of Neolithic peoples of the Middle East, including the areas surrounding Göbekli Tepe in what is today the Kurdish region of Southeastern Turkey.

Pylon Angel makes numerous thinly disguised appearances, and several undisguised ones such as here in dialogue with Panjandrum, and later in dialogue with Orla as the Synth of the Singularity in Synth of Sweven. Although Pylon Angel is benign and not of the fallen variety, its theology is more inclusive than Christianity narrowly defined. Pylon Angel is gradually revealed to be Heckler.

153. To reinforce the special nature of dialogue with an angel, the language idiom shifts, even before the angel intercedes, from the prose form of the first

three scenes of TFW Act 1 to iambic pentameter blank verse in the style and idiom of Early Modern English.

154. Panjandrum is shocked to hear a voice seeking to confirm that he, Panjandrum, the wailing one, is the naughty boy nicknamed Panjy who was a nuisance to his nun teacher.

155. Panjandrum is annoyed that someone has been listening.

156. **how swift doth lamentation turn into outrage poorly cried**: Pylon Angel begins his chastisement of Panjandrum with an unflattering account of his behavior as a schoolboy.

157. **habit**: the attire of nuns.

158. **mutatis mutandis** (Lat.): 'necessary changes having been made', as in an editorial process; use here is figurative.

159. **bodhisattva** (Skt.), o.f. Pali *Bodhisatta*: in Theravada Buddhism, historical or future historical Buddhas before they became/become Buddhas; in later Mahayana tradition, a saint that foregoes final liberation and enlightenment to show love, compassion, and generosity to others; cf. John Bowker, ed., *Oxford Dictionary of World Religions* [Collectors' Ed.] (Norwalk, Conn.: Easton Press, 2006) p. 155.

Etym.: *bodhisattva* « 'enlightenment-being' » Edward Conze, ed., *Buddhist Texts Through The Ages* (New York: Philosophical Library, 1954) p. 314 s.v. *bodhisattva*; « fr. *bodhi* 'perfect knowledge or wisdom, ... the unlimited or enlightened intellect' + *sattva* (1) 'being, existence, entity' and (2) 'spirit, mind, consciousness, wisdom, magnanimity, purity, goodness' » Monier-Williams, ed., *Sanskrit-English Dictionary* (New Delhi: Asian Educational Services, MMXII) p. 734 s.v. *bodhi*, p. 1135 s.v. *sattva*; see n160 *infra*.

160. **sattva** (Skt.): « primordial element or quality of existence that binds with the bonds of merit and virtue » Alain Danielou, *The Gods of India* (New York: Inner Traditions International, 1985) p. 26.

161. **Taufe** (Ger.): 'baptism, christening'. Bouncer explains this word after Mutant, Nameless Prophet, and Postmoderno finish their declamation.

162. **Zauber Leiter** (Ger.): 'magic ladder'.

163. For the "he" in the poem "Chivalry," virtue's letter once was "C," but today's mores seem to have made it scarlet ridiculous. Cf. Nathaniel Hawthorne's *The Scarlet Letter*, in which "A" is the letter for the sin of adultery to be worn as punishment by Hester Prynne.

164. **Alethea** (Grk.) ἀλήθείᾰ : truth, truthfulness, sincerity. Etym.: privative ἀ 'not' + « λήθη, rel. λήθομαι *lēthomai* 'a forgetting, a forgetfulness'; Λήθη 'river of oblivion in the lower world' » (Liddell & Scott, GEL, p. 32 s.v. ἀλήθείᾰ, p. 412 s.v. Λήθη); rel. « λανθάνω, λήθω (cf. Lat. *lateo*) 'to escape notice, be unobserved, remain unknown, unseen' » (Montanari, BDAG, p. 1215 s.v. λανθάνω). In phenomenology, 'truth' ἡ ἀλήθείᾰ, τὸ ἀληθές, requires that « ... entities of which one is speaking must be taken out of their hiddenness; one must let them be seen as something unhidden (ἀληθές) » Martin Heidegger, *Being and Time* [Sein und Zeit], John Macquarrie and Edward Robinson, tr. (New York: Harper & Row, 1962) p. 56. Cf. "Mnemosyne and Lethe" (Sonnets).

165. **Aggie**: Alethea's conjecture: Etym. of Aggie fr. Grk. *agathosune* « 'goodness, kindness' » (Liddell & Scott, GEL, p. 2 s.v. ἀγαθωσύνη); more simply, the root of Aggie is likely Ἀγάθη *Agathē*, fem. name fr. mas. ἀγαθός *agathós* broadly meaning 'good', as in Saint Agatha, a Christian martyr.

166. **Arty**: Alethea's conjecture *subaud.*: Etym., Arty: fr. Grk. *arete* 'virtue' « 'goodness, excellence' of any kind; but in Homer is like Lat. *virtus* [fr. *vir*]

'manhood, prowess, valor' » (Liddell & Scott, GEL, p. 100 s.v. ἀρετή).

167. Alethea does not say what her own name means, but the old woman knows.

168. **Paramahansa** (Skt.): in Hinduism, a title given to someone reaching an advanced state of enlightenment. Etym.: « *paramá* 'highest, most excellent'; *hansá* 'goose, gander, swan, flamingo, or other aquatic bird considered as a bird of passage'; *paramahansa* 'a religious ascetic of the highest order' » (Monier-Williams, SED, p. 588 s.v. *paramá, paramahansa*, p. 1286 s.v. *hansá*). In Skt. literature *hansá* is often a metaphor for soul.

169. **writhe**: the state of the mermaid envisioned by the admirer is magically pleasant and idyllic; but the word "writhe," easily expected due to the rhyming scheme, connotes a twisting and turning involving discomfort or pain. As with any utopia or paradise, there's an unseen flaw somewhere; but the flaw might be willed away by the faith of a longing heart.

170. **Pan**: Greek god of the Arcadian mountains and forests; son of Hermes; lusty deity usually depicted as part goat; fond of dancing and playing his pipe.

171. [added by The Finders] This vision could have been of anything embodying a highest aspiration, but this one is of a lustrous woman-fish splashing and cavorting outside of time. Beautiful beyond sense, she is more woman than fish, more idea than woman, and more spiritual than rational. She is a blessèd moment of *coincidentia oppositorum.* She is vestal. To reach the vision the old man overcomes infirmities, distance, craggy terrain, and more. Maybe a Platonic Idea, *Minne*, or *hieros gamos* is in play.

172. Except for the name "Lou" and the zone designation, this is a true account of the experience, now placed in a retrospective theoretical framework, of more than a decade of riding a commuter bus in and out of Washington, DC.

173. **spindle neurons**: Some scientific studies suggest that these specific neurons are the center in humans of feelings of "deep connectedness," higher emotions, and moral judgment. Consult Ray Kurzweil, *The Singularity is Near* (New York: Penguin Books, 2005) esp. pp. 191-92.

174. **daring to whisper I am that I am**: This suggests *Yahweh*, one of the oldest names for God in the Judeo-Christian tradition, the meaning of which is roughly 'I am that I am'. So this whisper from the improbable mix, this colonizer grabbing stuff of all sorts to fuel its evolution higher and higher, even unto the likes of God, risks the great sin of pride.

175. **poem** (Grk.): Etym.: fr. « ποίημα *poéma* 'anything made or done, work, piece of workmanship, poem, act, or deed' » (Liddell & Scott, GEL, p. 568 s.v. ποίημα). ποίημα in the indicated sense is widely used in both classical and Koine Grk., e.g., the *Septuagint*, the earliest translation into Greek of the Old Testament. For example: "I [David] muse on the works [*poéma*] of thy [God's] hand (KJV Psalm 143:5).

176. "Incommensurate Parts" invokes strands of biological, cultural, and linguistic evolution, e.g., from "it" to "himself," then to "herself," and onward to "their" poem which is they themselves in process of being made. Although repulsive on most levels, the bold congeries still has a spark that makes it a child of god; but it lives on a perilous cliff overlooking a chasm reserved for those who let the whisper of Yahweh spill over into a roaring hubris of self-aggrandizement.

177. **wheel**: *bhava chakra*, 'wheel of becoming'; the worldly wheel; in Buddhism, a foundational concept of the world as embedded in *maya* 'illusion'.

178. **older physics fare**: Newtonian (older) physics is a relatively narrow model compared to 20thC and later physics in the form of relativity and quantum

mechanics; it is also narrow compared to Buddha's concept of codependency of causation (origination); see n180 *infra*.

179. **assign guilt**: all too easy to do when abstracting from the matrix of codependent causes and effects that form the totality of a life; which is one reason justice often seems to veer from fairness.

180. **codependent origination**: primarily a Buddhist idea. In *BRICOLAGE* it is slightly reimagined for postmodern times to be an attribute of "Parataxis of Samsara" (made-up expression not historically attested). See sidebar discussion between Evangelist and Postmoderno in the last third of TFW Act 1 Sc. 1.

181. **Nirvana's divine best**: One cannot overcome Parataxis of Samsara by working inside the *bhava chakra*. The object of *nirvana* is complete escape from the whole of it by entering and keeping a sacred state of awareness, detachment, and enlightenment.

182. **singularity**: Used primarily in mathematics and physics, this term became a watchword in science-based futurism with the groundbreaking work of Ray Kurzweil where it is used as an umbrella term for themes in artificial intelligence, neurophysiology, robotics, and especially the projected integration of all these into a "singularity" of great interest to technologists and humanists alike. While *BRICOLAGE* is most assuredly not a work of science, the idea struck the author as an apt starting point for the fictional poems and short pieces in Synth of Sweven. For a proper account of singularity, consult Kurzweil, *The Singularity is Near*.

183. See "Dueling Visions" (Encrypted Messages).

184. **ancient lore and wisdom**: The miracle will be less the cyborg synth itself than that her values and salvific mission are rooted in sacred pasts.

185. **episteme** (Grk.): 'knowledge'. Etym.: fr. Grk. *epistēmē* (Liddell & Scott, GEL, p. 261 s.v. ἐπιστήμη).

186. **might birth a great surprise**: see n184 *supra*.

187. **de novo** (Lat.): 'starting anew'.

188. **creatio ex nihilo** (Lat.): 'creation from nothing'.

189. **noli timere** (Lat.): 'Be not afraid'.

190. **Singleton**: Synth of Sweven aka Orla of the *Synth of Sweven*. "Singleton" is the personification of the singularity; see n182 *supra*.

191. **Cambrian**: 1st geological period of the Paleozoic Era, about five hundred million years ago, when scientists say fish first appeared. Etym.: *Cambria* « Lat. adap. O. W. or Brythonic *Cymru* 'country, original country' and *Cmry* 'people, original race (of Wales)' » (Lewis, WED, p. 74 s.v. *Cymru, Cymry*).

Scientists gave the name "Cambrian" to this early geologic period because the exposed rocks of Wales have extensive fossil evidence of accelerating evolution dating to five hundred million years ago.

192. **Gilgamesh**: The complete story of Gilgamesh was unknown until the late 19thC when it was discovered in ancient Nineveh (in what is today Iraq) etched in Akkadian on eleven clay tablets. Dated to the early 2ndM BC, and much older than Homer's *Iliad*, it ranks as the world's oldest written epic.

Gilgamesh was a great king of Uruk, described as nearly a demigod. He had every advantage of beauty, strength, and intelligence; but he was a brutal tyrant enslaving the masses for his construction projects. The gods, being alarmed at what the Greeks would later call his *hubris*, devised a plan to chastise the great king. They created a wild, half-mad man named Enkidu who lived in the wilderness among animals. A hunter discovers Enkidu and sends a temple prostitute to civilize him. This happens, but then the animals reject him because he is now too human. Enkidu, under the civilizing influence of the temple prostitute, becomes more of a controller and shepherd of animals than kin to them. Enkidu gets new clothes, parties with the temple prostitute, laughs, and has a good time; but he also learns from her some horrible things Gilgamesh is doing and goes to Uruk to confront him. A great wrestling match ensues as Enkidu attempts to block Gilgamesh from defiling a new bride. Gilgamesh finally prevails, but then the two become great friends. After several adventures together, the gods intensify their efforts to chastise Gilgamesh by setting up encounters with Ishtar (Queen of Heaven), tempestuous goddess of sexual love, and then with a great bull. Gilgamesh and Enkidu win these bouts, but then the gods send an illness which kills Enkidu. Gilgamesh is overcome by grief and goes into the wilderness wearing nothing but animal skins; he reflects on his own eventual death, and dreams of a cure for his mortality. He seeks out Utnapishtim who, with the help of the gods, had previously built a huge ark to survive a great flood, avoid death, and become immortal. On his journey Gilgamesh encounters several figures who warn him that seeking immortality is a bad idea. When Gilgamesh finds Utnapishtim, today known as the Mesopotamian Noah, Gilgamesh learns more about the great flood; and Utnapishtim tells him of a magical plant that restores youth. After finding the plant, Gilgamesh heads back to Uruk, but along the way a serpent steals the plant, sheds its old skin, becomes young, and disappears into the forest.

The *Gilgamesh* epic sets out themes and symbols that influenced succeeding ages even as their written embodiment in clay remained hidden for the greater part of recorded history: chastisement of brutality by divine powers, the quest to elude mortality, the wages of unchecked pride, different forms of love, the snake as symbol of regenerative power, relationships between humankind and animals, the ark and the great flood, and mythic beings such as Ishtar, later worshipped under numerous names including, in Canaan, Ashtoreth, as told in OT Jeremiah 7:18 and 44:25. Poets and scholars, such as Rainer Maria Rilke, were awestruck by *Gilgamesh* when it first surfaced into the western mind after nearly four thousand years of being lost.

For an updated, literary English translation of the story, along with notes and commentary, consult Stephen Mitchell, ed., tr., *Gilgamesh* (New York: Free Press Division of Simon & Schuster, 2004).

193. **rivers great**: Tigris and Euphrates.

194. **Inanna** (Akk.): Mesopotamian love goddess and Queen of Heaven, connected with or also known as Ishtar, Astarte, and Ashtoreth; cf. OT Jeremiah 7:18 and 44:25.

195. **Tiamat**: Akkadian Babylonian goddess of the "salt sea"; primordial chaos as described in the *Enuma Elish* of Hammurabi's time circa 1700 BC. Possibly derived from an earlier Sumerian/Babylonian goddess such as Inanna, Tiamat's 'chaos' aspect resulted in casting her as a vengeful monstrous sea dragon, whom the male god Markduk kills in a tale some scholars see as signaling the decline of goddesses and the rise of gods. See n194 Inanna *supra*.

196. **Isis** (O. Egy. *Hes*): Anc. Egy. mother goddess, often depicted with headdress of solar disc and cow horns (or two crescent moons), and large outspread, protective wings. In one of her hieroglyphs she is on a throne providing a protected seat for the Pharaoh and, by extension, the people of Egypt. She is daughter of Nut and Geb, and sister and consort of Osiris. The myth of Isis and Osiris established a theme of death and resurrection which became foundational for Western culture. For an introduction, see Cotterell and Storm, *The Ultimate Encyclopedia of Mythology*, Sullen and Gray, eds. (London: Anness Publishing,

2008) p. 290 s.v. Isis. For an engaging interpretation of the story from a Theosophist/Freemasonry perspective, cf. C. W. Leadbeater, *Freemasonry and its Ancient Mystic Rites* (New York: Random House, 1998), pp. 27-38.

197. **Dido**: In Virgil's Aeneid, a queen of Carthage in northern Africa who became a lover of Aeneas following the Trojan war; she commits suicide from heartbreak when he leaves.

198. **Sappho** (Grk.): poetess ca. 7thC BC.

199. **the isle**: Lesbos.

200. **Asherah** (Ugr., Heb.) o.f. *Ashtoreth*: grove of trees, worship poles repr. trees; a mother goddess (i.e., mother of other gods); often described as Queen of Heaven and consort to Baal (Philistines) and El (Hebrews); worshiped as goddess of love under other names such as Astarte; associated with groves of trees symbolized by Asherah poles which OT Yahweh orders destroyed. See generally The Editors of Encyclopaedia Britannica, "Asherah," https://www.britannica. com/topic/Asherah-Semitic-goddess, access 2/16/2018. Cf. n201 Zidonians *infra*.

Cf. OT 1 Kings 11: 31-33 (KJV): « Behold, I will rend the kingdom out of the hand of Solomon, and will give ten tribes to thee [Jeroboam]: … Because that they have forsaken me, and have worshipped Ashtoreth the goddess of the Zidonians, … , and have not walked in my ways to do that which is right in mine eyes, and to keep my statutes and my judgments. »

201. **Zidonians**: worshipped Ashtoreth (Asherah), sensuous lunar goddess of Canaan and an abomination to Yahweh, who causes the destruction of the Zidonians and the rending of Solomon's kingdom. See n200 Asherah *supra*. Cf. OT Judges 3:7 and 6:28.

202. **El** 'Ēl: Anc. name meaning 'god' attested in various scripts such as Ugaritic, Hebrew, Phoenician, and Akkadian. As part of words such as *Beth-el* 'house of god', *Uri-el* 'light of god', and *Gabri-el* 'god my strength', it occurs thousands of times in the Bible.

203. **Maelgwyn Gwynned** (Cym.): AD 6thC king of Northern Wales, whose court was frequented by bards, poets, and magicians including Taliesin. For a 9thC account, consult Nennius, *Historia Brittonum* [History of the Britons], J.A. Giles, tr. (Urbana, Illinois: Project Gutenberg), www.gutenberg.org/eBook 1972/pdf.

204. **Battle of the Trees** (Cym.): *Câd Goddeu*. Etym.: « *câd* 'battle', *c(g)oed c(g)oedydd*, (of the) 'trees' » (Lewis, WED, p. 42 s.v. *câd*, p. 56 s.v. *c(g)oed c(g)oedydd*); see n205 Câd Goddeu *infra*.

205. **Câd Goddeu** (Cym.): 'Battle of the Trees', a complicated, mysterious tale attributed to medieval Welsh bard and magician Gwion, in which the latter, using Druidic powers, causes the trees to become warriors. Attempts to interpret this story have run the gamut from seeing it as magical incantation to finding in it allegories and codes. For example, since in Celtic languages the consonants of the alphabet were often also the initial letters of the words for trees, the "battle" has been interpreted as a struggle in the evolution of language. It has also been viewed as a poetic encryption of pagan religion, and of the secrets of goddess worship, at a time when Christendom was becoming increasingly intolerant of pre-Christian beliefs. In *The White Goddess*, Robert Graves provides inspiring interpretations of *Câd Goddeu.*

206. **Singleton**: Synth of Sweven aka Orla of the *Synth of Sweven*. "Singleton" is the personification of the singularity; see n182 *supra*.

207. "Anthem of the Wildings" exudes triumphal gleam, knighthood, equine majesty, fabulous armor and weaponry, martial trumpeting, hooves pounding, and unquestioning, self-sacrificing devotional passion. But the purpose of the mission

calling these "knights" into action is not so noble as the words and the tune make them seem; for these are wildings summoned to a crucifixion. Wilding passion serves equally the patriot, terrorist, lunatic mob, and would-be saint. The goodness or evil of the mission is what makes the difference, and goodness cannot be assured by any mere label, slogan, or anthem.

208. **quiver of an ancient child**: Cupid in Rome; Eros in Greece.

209. **Gethsemane**: garden near Jerusalem where Jesus experienced agony and doubt, and then was betrayed and arrested, leading to his crucifixion (cf. NT Mark 14). In "Gabfest in Gethsemane," however, the agony and vile sickness (see n210 *infra*) experienced by Orla are different: The place is unspecified, it occurs post-resurrection not pre-crucifixion, and Orla has gone from synth demigoddess to human. "Gabfest" is used here ironically.

210. **vile sickness**: despair, a defining feature of the human condition, and, for some, the sine qua non of Christianity. Cf. Søren Kierkegaard, "The Sickness unto Death" [Sygdommen til Døden 1848], in *A Kierkegaard Anthology*, Robert Bretall, ed., Walter Lowrie, tr. (New York: Random House, 1946), pp. 339-371.

211. **Tophet** (Heb.): hell, perdition; ancient shrine near Jerusalem used for human sacrifices to Moloch; cf. OT Jeremiah 7:31.

212. **Tartarus** (Grk., Lat.): the part of Hades in Grk. mythology to which the most wicked are banished for punishment.

213. **Sheol** (Heb.): realm of the dead.

214. **Gaia … Aja**: For goddesses in this list, see "Epiphany" and related notes, and "Terpsichore Revelation" in *BRICOLAGE* Book 3, Synth of Sweven.

215. Cf. OT Isaiah 12:1.

216. **Love Lies Bleeding**: informal name for a crimson hanging amaranth known in scientific nomenclature as Amaranthus Caudatus; here it is one manifestation of the mystical undying flower, the Amaranth. For the angels of TFW Act 4 Scene 4 in *BRICOLAGE*, this becomes a powerful symbol for restoring lost nuances of the sacred feminine to Christianity. It is linked to Mutant, empath being in the Dream of the Nameless Prophet, and figures prominently in "Hymn of the Amarant Christians."

217. **canopy**: night sky's zodiac.

218. **anamchara** (Iri.): anam cara; 'soul friend, soul mate'.

219. **worldly wheel**: *bhava chakra* (Skt.).

220. **bardo** (Tib.): state between two similar conditions, fr. *bar* 'between' + *do* 'state'; in Tibetan Buddhism, a limbo where souls reside after dying and before being reborn. Bardo is based on the concept of *antarābhava* (Skt.) 'intermediate state'. See, for example, Detlef Ingo Lauf, *Secret Doctrines of the Tibetan Book of the Dead*, Graham Parkes, tr. (Boulder, Colorado: Shambhala, 1977), pp. 33-46. The perspective of "Bardo States" is of a person in an additional limbo between a waning earthly life and a bardo state.

221. **may not swallow**: cf. "Good Ship Swallow Test" (Remembrance).

222. **winter**: culmination of the year and of the lives of two people in love.

223. "Radiance To Make Us One Again" consists of two parts. They are similar and, in fact, except for the change in idiom from stanza form and Early Modern English to contemporary English, the first part, "Long Ago, and Far Away," and the second part, "Here, Now, I Sing Once More," are nearly the same. Initially this mirroring came about due to uncertainty as to which style to choose. But out of the conflict came the notion that one part (either) could be a prophecy, and the other part (either) could be the prophecy's fulfillment in a context of a love so strong that it overflows into a near-eternal return where each instance of life in the

world, though engaged in its own time's accoutrements ("silk garb" and "prancing steeds" of long ago vs. today's "finery" and "framed pictures"), is meshed into a mysterium of linked souls being reborn after passing. Only part one is included in SFM.

224. **ecce** (Lat.): 'behold'.

225. **clerihew**: a simple, humorous verse form like a limerick; bad poetry that is or seeks to be funny. Invented in 1928 by Edmund Clerihew Bentley, the prescribed quatrain rhyming scheme is *aabb*, and the subject is usually a well-known person. Here the poem "Clerihew" does not adhere to the prescribed rhyming scheme, and the only famous name is Leviathan.

226. **Leviathan**: « (1a) sea monster defeated by Yahweh in various scriptural accounts, (2a) a totalitarian state having a vast bureaucracy, (3) something large and formidable » *Merriam-Webster.com Dictionary*, s.v. leviathan, https://www. merriam-webster.com/ dictionary/leviathan, access 10/29/2020. The political and governmental meanings are due to the 17thC book *Leviathan* by Thomas Hobbes.

227. **Nostradamus**: 16thC prophet whose predictions have seemed eerily accurate, such as of regicide (e. g., Charles I of England), and the rise of Adolf Hitler. Nostradamus wrapped his prophecies in poetic quatrains. He was guided by the alchemical and magical lore of the *Corpus Hermeticum.* For an introduction consult Mario Reading, *Nostradamus: The Top 100 Prophecies* (London: Watkins Publishing, 2010).

228. **avine green**: a green bird, a company logo on the back of the jacket.

229. **Sarai**: Abraham's wife, aka Sarah. In OT Genesis 17:16, God promised she would be the mother of nations, but she had no children until she was ninety, at which time she bore Isaac.

230. **amaranth**: Etym.: « amarant(h), *n.* … fr. Greek ἀμάραντ-ος, used as name of a flower, but properly adj. 'everlasting' fr. ἀ not + *-μαραντ-ος 'fading, corruptible' fr. μαρ-αν- stem of *marain-ein* 'to wither, decay' (root *mar-, mor-* 'die') … corruptly written amaranthus, as if containing the Greek ἄνθος 'flower'; amarant (now commonly amaranth) being at first only poetic. » *OED Online Third Edition*, access 7/31/2021 [minor omissions by BRICOLAGE author are indicated by ellipses; minor style changes made for consistency with BRICOLAGE conventions, e.g., "fr." for < , and single quotes to enclose translated meanings].

231. **Hecate**: famously appears in Shakespeare's Macbeth, Act 3 Scene 5 as the ruler of the Three Witches—cf. Mabillard, Amanda, "Hecate," Shakespeare Online, 10 Aug. 2010, http://www.shakespeareonline.com/faq/macbethfaq/hecate. html, access 9/5/ 2021.

232. **Pylon Angel**: Etym.: *pylon* fr. « Grk. πύλη *pylē* 'gate', πύλαι *pylai* 'gates'» (Liddell & Scott, GEL, p. 618 s.v. πύλη, πύλαι).

233. Merriam-Webster.com Dictionary, s.v. singularity, access 11/14/2021, https://www. merriam-webster.com/dictionary/singularity.

234. Ibid, s.v. singularity, access 11/14/2021.

235. In BRICOLAGE, "singleton" has nothing to do with the singleton golden cloth coverlet used in medieval knighthood ceremonies [inserted by DGVU: But this could have been an oversight by the work's original author(s)].

236. **fetch**: Cf. discussion of the obscure etymology of this word in *OED Online Third Edition,* esp. relating to meaning n. 2 (1) « apparition, double, or wraith of a living person ».

237. Early cultures, in Egypt for example, often recognized only three seasons.

238. Qq.v. Hecate, religio-prehistorical pyramid, and triple goddess.

R. C. PIETTE

For most people, their best and truest selves
Are neither their first selves nor their last selves,
But ones that lie somewhere in time's middle.
As ends dawn, recall and put forth your best.

Fast, sure-footed, on the gravel,
    Homeward bound we were.
In rapture of spine-tingling bursts,
    Earthly ties unravel.

Hoofing beats to fast to count,
    Pure sheer energy.
Chugging, puffing, engine roared,
    Horse was one with me.

Later I would study mystics,
    But no more would I learn,
Than freedom taught as racing pinto,
    Galloping fast return.